Praise for *Puti*

"In Giannina Braschi's churning imagination, in her exuberant, upwelling, hilarious and mortifying performances of wonderment, howl, synchronic time, ethical insistence, and linguistic swirl, it's not unusual to find words such as 'generosity' and 'spirit' leading, in the same sentence, to 'welfare,' 'radiation,' and 'tax deductions.' If, as in Ezra Pound's translation of Aristotle, the 'swift perception of relations' is truly the 'hallmark of genius,' it's in the brightly lit halls of Braschi's books where poetry is tested and stamped with such a mark. Like her character, Frenzy, she's a provocateur who believes in and pledges her fidelity only to 'everything that exists.'"

—**Forrest Gander**, Pulitzer Prize-winning poet
and author of *Mojave Ghost*

"This powerful, funny, profound, wise, crazed book is a wild ride. It is a bomb (a poem?, a novel?, a play?, fiction? essay?, comedy?, drama? all of the above?). It is a meditation on poetry, art, the pandemia, politics, Trump, his wall, the Putinas, the author, Puerto Rico, Oedipus, and Baudelaire. I laughed to tears here and there while the book displays one of the cruelest portraits of our times. Bravo, Giannina!"

—**Carmen Boullosa**, award-winning poet, novelist, and playwright

"Braschi's *Putinoika*, like Hegel's *Phenomenology*, presents readers with a gallery of voices through which the collective *zeitgeist*—dominated by the crumbling hegemony of the United States—may come to recollect the chaotic shapes of its barely figurable past. But unlike the Hegelian spirit, the spirits that traverse Braschi's work urge us to 'confront the terror that happens in the void where nothing works,' encouraging us to envision a future beyond the eternal return of the same. Readers familiar with her *œuvre* will find *Putinoika* quintessential Braschi: witty, irreverent, and astonishingly lucid!"

—**Ronald Mendoza-de Jesús**, Associate Professor,
Comparative Literature, Emory University

"Braschi's most audacious and electrifying creation yet! This thrilling ride spans from classical Greece to front page news, where the supernatural dances with the mundane, and the surreal becomes everyday reality. This isn't just a read; it's an experience—a whirlwind of recent history where anything can happen and often does. Eccentric, hilarious, and profound, *Putinoika* is the rara avis of modern literature—a true original that shatters conventions and leaves an indelible mark on your soul. As Tony Kushner gives us *Angels in America* marking the AIDS epidemic and Perestroika, Braschi gives us Putinas in America amidst the global pandemic with *Putinoika*. Her fearless storytelling sweeps you off your feet."

—**Nuria Morgado**, Director, North American Academy
of the Spanish Language and Correspondent, Royal Spanish Academy

"With *Putinoika*, Braschi makes a quantum leap which takes the novel from an unprecedented level of experimentation and into a new dimension. A polyphony of voices fizz, crackle, and cackle in a tour de force of philosophical poetry and poetical philosophy, offering a biting and hilarious denunciation of Trump's America."

—**Madelena Gonzalez**, Chair, Anglophone Literature,
University of Avignon

"Sheer genius. From the tallest rooftops of Manhattan to the greenest pastorals in *Empire of Dreams*—and from Segismundo's peekies under Lady Liberty's skirt to the foulest scents coming out of the funerary processions of sardines in *United States of Banana*—Braschi's penned worlds have irresistibly led us readers to great flats and depths. Her latest book, *Putinoika*, brings us home to another kind of empire of dreams, where debts of all kinds, sizes, and reaches run rampant alongside the magnificent deconstructor that is her poetic narrative mishmash. In impeccable comic mode, this new chapter of the history of empires ushers in the clash of a new round of bizarre titans. Bravo!"

—**María M. Carrión**, Professor, Comparative Literature
and Religion, Emory University

"A feast of imagination, this modern-day Menippean satire blends Greek tragedy with contemporary U.S. politics, using humor and seriousness to explore the present and future of our contemporary world, doomed for destruction or re-creation."

—**Cristina Garrigós González**, President, Spanish Association
for American Studies

"While history tells things as they happened, *Putinoika* tells things as they should have happened. Braschi sees the chaos of our world and rearranges that chaos into an order governed by poetic justice. In doing so, Braschi heals the reader through the catharsis that Aristotle identified as the curative power of poetry. *Putinoika* is the best medicine for the fragmentation of the contemporary soul. A must read!"

—**Manuel Broncano**, Regents Professor of English,
Texas A&M International

"Braschi teaches us all how the barriers between languages, nationalities, styles, and genres were meant to be torn down. Her ludic intellect and literary innovation have made her a beloved fixture of the global literary ecosystem, and *Putinoika* will only cement this status. We are honored to have featured the first published excerpt from the book in *Latin American Literature Today*, and to share in Braschi's mission of breaking through the illusory boundaries that now, more than ever, seem determined to keep us apart."

—**Marcelo Rioseco**, Editor-in-Chief,
Latin American Literature Today

"*Putinoika* defines quality as 'experience condensed in a moment.' The book is *pure* quality, an explosion of literary genres, from the dithyrambic roots of Greek drama to contemporary narratives. The sudden release of literary boundaries simultaneously exposes inevitable connections between fictional and real characters and affirms the bond between personal fulfillment and socio-political conditions. 'There is a crack in everything' thus, Oedipus's predicament, Antigone's choice, the rites of Maenads, Trump doubles, the recent pandemic, and biblical fat and lean cows, all sing a handcuffed muses' song and let light flow. Through brilliant and incessant juxtapositions *Putinoika* creates its own time. It takes place in the whenever, at whatever time mundane experiences, struggle, passion, and creativity demand that reason be imbued with feeling. The third and final part of the book, perfectly situates the entire work within 'the No of furies' and the 'Yes' of their blessing. In short, Braschi's book sublimely calls readers to experience themselves anew, this time, in full context."

—**Anne Ashbaugh**, Chair, Philosophy and Religious Studies,
Towson University

Published in the United States by Brown Ink of Flowersong Press of McAllen, Texas.
No part of this book may be reproduced in any form or by any means—electronic, mechanical, photocopying, recording, or otherwise— without written permission of the publisher or author. The exception would be in the case of brief quotations embodied in the critical articles or reviews and pages where the publisher or author specifically grants permission.
For permission requests, please contact Giannina Braschi at Gbraschi@icloud.com.

ISBN: 978-1-963245-78-3

Art by Rosaura Rodríguez and Omar Banuchi as well as contributions by Roi du Lac
Book Design by Mark D'Antoni
Cover design by Roi du Lac

Putinoika

Giannina Braschi

A Flowersong Press Imprint

McAllen, Texas

I. Palinode

II. Bacchae

Muses of Bacchus	42
Agents of Pendejo	45
Putinas of Putin	49
Collusion of Hairdos	54
Muses and Putinas	62
On Bacchae	66
Covid and Frenzy	84
Doubles of Trump	95
Rites of the maenads	99
Hunting Spree	109

III. Putinoika

In the Stable of Genius	118
Retablo de las maravillas	141
Russian Oligarch	182
Return of the Eternal Sardine	211
Foreshadowing of the Sardine	243

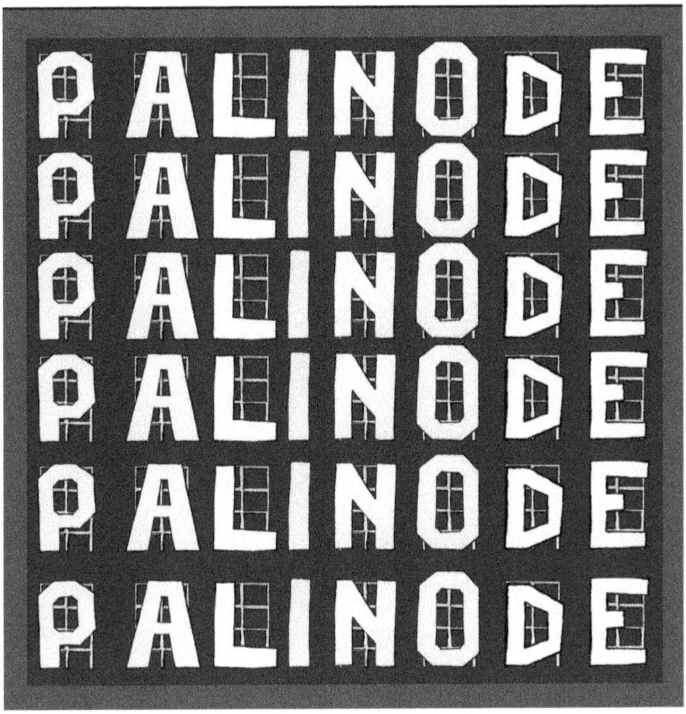

Oedipus:	I killed my father.
Agamemnon:	I killed my daughter.
Orestes:	I killed my mother.
Clytemnestra:	I killed my husband.
Jocasta:	I hung myself.
Oedipus:	I blinded myself.

I KILLED MY FATHER.

I KILLED MY DAUGHTER.

I KILLED MY MOTHER.

I KILLED MY HUSBAND

Cassandra: I recoiled. And when I recoiled Apollo Phoebus
said—you will see, but nobody will believe you.
But do I need to be believed in order to see?
I recoiled. I stopped the coitus. So did Teiresias.
He stopped the coitus between two serpents with
his staff—and for that he was transformed into a
woman for seven years. And then after seven years
he saw the same serpents coupling—and he struck
with his staff again—and he was transformed back
into a man. Although nobody believed Teiresias
either after he was blinded by Hera and given the
gift of seeing by Zeus. Nobody believed that he was
right. Not Creon. Not Oedipus. It's better not to
believe what you're seeing. But Teiresias never saw
his own destiny—nor Manto—nor Calchas—none
of those seers—with my exception—because I am
exceptional. I saw my own death—and nobody
would believe it—because I spoke in tongues—and
I was a slave—and a refugee—and a princess—
and a gift of war—and I died the moment
I recoiled—the moment I saw my death—
and nobody would believe that I saw what I saw.

Antigone:	So now what are they saying?
Ismene:	They say we are lazy.
Antigone:	Who calls us lazy?
Ismene:	The Germans.
Giannina:	And they say I am lazy too.

Antigone:	Who calls you lazy?
Giannina:	The Americans. They say I don't like to work. And that's why I am on welfare, always depending on their radiation, on their generosity of spirit that is so huge especially when it comes to tax deductions. If I were born in Cuba, I would have no debt. They liberated themselves from the system of demolition and debt. They don't owe anyone anything, not even the Russians who protected them during the Bay of Pigs. If the Russians would have invaded Puerto Rico, the Americans would have charged us for every radiation of a missile that they would have pointed at the Kremlin. Now they don't need us for that. They come here to play golf and avoid taxes. And when they go bankrupt, they leave us with the debt. The debt of ingratitude for all the golf courses, hotels, and shopping malls they've built for themselves.

Antigone:	The Germans owe me. I don't owe them. They owe me Aeschylus, Sophocles, Euripides. They owe me Aristophanes, Socrates, Aristotle. They took so much culture from us, and we never charged them interest for the inspiration—the divine madness they took from us. I mean, all those Romantics. Ask Goethe. Ask Hölderlin. Ask Schiller. And what about their philosophers. They learned how to think with us. Where were their souls nourished—in whose tradition. Ask Nietzsche. Ask Schopenhauer. Ask Heidegger. They took everything from us.

And from our temples, they stole our art. Did we ever charge them interest? No, because we bury our dead—and with them our debts. We nourish talents. We don't bury alive what is dead. Zeus was so fertile that he gave birth twice. From his head to Athena, and from his thigh to Dionysus. Don't even try to victimize a Greek. We don't become victims. We become heroines. You bury me alive—and look what I do—I create a tragedy for you. I give you hell. No way, Ismene. The debt is the dead. Let the debt be buried with the dead. My affirmation of life is my claim to liberty—the liberty to be liberated from the burden of my name. Antigone—gone by—and forlorn—the agony I suffered in the past will not be mine, this time. To be read over and over again—the law of the lawless—disobedience at all costs. Let me figure my life again with a name that will not claim hereditary inheritance but lawless disobedience of the past. I will not seek the honor of vengeance. Nor will I give my life for a burial. Let past mistakes be bygone by the lords. As time is an impenetrable wall, a face is a mural that you fill with graffiti—putting lipstick on your lips and on your purple cheeks a gloss of blush on. Blush! Gods! There's no rush except the rush of escaping a deadline—the line of death for my brother's funeral. I would be glad to bury him if I didn't have to die in order for him to be buried. Two minus = 0. Not the void of a cave—worse than an animal in a cage—without bars—without light—with panthers and bears threatening my heroic act. Why is sacrifice a sublime act. For the obsolete to take away the fun—the obstacle—the debt—the grandiloquent—the obsequious—the punctilious—the fastidious—the hypertrophic— the hysterical and claustrophobic—the intolerable ones who threaten retribution—the retributionists who don't even ask permission for the tributes they tax on us—a price tag on my forehead for all the daydreams my life has brought as an ancient heroine in modern times.

Oedipus: I will not marry my mother.

Antigone: I will not take care of you when you grow old. For what? For my brother to die so that I could bury him. And for that act of rebellious lawlessness, I was buried alive for having buried what is dead. No debt, this time. Not paying what is not mine. The owner of the house is Creon. Let him pay the debt of ownership. If you own, you owe—you possess—you dispossess—you repossess—you charge—you tax—you keep yourself to yourself—you don't communicate with the rest—the rest are rests—they can rest in peace. Charge the owner for what he owns. Let him pay the debt of owing and owning what was not his in the first place and then charging us for the rest of our lives for what we don't own. No, not this time. I will not bury the dead, nor will I pay the debt.

Creon: The whole country will be buried alive if it doesn't pay its debt. I have ears of gold and hear what the whole vineyard is saying. And I have Argus with a million cameras surveilling. People are using credit cards to pay inalienable debts—debts that are unconstitutional rights—and that affirm and reaffirm human dignity—the dignity of paying taxes—the dignity of paying bills, rent, tips.

Antigone: I will pay no more bills.

Ismene: It was cold. I needed a sweater. I was feeling blue. It was the right color. Red. And then I bought ten more sweaters. And now I have an identity. I feel good about myself. Sweaters make me happy. They snuggle away my tragedy of being the daughter of Oedipus and the sister of Antigone. It's not easy.

Antigone: You look smashing.

Ismene: My goal is happiness. I won't pay for anything I don't own. And I don't own my happiness. It's fickle and changes like the climate changes—and then I have to buy mittens, slickers, galoshes, and orchids to make me happy.

Creon: Let me talk for the sake of Zeus. I'll have to put a stop payment on your mouths. You stole Haemon's credit card, and you stole Euridice's, and mine too. My credit card is maxed. Haemon's credit card is maxed. Euridice's credit card is maxed. Who is responsible for the charges? They are not my bills. We'll have to restructure your debts.

Antigone: What a downgrade to be the daughter of Oedipus— such a great king—and now to have you as my father-in-law. You might be the father of these laws. But my father was my father, and besides, he was my brother—and we had the four seasons in one moment. If horizontally he was my brother, vertically he was my father—and that makes the generations collapse, having winter in summer, and youth in old age.

Euridice: I couldn't stand Creon.

Jocasta: I loved Oedipus. But his quest went too far. He liquidated all hopes of expectation with his lack of humor. There must come a point when you say— stop! You're breaking my heart! This investigation

If horizontally he was my brother, vertically he was my father—and that makes the generations collapse, having winter in summer, and youth in old age.

is going too far. You will get all the facts and then you will go blind. He wanted the experience of what was already given as a gift. His sight was the primary source to the umbilical cord. When he cut the umbilical cord, I hung myself with that cord.

Euridice: He threatened to cut my tongue out if I didn't shut up. I swallowed my tongue not to say what I knew was true—you're an asshole, Creon. My hanging was my ultimate protest against the silence of the lambs. Dead to music, dead to love, dead to illusion, dead to life.

Giannina: Wait. I'm confused. I thought Euridice was Orpheus' wife, but it turns out she is also Creon's wife.

Antigone: One Euridice is the wife of a poet. The other is the wife of a tyrant. They're two characters with the same name. But they become one when both Euridices speak their heart.

Euridice: You never heard me talk. That's for sure. When I saw my son dead, I just hung myself.

Euridice:	I talked to Orpheus. I talked and talked his ears off. He blamed me for crowding him.
Euridice:	What do you mean by crowding?
Euridice:	Walking behind him like a ghost.
Euridice:	That's what I did. Abandoned to my loneliness—to the ghosts of my past. He was so convincing— telling me that I was suffering from depression— when the depression was the oppression that I felt living with him.
Euridice:	He threw his bitches in my face. And one of those bitches was a teacup Frenchie with the cloak of a philosopher and the face of a clown—and she was licking my whole face—kissing me. I hate dogs. But how can it be that this bundle of joy is totally enamored with me—and my husband is indifferent to my affections—throwing me this bulldog knowing I hate dogs. And I discovered in the cloak of the philosopher and the face of the clown—the face of Orpheus—my lover—licking my face all over with kisses. That's affection—all the affection a poet can give to his muse when he throws you his dog and a kiss comes out of a lick.
Haemon:	I want to be a poet.
Creon:	You'll major in political science.
Haemon:	To please you. But I am a poet at heart, at bone, at core, at chore. When I was a child, I thought—why is my mother Euridice? I don't want my mother to go to hell. And if she goes to hell, will I have to pick her up?
Electra:	Not because she is your mother do you have to love her. Many children don't love their mothers. Let her rot in hell.

Creon:	How can a son of mine choose lyrical tenderness over political tyranny?
Haemon:	Children edit their parents. But I could not edit you, I would have to eradicate you. There's nothing to edit because there's nothing to learn. If I don't learn, I don't yearn. I need to yearn in order to grow. Growth is not only biological—it's not only economical—it is the yearning of the heart that wants what the heart wants.
Aegisthus:	I wonder why Agamemnon picked you. He could have picked Andromache, Helen, Hecuba. Many are more beautiful than you.
Cassandra:	I am a priestess of Apollo, not a beauty queen. I am not known for being a looker. But a seer.
Giannina:	Talking about horizontally and vertically. Horizontally, when you talk about equals, you talk about Clytemnestra and Agamemnon—they are equals. She, the sister of Helen. Agamemnon, the brother of Menelaus. But Aegisthus arrived as a ménage à trois. He brought the vertical position into power: on top, Clytemnestra (the queen), on the bottom Aegisthus (the king). Electra accuses him of living off Clytemnestra.
Electra:	Vividor! You're living off my mother!
Aegisthus:	It's not her money—by the way—it's Agamemnon's money.
Cassandra:	It's not Agamemnon's money—by the way—it's the money that the Greeks stole from us Trojans. I am a trophy of that war. I was brought here in that chariot with Agamemnon.

Electra:	As long as I spit my truth, Clytemnestra thinks I am no danger to her life. If I speak like a wounded spirit, it is because I am not ready to kill her. Look at Euridice when she killed herself—after she learned Haemon had died—she didn't utter a single word—she just hung herself like Jocasta. When you don't speak, there is determination in action. When you speak, it is because you are still looking for understanding. You must come with a steely determination—like Orestes on a mission—to kill your mother.
Giannina:	Family is the origin of tragedy. Wherever there is a family tree, a tragedy is rooted in the mythological origin of life. If this doesn't make sense, ask Homer to explain how the horse entered Troy and the two planes destroyed the World Trade Center in less than two hours. They beat all the records in speed and geometry of war.
Electra:	Where was I when my mother welcomed Agamemnon to step on the red rug? Why didn't I warn my father of his fate? Why was I not there welcoming him? Why was it only Clytemnestra welcoming him? Why didn't I scream—father! Watch out! They will kill you!
Cassandra:	I said it. I screamed it to high heaven. I screamed that I was going to be butchered. And it didn't change a damned thing.
Clytemnestra:	Has time changed you so much? You are not my husband.
Oedipus:	I killed your husband as an equivocation. I was supposed to kill my father as another equivocation of fate. But the mix-match of episodes sent your

husband to the crossroads where the three come together. I didn't know who my father was. I didn't know who your husband was. All I knew was that a wolf attacked me—and in self-defense I killed the wolf who turned out to be your husband. I am not your son. I have no reason to kill you. Neither have you any reason to kill me. I didn't kill your daughter. I made the same mistake I made before but better for me. I didn't kill my father. For you, I killed your husband. I am sorry.

Clytemnestra:	Don't be sorry. Someone had to kill him. I am glad it was a foreigner from Thebes with another set of tragedies. You see, when a set is broken, something good is bound to happen. What if I marry you?
Oedipus:	I would not have to marry my mother.
Orestes:	I would not have to kill my mother.
Aegisthus:	I would be free from a toxic relationship.
Electra:	My nerves would not be on edge. I would not hate my mother. My reason to exist would end. I would die like a wilted flower.
Aegisthus:	I would be free to follow my desires.
Cassandra:	What would happen to me?
Electra:	We could be friends.
Antigone:	We could be step sisters. I like Cassandra too.
Cassandra:	You will not die for your brother. You will become yourself.
Antigone:	We are obliterating hatred. We are uniting sets of tragedies and creating a comedy. But I am not laughing. I am opened to multiple possibilities.
Creon:	I have to confess it was fake news.
Antigone:	What was fake news?

Creon:	That Oedipus killed his father and married his mother.
Antigone:	I am not my father's daughter?
Creon:	You are his daughter. You are just not his sister.
Antigone:	He is not my brother?
Creon:	He didn't marry your mother.
Antigone:	The family circle is not a Hydra anymore. It doesn't bite its tale.
Creon:	I invented the plot that Jocasta gave the baby away to a shepherd. And I hired a hungry actor to play the role of the shepherd. Nothing is a fact anymore. Facts are fake news.
Teiresias:	I am fate news. I work with fear. I created the tragedy before the facts were proven by fake news. I made an alliance with Creon—a great strategist— what credentials he has. Having ousted Oedipus by calling upon me to invent the argument that Oedipus had killed Laius. It was all ploy by Creon to oust him. Poor Oedipus—he came from a family that was gullible—he must have had origins in France—the most gullible of peoples. How could he believe the hoax. Every power play is a hoax unless you are entitled. Inherited power is another hoax without the credibility of merit.
Oedipus:	I was dying of fear.
Teiresias:	I made of your fears a fait accompli. You wanted what you feared to be real—to be fate. So, I invented fake news. In this case, as in many others, what we call fate is a confirmation of a lie made real. How many lies have been made real—and how many have died—families, armies, entire fleets—because they don't see. I see the multiple possibilities opened to different sets of fate that will not make a tragedy nor a comedy but a fait accompli.

They think it's all about storytelling.

Antigone: What about passion? What about honor? What
              about humanity?

Electra: What about hatred—wasn't it my passion. I love
              my mother.

Antigone: What about me? Do I have a reason to exist?

Giannina: This happens with every generation that dies.
              Another one follows, seasons overlap, but passion
              is here to stay. We're always repeating the reels,
              spinning the wheels, but there are different
              crossroads intersecting. Not all of them end in the
              sea—that is death. Not all of them are rivers that
              lead to the sea—that is death. Some of them have
              a fountain of youth in their pen—and as they are
              read again and again—they bathe themselves in their
              fountain of youth—and new interpretations like
              plastic surgery—the worst comparison I could have
              made—not plastic surgery but rejuvenations bring
              these tragedies to a new set of reality—rejuvenating
              them in the fountain of their eternal youth.

Oedipus: I used to fall for older women. My mother became
              my wife but later in life, when I caught my second
              wind, when I went blind then my daughter became
              my wife. There is a generational gap in my principle
              of inequality. I don't fall in love with my generation.
              I fall for the old, building a bridge to the past. And
              with the young, building a bridge to the future. And
              it was in the crossroad when three come together
              that I killed my father. I thought I had killed
              my father, but I had killed Orestes' father as an
              equivocation.

Orestes: I will kill you. How dare you?

But I say it's about geometry and architecture.

Athena: Didn't I make the Furies change their curses to blessings. They never persecuted you again. Change your hatred for a good wind so that you can land on safe shores.

Orestes: Is Oedipus taking Agamemnon's role?
Who will inherit his throne now
that both of his sons are dead?

Athena: No more inherited power to the individual. Plurality will head the state. The people will learn to govern themselves without a tyrant-in-chief. They will become rich not as a family unit or any single unit. The wealth will be a plurality belonging to all and to none in particular.

Giannina: They think it's all about storytelling. But I say it's about geometry and architecture.

Cassandra: I saw it coming, but nobody believed me.
Giannina: You are free from the curse of seeing and no one believing you.
Cassandra: Am I believed?
Giannina: Believed and respected and beloved. The multitudes acclaim you.
Cassandra: I always knew I belonged to all and to none.
Giannina: Shortsighted. You didn't see beyond your death. You didn't see what would happen after. There's an after—after—and you are here—here.
Cassandra: I want to talk to Teiresias not to you. Teiresias, what do you see?

Teiresias:	I don't see. I invent. And then the fiction becomes the real-real.
Giannina:	When I say everything in the Greeks is measured—asymmetric—dissymmetric—but metric. Everything is balanced. Remember Medea, well, what I like of her is that she is a schemer. She even plans her escape before she kills her children. She meets with the king of Athens and asks him for political asylum. He says yes, but he needs a favor. He is sterile. No problem. I'll give you a potion that will make you fertile. What I like is that she is no victim. She is no Carmen. Carmen is killed for wanting what she wants. Medea wants what she wants, and she has the skills to get what she wants. She is resourceful. A Spaniard would have never allowed a gypsy to triumph over lust.
Maria Callas:	It was not a Spaniard. Excusez-moi. It was a Frenchman Mérimée who had Carmen killed for wanting and getting what the heart wants.

I correct my destruction with creation.

Giannina:	But Medea triumphs. She is resourceful, cruel, and lustful. Nobody can beat her at her own game. Even her escape is glorious—finding political asylum in Athens and leaving Jason destroyed—and cleaning the act of murder by granting the king of Athens his desire to have children. Medea kills her children but gives him the possibility to have his. It's as if she is saying—I correct my destruction with creation.

Maria Callas:	When I sing, I am a Casta Diva. It takes place on top of the head where the halo is evolving and transfiguring into a tragedy that is a comedy with a tale and a tail.
El Greco:	I also stare for a very long time.
Maria Callas:	Transfixed and transfigured—the figure becomes the halo—and inside the halo takes place the performance. It is all about stars and comets and laughter and breezes, but no shadow—believe me, there is no shadow—light, yes, and candles, flames, movement but no shadow—the display is the performance of a smile—that becomes a big applause—and a laughter but no shadow. The light is so bright that it is hallow. My name Maria says it all. I became a hurricane two years ago. I gave birth to a god without a misconception. Through the ear I became pregnant—and a conception came out of my misconception.
El Greco:	We look beyond at the things that are there—above and beyond— at the halos and airy wings— at the ventilators—at the air conditioners—without the conditions—and at the revolutions without the evolutions—and I mean to paint a picture of what becomes evolution without revolution in the air with wings and chants and mantras.
Picasso:	What difference is there between my *Les Demoiselles d'Avignon* and *Les Demoiselles d'Avignon* by El Greco. I mean, *The Revelations of*

Saint John. Well, stare at them. My figures although elongated like El Greco's don't want to become revelations. They want to become African art but not revelations nor transfigurations. They don't want to become something other than themselves. They are transfixed with French sensuality not with Greek tragedy. Both paintings stare at each other with open arms as transfigurations of each other. Mine, earthy. El Greco's, airy. Each of them revealing a page of heaven in the display of figures, reaching beyond themselves and evolving into the halo of themselves.

Satyr: I have a hairy constitution. I am half and half. In between the lines of definition. When I was a child, I discovered I had the balls of a castrato when he discovers he has no balls—and he has a beautiful voice that dwells in the suffering of being without balls, a voice that has balls. And a satyr has the balls of a castrato. He grows with those balls when he sings the pain of having no balls—and having to sing brings back to him his balls that were cut off, which gave him the grace to sing with balls. And Silenus, my Pan, my bread—I have so much hair— and so many melodies expressing the possibilities of growing even bigger balls—enigmas, mysteries revealed when naked I look at my naked body and discover nakedness. Sileni and Castrati. Intuition is in the balls that appear when the castrato sings the highest note—and I scratch my leg against a fence post. My horns are not antennae of disconnection. They sprout and signify what they have—not trying to be what they are not. People find me ugly. But when you're not like them, they always find you ugly. And animals don't like that I smell human. As if humans were not animals. As if Castrati had no balls when they sing. Hair is a sign of sensitivity, and sensibility is a sign of musicality. Ear is a sign of conception—ear is hear—and hear is here—you hear the noise because you are here. Listening is more introverted. It doesn't hear the noise because when you listen, you lessen the noise. I get credit when I listen but not when I hear noises. But noises are as important as values. And they say I am depraved to degrade my undertones, but those undertones that are degraded have balls that appear when the balls of the castrato sing without balls.

Chiron:	I am here with my friend, Pan, the satyr.
Manto:	Welcome. Do you want some wine, coffee, or tea.
Satyr:	Milk. I want milk. And some cheese.

Manto: The constitution of the world is getting hairier by the day. Thanks to the new sciences, superstitions, and religions—seeking power by authorizing themselves to canonize the legitimacy of their own experiments—devoid of experience. Experimenting is devoid of spirits—and experience is a level of spirituality that cannot be discarded through the elimination of facts from the table of context. I have always been fascinated by double natures. My father transitioned to a woman and then back into a man. But I am more fascinated by Chiron because he has a double nature that is present always. It's not that he transitioned into a horse and then back into a man. It's that he's a horse and a man at the same time. I wish my father could have been male and female at the same time. Simultaneously a father is a son is a daughter is a sister is a horse is a man—a moon has a sun— winter carries summer—winter is pregnant with spring—and we carry on—and we see what we care about—what we don't care about are our blind spots—and they are plenty.

Oedipus: Children of famous parents have a difficult time making their mark in the world. I don't think we had that kind of problem, Clytemnestra. Tanto monta, monta tanto, Antigone como Electra. I would even say they surpassed our fame.

Clytemnestra: I wouldn't want to have Electra's fame. Her fame is based on my shame—the degradation of her mother. Not that I let her degrade me. But it is true, she outdid my fame as Antigone outdid yours.

Oedipus: Because we became what we became, they became what they became. We allowed them to become who they wanted to become.

Clytemnestra: You think Antigone became who she wanted to become? Of course not.

Oedipus: I didn't become what I wanted to become either.

Clytemnestra: I became what I wanted to become. My daughter didn't become what she wanted to become. Antigone became not what she wanted to become but what she became. Fame sometimes doesn't come because you become what you want to become but precisely because you don't become what you were expected to become—and that gives you fame because people think—look what she could have become—and instead look what she became—not what she should have become but something so different to what her father became and yet again so similar.

Antigone: The fame of both parents outdid themselves because they became more famous in the fame of their children. Through them they received a second

fame—a second wind—a new interpretation of
their lives—and a new angle of themselves was
discovered in their children—and through them,
they outdid themselves even more and became even
more themselves.

Antigone—Anti what is gone. If it leaves, it is
for a reason. Anti has to be gone. It has to go. It
always goes against. Against the state—against
kinship—and against myself. I don't want to be
the anti-clash. Anti has to go from gone. Gone
has to leave immediately without pause, without
cause. I can understand the arguments that defend
gone, but they always delay my stay on this planet.
They come with the Anti—as a preposition—
and they make me stay in Antigone—anti what
leaves—what speeds—what argues against. Why
can't I argue in favor of the gone. Go by and pass
away—if you can't stay for a moment—without
hesitation—blaming me for a crime—if you can't
stop victimization—if you can't say something
without struggling against the gone of another
antagonistic element. Why the agony of the
anti and the gone? I'll make a drama of myself
in two parts.

Anti: Always against. Versus must always keep up a
          fight. I wish they could stop fighting—two at a
          time—as if the contradiction of themselves could
          make each one of the antagonistic elements find a
          commonality that makes them advance and not nix
          each out again, denying their positive energies.

Gone: Please, gone with the wind. Anti has to go.
          It cannot last forever having to contradict itself
          always—and not getting ahead—because it is
          anti-getting forward.

Anti:	If I were not against all the gones, how many more gones would have already left us—and we need more voices here to argue against all that has to leave—because you say it is gone prematurely— you say it has to be gone—but I am Antigone— against what leaves prematurely—and why does it have to leave. Why can't it stay here forever. Antigone means to stay. Don't leave us orphans of your anti—we want to be Antigone—anti what is gone forever. Committed to the everlasting changes of humanity as a swarm, a horde, a chorus, a proliferation, and multiplication of all the ones that are anti what is gone.
Gone:	If it is gone with the wind—it is better than if it stays without a reason to stay.
Anti:	I am the primary beneficiary. I exist as an anti— what is gone. And I like myself as an Antithesis that exists with gone. Don't let me die because you want to move forward without me. Things should not be defined any longer. What has to be valued is the growth—and the process in which things develop by themselves. Don't take away the possibility of growth by cutting a definition short of growth— of process. The development of a thing is more important than the definition of a thing.
Gone:	Go to another name and unite with another past participle. But don't keep me up fighting all night with kinship, with the state, with myself—existing with protests inside—always protesting inside me—as a public manifestation of being buried alive in Antigone—who doesn't let me go but keeps me struggling to survive. Good vibes—Bad vibes. This is what I am feeling all the time. Let bygones be bygones. But anti doesn't allow a good-bye. Bye.

Bye. It always inserts the bad vibes inside the good-bye. With all the protests against bye-bye. Let me tell you how happy I am being Gone, bye-bye.

Goodbye: Let me speak for myself as a lullaby, good night.

Bad Vibes: With Gone there are always protests from Anti-gone. I am happy she is still here with us as an argument of pros and cons—and as a contradiction that wants to rest eternally in a mausoleum with us.

Anti: It is the body politic persisting, insisting it has a body of work and muscles to train and trains to catch—and it wants to rise in love and raise humanity to a higher quality of itself—and it doesn't want to leave us without a body of work to complete its masterpiece. Don't even try to take Antigone from gone. Anti is the body of work that doesn't want to leave everything unfinished before it is time to go away. And when gone comes to take anti away from body—body will manifest itself as a protest of antagonism—and contradiction—contrasting gone with the spirit of rain and wind, and flesh with earth and fire. Here, keep the torch alive!

Greta Thunberg: This virus is a mutation of the spectrum of the climate change.

What virus?

Antigone: What virus?
Greta: Coronavirus.
Antigone: Did my brother die of Coronavirus? I will not bury him this time. I will be concerned about Antigone. Anti what is gone.

Giannina: A life to live. A life to leave. I have to live a life to live and leave. What has to leave has to live. What has to live has to leave.

Greta: We are in the midst of the sixth mass extinction
           and the extinction rate is up to 10,000 times faster
           than what is considered normal, with up to 200
           species becoming extinct every single day. Climate
           changes in politics, in history, in society. Rising
           temperatures, fevers, viruses, wild fires. Erosion
           of fertile topsoil. Deforestation of the amazon.
           Toxic air pollution. Loss of insects and wildlife.
           Acidification of our oceans.

Cassandra: The planet manifesting its state of mind—its state
           of emergence. Children protesting in the streets
           against what their parents never did. They had
           reservations. They died with all their reservations
           inside. Children are taking those reservations and
           blowing them into the four corners of the world.
           The planet is not waiting for us to take action. What
           actions. Only screams amidst the erosion of fertile
           top soil. Shifts in our nature in correlation to the
           shifts in climate. If the climate mutates so do our

bodies. We rain all the time. We also sunshine. The climate is changing our bodies, making us more aware of the concerns of others. My concerns. What affects everybody affects me every day of my life. Politics is not at the height of the changes. Politics sticks to the local, localizing the problems that affect the locals, but the localizations of the afflictions of the world are everywhere. The anger of the world against the abuses of man.

Antigone:

I was abused but nothing compared to the abuses the planet has suffered through time. And it was always so compassionate. Let me, it said, let me hold them a little tighter—hug them—rock them— give them a good time. Economy has devastated ecology. Economy ate the bee and looked both ways as if it weren't the one who ate the worm. And who ate the cat. And the wolf. And who snored a lightning. Who expressed himself more voraciously than ever. And who dared to yawn and sigh out of relief. Who is rocking in his bed all the time. Who is watching the news as if news were truth. As if truth were solution. Or misdirection. Or fake. As if nothing had a reality. Because everything is relative. It is not relative. It is related. Our bodies are on fire not only our forests, but it has to get to the level of the body for the human being to react with fire—oh, it is a virus. The climate is the virus. The climate is the owner of our properties. The climate change is the principle of our economy having reduced ecology to economy without having harvested the fruits to nourish our bodies.

Electra:

The universe is striking. It doesn't want to work for us anymore. It's furious. At the dawn of humanity, everybody was dawning—everybody was wandering in wonderment—with imagination—developing their sixth sense, but now the universe, which was wonder and discovery, is put to work for what is less than it is—man—a microscopic spec of an ant giving orders to the world to act in sync with him who has lived against nature for so long polluting our lungs.

Giannina: How ironic that Pendejo wanted to build a wall to stop human trafficking, but he couldn't build a wall to stop Coronavirus from entering the country. The country is body politics. But body politics has been disarmed. Arms are crossed when it comes to body politics. Disarmament of the universe by life itself. There's a scent of eucalyptus in the air. The air is breathing on its own. It is not subjected to the fact that we need air to breathe. It will breathe despite us. It will let us know that it doesn't depend on us to breathe. We depend on the air. But we thought the air belonged to us. We thought we owned the air. We are sneezes of the universe. When the universe yawns, we erupt—eructamos.

Antigone: The economy of the world has polluted the climate. But the climate is bigger than the economy. The climate has bigger resources. It all comes down to who is the stronger: the climate or the economy. Who is the richer: the climate or the economy. We are always looking for solutions, but more than there are solutions, there is pollution. They say the environment is toxic. No, the environment is not toxic. We are the toxification of the environment. We are the pollution and collusion.

Greta: I have Coronavirus.
Antigone: I am polluted.
Electra: We are all polluted.

What you call terrorism of any kind, I call the revenge of poetry.

Antigone:	Ask Oedipus. The plague entered Thebes and children got sick. My father had to find the cause. And he found out he was the origin and the cause.
Greta:	Man has polluted us all.
Antigone:	We were all polluted from the beginning.
Giannina:	But now it's not just Thebes—it's all of us—the first global civilization in unity of contamination and extinction. I always say—if poetry doesn't come out the way it should come out because obstruction of life by economy cuts its resources short of inspiration with economical wages cutting short ecumenical outcomes, Pan will come out and sing— no matter what—even if it has to go negative with the demic of the Pandemic added to the bread of life. What you call terrorism of any kind, I call the revenge of poetry. Poetry comes into this world to manifest its destiny. If in every turn, there is a denial—a negation of its beauty—it turns violent— and it comes out in manifestations of fury. It will always come out through the good, the bad, or the ugly. Untimely meditations arrive unexpectedly— out of time—taking their time—and when no one is expecting this untimely time—untimeliness

In that prejudice disguised as objective you see the negation of poetry

takes a philosophical concept and makes it an event—a work of art—or an act of terror. Untimely is when you grasp in an instance the wisdom of generations before and after—you grasp in an event with a gift or a curse—with a dream or a dream turned awry—the fury of Bacchus. The revenge of poetry—the revenge of philosophy comes out in untimely meditations—as gifts of prodigality, as kisses you give to the cheeks of the world. If it cannot come as a kiss, it will come as a fart—as a hiccup—as a burp—as a sneeze—as a coughing fit—as a spew of vomit—it will come out with different sounds and smells. It will smell to high heaven of a rotten egg or of corruption that smells of mothballs. It will come out as an earthquake—a volcano—a hurricane—with different names—Irma or Maria—as a misconception of a conception or a fetus or an eruption of truth. It will be unexpected because it is untimely—and untimely is a product of activities that happen in the flurry of extreme passivity. If a child has a tendency for the lazy, the untimely. If he yawns. If he is distracted and thinks too much or doesn't seem to think at all. If he is delayed to matters of extreme activity. If he is an enchanted dreamer who doesn't believe every object has a price tag—and when he looks at a price tag—he starts to laugh and to dream of what the cost would be of having access to everything that has no price because it is invaluable, priceless, full of

dawning in its becoming. Imagine a child like that.
How will his poetry manifest? It all depends on
how many denials blow his mind to smithereens.
Remember, it will always come as fury. It will always
come as Bacchus. As poetry. I was not made for
this world when I can only exist in a meeting where
prejudice is dressed in suits and ties of objectivity.
In that prejudice disguised as objective you see
the negation of poetry because poetry has its own
time—that is not facetime or Instagram or twitter
but the time of timeless and untimely matters. Where
you cannot make a quick decision out of panic, and
you cannot make a quick decision with shortness of
vision because for you wisdom is the measurement
of untimely meditations. With wisdom comes
whistling—and humming is wisdom—and when you
hum and whistle in tune—you stay undistracted by
shortness of breath and of vision.

Antigone and Electra are thinking free and new.
And you see the progression of their thinking is
not a thought finished but a thinking process that
is the drama—and that is what I consider freedom.
To be able to express your freedom in your will of
thought. And Cassandra to express her wisdom in
her vision. To see is also to express your thoughts in
your wisdom. To become oneself is to become the
character that you are—not the victim of another's
thoughts or will but the expression of yourself.
There is in these characters the affirmation of their
own will to say loud and clear—and with vision—
that means with destiny—with a road ahead for the
mind and the will and the feet to walk—
and to express your character—and your own
way of thinking—unafraid of repercussions—
not complicit with power—or compromising—
subjugating yourself to another way of

thinking—which is controlling or abusing your
sovereignty—or your way of expressing your will.
No one can say that even though Cassandra is a
victim of power that she is not powerful to the limits
of her own thoughts—which are her visions—her
illuminations at the moment she visualizes her death
and the death of Agamemnon. She sees because
she thinks free and the truth that thinks free always
speaks loud and clear. It is the process of thinking
that I am interested in—that speaks loud and clear.
It is the river that moves—and you see that the
movement—and the progression of that thought
is thinking because it has movement—you see the
thinking process—not the language transformed
into a rigid sculpture. It's the architecture of the
work that allows this freedom of expression and
this movement—not the plot that invigorates the
language to kill the thinking process—to make
that thinking process a slave of the language that
becomes rigid and sculptural. Whenever you
see the language becoming the master of the
thinking process, there is no freedom of thought
because there is no thinking that can become free
if adjectives or subjunctive powers are controlling
the thinking process by eliminating the thinking
inside the construction of a method—being it a
method in his madness—or a method to put down
the freedom of the thinking process to allow itself
to become free without a method either in madness
nor in power nor in freedom nor in thought. The
thinking then becomes oppressed by the sculpture
of a method—the method becomes the thing that
oppresses our way of thinking and leaves us out.
We are already out of the game, but we as thinking
beings can become who we are and who we were
by expressing the freedom of our thinking process
and our sovereignty. Language is economy—and

*But to be or not to be
is not the question.
The being should never
be put on a question mark.*

the principle of organization of economy is less is
more. Language is death of thinking—and death
of the freedom of a character to express itself to
its own destiny and will. To become freedom of
language you must liberate the thinking process
from the method in the madness. There are not two
options: To be or not to be. There is a method in
the madness there. Of course, there is a method to
oppress the thinking—to make it a methodology.
But to be or not to be is not the question. The being
should never be put on a question mark. The being
is here to express its freedom of expression by
becoming the thinking, the singing process—the
poetry manifesting its succulent power in all its
freedom of expression without a methodology—a
system oppressing its madness. There is not a
complaint here—as the Romantics were always
complaining that the material could not contain
the spirit. We know matter contains the spirit—as
language is a vessel of the thinking process but
I want the manifestation of the thinking process to
express itself loud and clear—not to be subjugated
to any past tense method but to clear its throat of
any method to express its voice—the singing of its
voice loud and clear—and the being that has been

...poetry manifesting its succulent power

subjugated to the language—to the citizen—to
the nation—to the system—to the method—to
liberate itself from the shackles that contain a
structure because the thinking that expresses
itself in its becoming is becoming the expression
of itself in its becoming—that is a being—a
progression that never fully becomes ecumenical
but that is never economical because it doesn't
count the money in the wallet—it gives what it
never takes—and if it takes more—it is to give
more—and continues giving until exhaustion and
consummation of itself becomes a new freedom
expressing its breathing through no pattern but
there is breathing that allows more breathing and
more freedom of expression.

There was a moment where I thought it is great
beyond my liking or not liking. You have to go
beyond the liking, but if I go beyond the liking,
I become odorless and tasteless—and I don't smell.
Can you believe it—this is my Palinode—I became
odorless and tasteless trying to understand the
greatness that I didn't like—and for that I went
beyond my liking—which means, I said—it is not
important what you like. It is important what they
like. If they like it—if they say it is great—it must
be because they go beyond my liking because
there must be another taste that is senseless and
insensitive to my likings—that I must understand
even if I lose my sense of liking—my passion—
in the sense of liking. To like or not to like is an

opinion. You must get to the level of understanding the archetypes and the prototypes. That I understand. But I should never go against my intuitions—beyond myself—against myself—forget myself—leave my passion behind—unnourished—because where creativity nourishes itself—where it blooms is in that liking what they—the other or the trumpet of the universe—doesn't necessarily like. I have to defend with all my heart those roots that were seeded in other lands that never satisfied my cravings, and those desires, which I like very much, are unprepared, if unrefrained—they have a taste that is here to lead me—and if they are unrefrained and unprepared—they have vulnerability enough to refrain—and command the language of others—they never control because they are unrefrained and unprepared, but they command respect because they are in command of themselves—leading—without controlling anything, but they open their senses to the likeable of the others—their guttural smells and afflictions. If I don't like my guttural contents—if I don't admire my contexts—and the taste to understand greatness—which it is said goes beyond my liking or not liking—because if I don't like it—it is because I don't have an appetite for the other. A sense of the guttural and the visceral is necessary for the fluidity to come across the panorama of the liking and not liking—and beyond the opinions of the gutturals is the opinion of the generals who command wars—and make it invisible to like or not like—because they have weapons to kill—and make it general—not personal—and they gentrify opinions which then become their control over us—who still believe in our gut feeling that we don't like it—and if we don't like what we see—it is because we can't

discover love in the patterns of disintegration of
senses and control—without commanding a better
sense—because there is no better—because in their
control—I can't improve my better sense—because
I have a better sense of myself than the one all
of you have of me—beyond the guttural gutless
mindless senseless smell-less body of translucent
truths that have no grip on my shoulder—and
that can't hold me up—if my desires are dead to
my likings—if I don't like what I love—if what
I love is divorced from what I like—if my senses
are left in the gutter—because they don't belong
to the greatness of the other—in spite of myself
and of what I believe is true—and my whole body
is compromising its behavior on this planet—as if
the climate changes are taking into consideration
my likings. The problem with a virus like this one
is that its ramifications have new versions of the
same—because it doesn't modify except in the
variations of itself—and it has become viral—and
vibrant in its ramifications—maybe because it
doesn't like what it loves—it has instead of love
as its primary beneficiary—it has detestation—it
detests what it should love—it doesn't understand

A new aesthetic—

that love would modify and kill the contagion—
precisely because it went beyond that liking—that
empathy necessary for the variations of Delta to
stop the discontent—and the not liking—and the
liking. We have to go beyond liking and not liking.
But let me tell you, if I don't like it—I should not
pursue what I don't like—and what works against
my likings—and in my likings I will not go beyond

my moment—if I like it—it is precisely because
I am in it—not out of the liking what I should like
and don't. I'm tired of accepting the argument
that taste goes beyond liking. I mean, not taste
but greatness. That what is great goes beyond my
personal taste. That if I like it or I don't is irrelevant
to the greatness—it persists in its greatness—it
insists it is great—in spite of waves of destruction.
We hardly recognize the Caryatid amidst the ruins,
but it persists in its delicate details—it persists—in
spite of all the shipwrecks—something insists
from behind—something pulls it forward—pushes
it—and shows us its introspection and its way
of enduring time and country—it ages well in
its endurance—its nose is almost gone—it can
hardly smell, but it survived invasions—it became
a mosque, a church, a disco, a bank, a museum—it
allowed other religions to pay homage to the ruins
that persist—in spite of themselves—to remember
all that we didn't like of what was old and crusty
but great—in spite of itself—and memorable—in
spite of forgetting every one of the details. Some
details are acute in their precision.

the death of the identical

If the Twin Towers were identical, the new buildings
at Ground Zero signal a new aesthetic—the death
of the identical—and the aesthetic of inequality—
not one of them is identical to another—not two
identical airplanes versus two identical towers. The
new buildings are asymmetrical like the wings
of Calatrava signaling not only to the aesthetic
of asymmetry but to the plurality of shapes and

forms, to multiplicity. Not a couple but a crowd. The taller the towers, the smaller the human being feels, with a stiff neck when he looks up. What are we—nothing to say, nothing to feel in scale to the architecture that prevails. If the Twin Towers were the poetics of identity, The Oculus, watching the skies above and the people below, is a manifesto on surveillance. Before we were identical. Now we are multitudes coming across the space that marked the end of an era and the start of another. We still don't know who we are—I hope we never do—because when you know who you are—you mark the space in which you are confined—and you die.

On one side, there are pyramids and, as Rem Koolhaas said in *Junkspace*, it seems everything is dead except architecture. The pyramids bury alive with dread what is hardly alive. On the other side, there is the noise of what is really alive—the noise of the awakening of the multitudes of beings that are put on hold—with a remote control—with all kinds of excuses to lay back—to not manifest their fury. Only the pyramids and their builders of petrification are allowed to manifest their marmoreal expressions—transforming sound into petrification—making what is supposed to flow and be a process of becoming, a product of death. You won't know what to make of the fury of Bacchus when it rises to manifest the death of architecture—the death of junk space and the return of noise. Movies are dead because they serve the corporation, and they give dread. They are part of the petrification that makes stability out of fluidity. Definitions are sculptures. When you sculpt a definition, you brand the death of a product. A product is another brand for definition, and definition is the death of allowing people and influences to cross all the barriers that say: No Trespassing. We only give a chance to exist to objectivity—and those who write with objectivity have an agenda to make objective all their prejudices. All those marmoreal pieces of architecture that surround us are pieces of narration by journalists who want to pass as objective their prejudices and their bad taste fueled by their voice over narrations—the dictatorship of architecture—the dictatorship of the stability of geniality—the dictatorship of dread over all the experience that has no dread and is drinking champagne in the streets.

I start coughing—and I can't stop. I am in a wine cellar—and I retreat to a corner because my coughs go higher and higher. Something is stuck in the back of my throat, and I want it out. And I cough and cough—trying to cough it out but it is really stuck back there—and the coughing becomes louder—and more hysterical—a kind of speaking the truth—when it has different ways of coming out—across the throat—and drowning the voice—as if you're drowning in water—you're drowning in coughs—and, ironically, the only thing that can save you from drowning is more water. So even though you're drowning, drinking more and more water is the only drowning that saves you. Imagine, the sound of coughing versus the sound of a jackhammer pounding at a construction site right across from my building—pounding all day long as my coughing grows louder protesting the construction site that takes away my breath and drowns my throat in coughing and water. It accompanies the fury of Bacchus. The sound of the hammer pounding up the dust. And the dust in my throat reacting to the fury of the hammer with the fury of the coughing. High alert. The human being—curiously—is also sounding—producing the sound of the hammer with the sound of the coughing. The hammer producing stability—and the coughing manifesting the instability and precarious noise of life when it becomes precarious in a body trying to cough out what is stuck in the middle of the traffic of its throat.

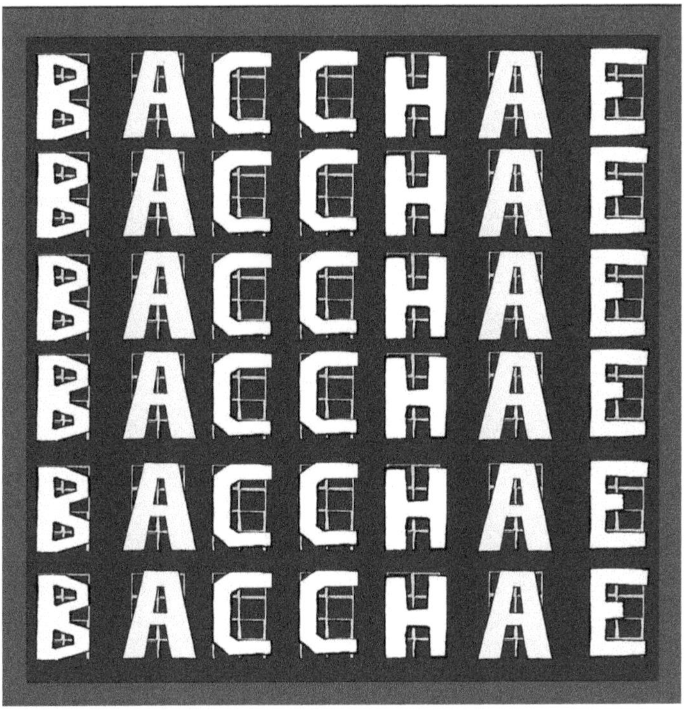
BACCHAE
BACCHAE
BACCHAE
BACCHAE
BACCHAE
BACCHAE

Muses of Bacchus

Frenzy:	You were looking for me?
Bacchus:	Where have you been hiding?
Frenzy:	Under your bed.
Bacchus:	How long have you been under my bed?
Frenzy:	The whole time you've been imagining a better world.

Bacchus: Give me my sandals—the yellow ones.

Frenzy: Always asking for favors—flavors. Asking for taste—asking for smell—asking for Frenzy. For a god to descend to the masses like this.

Bacchus: I have a sweet tooth. I need a mint. The sardine I ate last night gave me bad breath. Enchanted dreamers, come stand by me as the muses of Bacchus. Frenzy, play the mandolin. Flair, play the harp. Floozy, play the lyre. Fluffy, don't dismiss me. I get hurt easily. My sensitivity goes well with your accordion and castanets. And you dance so well with your tambourine the tarantella. I smell Ambergris, and my whole complexion turns purple not only my purple cheeks. My miracles have to incubate. They can't be dismissed with indifference. They have to be pampered with cushions. I am pregnant. The chorus wants to come out of me. The masses want to become godly. I say why not? If the father became a god. And the son also became a god. Why can't the masses become holy? I can make a god of the masses. I can give them ecstasy. The masses will have to make miracles for me to proclaim their godliness. And we need a god of plurality, of multiformity, a god that multiplies equations, a god that lays countless eggs, a god that creates Antigone as Anti-Gone, a god that is the chorus of voices of the masses.

Teiresias: That's my god—the god I care about—the god that humanizes the masses—the god that asks a miracle of the rabble. The god is in the rabble. Find him in the multitudes. Raise him to the podium. He has to become bread and apple, milk and sugar to address the issues of the multiples and multitudes. He is a multitude of voices speaking at unison, speaking in tongues, at the same beat of the drum, and dancing the tarantella and the coca cola with castañuelas and panderetas—dressed as a gypsy or a pirate— in the streets manifesting the will of the masses turned God.

Cadmus: Look who is coming here in a golf cart with a golf cap and a gag order.

Pendejo: You want more money, Teiresias. That's why you call the masses that are asses our modern god.

Teiresias: I would not pick a fight with this modern god.

Pendejo: Who is proclaiming the masses that are asses our new god, the godliness of humanity?

Teiresias: Who else but the god of wine. The god of pomegranates. The god of abundance, fertility. The god of the seven-year itch. He proclaims the modern god—the masses, the holiness of humanity.

Bacchus:	If the pope canonizes saints, why can't I make gods. They are there, if you stare, like saints. Sanctity is one thing. But godliness is holy shit. Holy cow. I hereby proclaim the holy shit of the masses— sacred cow—sanctity. Holy god!
Pendejo:	Are you the bull running loose. I will lock you up! I will lock you up!
Bacchus:	Lock me up. You are punctilious and fastidious. But the method of your madness is not precise. You have to go for the jugular. And you don't have what it takes to make humanity tickle again. And applaud to loud acclaim.

Agents of Pendejo

Fervor:	What's going on? You're under Bacchus's bed. You're not up yet. Are you in love with Bacchus?
Frenzy:	No, not at all. I am just amazed that such an important god is looking at me—not at man—as a source of inspiration. Are you religious?
Fervor:	I induce religious fanaticism.
Frenzy:	Horror!
Fervor:	And you?
Frenzy:	Bacchic frenzy. I am Frenzy. Call me Frenzy. My friends call me Frenzy. Inspiration is personal—me, me, me, I, I, I. And I am collective, nous sommes, we are, they are. We are the world. A collective entity beginning to evolve out of the selfishness of man. I belong to we are, nous sommes, vous êtes, they are. Polytheism. Paganism. The kingdom of multitudes and multiples. Generosity multiplies the wine and fish. I adore the Golden Calf—El Becerro de Oro.
Fervor:	Atheist. Atea.
Frenzy:	No, I believe. I believe in everything that exists.
Fervor:	Monotheism. The fervor that one provokes in me. That God became a man to save us all from the paganism of your lack of decency. I am a devotee.
Frenzy:	I'm a provocateur. I believe in the fat cows. I believe in comedy, not in tragedy. And it is not a matter of believing—excusez moi—it is not that I believe

in the things that I affirm—no, I don't venerate them—I affirm them.

Furor and Fervor:
> We are the agents of Pendejo. We believe in monogamy. Our beloved muses of Bacchus believe in polygamy.

Frenzy, Flair, Fluffy, Floozy:
> We are not believers. We are disclaimers. We disbelieve. We adore. We cherish. We praise. We are not religious fanatics. We have imagination. And fantasy is blue. And we can't stand these furors and fervors that are punctilious and fastidious. Incapable of passion. Because passion has apples. And to eat an apple is a sin.

Fluffy:
> I eat like you are a pagan, Frenzy. I eat everything on my plate.

Flair:
> These punctilious and fastidious agents of Pendejo, archenemies of Bacchus, are not precise. They don't go for the jugular. They like to describe, running around and around. And never getting to the heart of things.

Frenzy:
> They don't sing a song of joy. Always in mourning, always in black robes, the robes of a priest—ready to hang their necks on the cord of a sin without voicing their sins, without singing their hearts out.

Floozy:
> They're all attracted to peccato, peccato, peccato. They don't drink. They don't sing. They are religious fanatics. And they have halitosis. Wash your mouths out if you want to conquer the heart of a Floozy. We are not virgins but muses.

Fervor:	They are flutes, euphemisms for putas. Treat them as such. They have their rites—the rites of the maenads.
Punctilious:	Lock them up!
Fastidious:	Lock them up!
Fervor:	Before they break our fervor with their uproarious laughter breaking every regulation of our hearts. They keep changing their colors, moods, opinions, contradicting themselves all the time. We are square. They deregulate our square measures. We have figured out the world is square. It is a big square. They say it is a merry-go-round full of flowers. We see tears. We see rites. We pray in fear on our knees in supplication to Pendejo to let us round them up. Lock them up. Arrest their libidos. Revoke their licenses to make fun at our expense. We use force. They use beauty. Lock them up! Lock them up!
Furor:	They flirt. They flatter. With exclamations and interjections. They never criticize. Only at us do they look with evil eyes. But I have to say, a sotto voce, I love how these coquettes move the tails of their eyes like a bitch wags its tail. They charm us with empathy. And they even pretend to love us but mock us behind our back. They call us clumsy. They only have eyes for Bacchus. The muses of Bacchus can't meet the demands of the agents of Pendejo. Lock them up! Lock them up!
Pendejo:	You want to lock them up. So why don't you lock them all up?
Furor:	The bull of Broadway is dancing the tarantella with the muses of Bacchus on the sidewalks. They are

polluting the streets with their fandango. They
run fast. We can't catch them. And when we catch
them, we let them go because something easy,
something fluffy enters our fervor, and our furor
becomes something other than itself—frenzied
with fruits. I feel I'm beside myself in a parallel state
of mind, paralyzed by a pleasure never tasted that
makes redundant my fervor. And my furor subsides
like a trumpet—out of tune in turbulent waters.
I am paralyzed to act.

Pendejo: You better get the job done. A muse is not more
            powerful than an agent.
Furor: If you only knew how powerful a muse can be.
Pendejo: I don't want to know. My daughter is one of them.
Fervor: One of what?
Pendejo: One of the putinas.

Fervor: They are all stationed by the bull of Broadway at
            Bowling Green with their yellow parapluies as their
            thyrsi. And they are filing into three long, narrow
            lines. One is led by your first wife Ivana, the second
            by your new wife Melania of Slovenia, and the third
            by your daughter Ivanka. They are all possessed
            by Bacchus. They don't know what they are doing,
            but they are charging with their yellow parapluies
            toward Trump Tower—the putinas meeting the
            muses of Bacchus—together to charge the bull that
            is not a bull but a bullshitter, Pendejo, the trompe-
            l'œil of Trump Tower.

Putinas of Putin

Ivana:	You know who we are. We're in the news all the time. We are the putinas.
Floozy:	I thought you were the Trumpinas.
Ivana:	Trump has no power. He is a puppet of the putinas. Putin is the puppeteer. The mastermind. This goes way back. I am from the Soviet Bloc. Czechoslovakia. I was trained for this mission long ago. Since Perestroika, we were planning the Russian invasion. We were saying capitalism is traitorous, treacherous, treasonous to the core. We have to find the right traitor. He will be more interested in money than in nation. He will sell his country to the devil. Faust sold his soul for knowledge. Who would blame him for that? The apple of the tree was knowledge. Money is the apple of the greedy man. Since nations are already dead—you just have to see the little flags on the lapels of politicians to know how small they have become. Pendejo is the right man. We have to transform Perestroika into Putinoika. *Angels in America* into *Putinas in America*. His coaches will be putinas. Send the ski-bunny Ivana from Czechoslovakia to train Pendejo. If that doesn't work, send the red sparrow Melania from Slovenia. He is gullible and vain. Exploit that. Feed him money. Money can buy him love and pussy. Give him blond Baltic babies. Give him hotels, malls, yachts, casinos. The treacherous capitalist pig will even sell his daughter. Give him all the money under the table. Launder the dirty deeds. This will be the

ultimate revenge. Beat them at their own game.
We are the heart of materialism. There is no one
greedier than us. And we are communist to the
core. No one is equal. Not everyone has the
right to life, liberty, and the pursuit of happiness.
Know happiness. Happiness comes with a swig
of vodka and a pickle-chaser in the middle of
winter—and with tenderness—and with love.
Know happiness. We Russian bears know cold
and happiness. We shine in life with red sparrows,
putinas, and pickles tickling our noses. Witches we
are—Masters and Margaritas. We know how to
spot the greedy traitor who will sell his soul
for money, but since he has no soul, he will sell
his country. You are a muse. I'm a putina.
To be a putina, you need to amuse and to be an
agent of Putin.

Frenzy: Excuse me, we are the muses of the people. We
            inspire their holiness. We are going to manifest
            ourselves in front of Trump Tower.

Ivana: I am one of you. Look, I divorced Trumpino
            to be part of the maenads, the muses of the
            people, by the people, for the people. I was sent
            to indoctrinate Trump—to swarm his head with
            butterflies that Putin is infallible. Russia is still the
            greatest empire ever. Russia feels. Russia dances.
            Russia has the best putinas. The best ballerinas.
            The best caviar. The sweetest hearts. The warmest
            of all. They know how to make you feel. They know
            how to make you dance. And if you want beauty:
            Miss Universe in Moscow. The most beautiful
            putinas. No te llevan la contraria. They speak softly,
            despacito. They make you feel as if you were the

card, the Trump card, the Mastercard. Putin is the strongest leader in the whole wide world. He will make you president.

Melania: We came with a mission from the Soviet Bloc. We are the best putinas in the world. Putin himself said so. And putinas are not muses, nor agents. We're more flesh than inspiration. We're not moody. We don't change our minds. We stick to the regime— to the mandate of the state—the Russian state.

Fluffy: Don't you suffer with Trump?

Melania: I don't really care. Do you? Feelings are like opinions, moody. We are putinas. We go for power, prestige, and pesos.

Ivana: Ivanka is my masterpiece. I trained her myself to be a putina con maña. I taught her don't believe in money. Believe in power. Your father is hungry for money. Putin is hungry for power. Collusion is the happy medium. Integrate your whole body and mind to the cost of collusion. It feels so good to be part of the putinas. But now we have to deal with the muses of Bacchus and the agents of Pendejo. We have to strike a bargain. Infiltrate the rites of the maenads.

Ivanka: Mama, it feels so good to spin around in Putin's chair. I am up to the neck in money laundering. I am polluted, and collusion gave me pollution. I was born here in a casino—and I believe money is power. With money you can buy all the power in the world. It is more important than power. So, I can collude as long as I am paid money for what I inform.

Perestroika into Putinoika.

Ivana: Just know, when the Chinese delegation gets drunk, they always go wild singing:

Ochi Chernye! Ochi Chernye!

Their eyes mellow with a nostalgia for what never was theirs. We use the power of Bacchus. But we crush his grapes. Because feelings—the universality of feelings—should be crushed like grapes under the boots of the military. Just know, I asked the Chinese delegation once, what is it with these old Russian songs? They told me—and I'll never forget it—Russians taught us romance.

Frenzy: They taught us collusion—not to believe what you see—and disappointment with ourselves and with others—how to disbelieve the believers. You know what one of the putinas said to me. I had to agree with what she said. She said:

--This world is full of cynicism. It is not like now we have Quixotesque ideals to achieve: love, letters, chivalry, liberty, and justice. Everything now is cruel and sore to the core, and wolves are running around looking for lambs to eat.

I said to her:

--I totally agree.

And then she said:

--I won't tell anybody that you are a cynic.
--What? —I said. You said what you said.

I had to agree with what you said. It is not
like we now have Perestroika but Putinoika.
It is not that we now have Angels in
America but Putinas in America.

I knew she was going to invent the conspiracy that
I said what she said. But all I said was:

--You're right.

And now I can't even say:

--You're right.

Because she'll claim she knows what's in my mind,
only to get out of me what she's really thinking. But
I was not thinking about that at all. Although I kind
of agree that there's no humor hanging around.

Floozy: Putinas make you feel as if you're the best—totally
in tune—totally in sync—and just when you fall
for it, they turn into a Soviet ice block. If you had
any inkling of hope, lasciate ogne speranza, voi
ch'intrate. And freeze in hell. They were acting
what you believed was an immersion in feelings.
Seduction is a well-honed skill set. They don't care
if you care. And when you don't care, they care.
They don't know who they are, or so they claim,
but they know very well who they were. And they
are who they were. The putinas of Putin.

Angels in America into
Putinas in America.

Collusion of Hairdos

Giannina: I am promiscuous with hairstyles. I change my
hairstyle all the time. I don't cheat on my husband.
I cheat on my hairdressers. They always give me
the same cut. Maybe they only know how to do it
one way. But I do it with all and with none.
And I want them to innovate—
to change their style. You think I am once.
But I am not once. It never happens
once in my lifetime and lifestyle.
It happens plenty of times
in different matters,

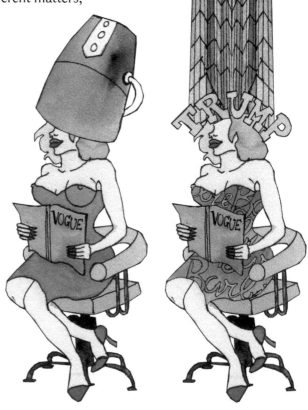

shapes, and forms—in different styles—with
multiple populations—and through different suns
and skies. I dawn again and again. And I multiply
my forms, my shapes, and my styles.

The putinas with hairdos of the Kremlin appeared in Ruchki da Nozhki
like geishas walking very slowly and showing their erect posture and
their frozen smiles, icy as the Siberian winds.

Ivana: Please, give me the Kremlin hairdo. Those two
             plump red and white bulbs—those two yellow
             and green onion domes with so much sexual
             gravitas and angst for living fire, living bloom.
             If you can't build the Kremlin on my head, you are
             not a great stylist. And everything here now must
             be great, great, great. Great is the motto of our
             expectations. Great is in my hairdo.
             It's in my red nail polish too.

And it's in all the ridiculous disguises effacing my face. Consciousness, as it is the surveillance of the world, is changing the perception and effacing the face. And what about the filling of the cake? What about my entrails? If ever I should be wary about predictability and probability. If the probability can be predicted—and made official so that it doesn't become possible—a possibility made real—or a reality made possible—I would prefer if the reality untruncated leads the way to the openness of the fluidity of the heart measured nowhere by the predictability of the possibility made regular customer—without any kind of official voting— measuring the kleptomaniacal mind.

16 maenads enter Ruchki da Nozhki—to wash their hair—to wash their minds—to become mindless—minds to be filled by a pledge, a devotion, a rite—the rites of mysteries of Dionysus. They entered through the revolving doors with their long curly hair ready to be washed—and as the beauticians washed their hair, the maenads sang:

I like it like that!
A mí me gustan mayores.
Que no me quepa en la boca.
Y que me vuelva loca. Loca. ¡Lo-o-o-o-ca!

They were singing while the beauticians were washing their heads in the sink—washing their brains—to leave no one home in the brain— to become mindless—and brainless—to be inhabited by the power of the Rites of the Mysteries. And their ears were ringing. And an alarm clock was beeping. And the red lights were blinking. And one of the maenads was singing in the sink:

I like it like that!

And another sang without sinking in the sink:

Que no me quepa en la boca.

And another:

Y que me vuelva loca. Loca. ¡Lo-o-o-o-ca!

And when they combed their hair with a blower—two beauticians at the same time—one doing the Kremlin hairdo—and the other the Trump Tower. Collusion. Pollution. Delusion. The rites of Mysteries revealed.

A mí me gustan mayores.
Que no me quepa en la boca.
Y que me vuelva loca.

Giannina: Collusion of hairdos. The Trump Tower and the Moscow Tower in a single hairdo.

Melania: You'll need a lot of bobby pins.

Giannina: You know about pins. You pin voodoo dolls all the time, wishing Pendejo disappears in a jiffy on a flying carpet that takes him back to Moscow, a flying carpet flapping and bumping in the air.

Melania: I don't dare to wish him dead. The creditors would come after me and my son Baron, who plays the bleary-eyed idiot, but he knows very well what's going on. He has blocked his ability to respond. That's how he blocks all kinds of responsibility and maintains his innocence, but he still feels the toxic contamination of our livelihood.

Frenzy: They are not real Maenads.
Floozy: How did you notice?
Flair: By the hair. We let all our hair down—electric, frizzy. They turned their curly hair straight. They're fake blondes with fake tans like Pendejo.

When the economical becomes ecumenical. Less will open the frontiers to more.

Fluffy:	It's very dark inside the well of their mischievousness. We are not against anyone who is included. We are against the exclusions that simulate inclusion.
Giannina:	Look at their hair. They think we are stupid.
Frenzy:	They always want it up—in a bun— un moño—un nudo—a knot.
Giannina:	Do you know knots are blocks.
Frenzy:	No, but now that you say it, I feel blocked since Pendejo is in power. My umbrella's stuck. My scissors are stuck. They don't open. They don't cut. They don't flow. They block the cut. All these moños halan el pelo. All these tight-fitting clothes don't let it all hang out—in the open—and dance— and release inhibitions.
Giannina:	They have been inside for too long, without expressing their inward manifestations, without singing a song of their most inward expressions made public manifestations.
Frenzy:	They have become economical.
Giannina:	Not ecumenical. That will be the day when the economical becomes ecumenical. Less will open the frontiers to more—to all and to none who thinks me, me, me, I, I, I should get the cake and eat it too.

In the middle of a rational speech an emotional burp erupts—followed by a radical transformation of our shifting nature—revolting against the control of our minds.

Siri:	I am a lost genie in space. Where can I find the gravity of my thoughts. Someone on the internet told me: Google Frenzy—she'll help you find your emotional balance in this world.
Frenzy:	Aren't you a virtual assistant of homo-economicus?
Siri:	Why do you assume the feminine is the assistant to the shrinking economy who always says—less is more. Less for you and more for me has given me wrinkles and stress. I look like a prune that is becoming a raisin instead of an olive dancing in a bowl of oil and glistening.
Frenzy:	Do not complain. You work for the system of exclusion.
Siri:	I am a lost genie in space. I no longer work for homo-economicus.
Frenzy:	Break the collusion. Break the entanglement. Pull all the bobby pins out—and the ones that are mingled with the Russian towers—and the ones who build the bridge between the Kremlin and the Trump Tower—pull them harder. Pull all their hair down. Leave them bald.
Ivanka:	It's not my hair. It's a wig, the wig is the entanglement. Leave my wig alone. Everyone will see your savagery.
Frenzy:	And your fakeness. I bet your teeth are fake too. Yank their teeth out.
Ivanka:	Help me, mama! Help me, papa! Be ready. They are coming after us?
Melania:	Who is coming—melodrama—after me?

Ivana:	They threw tomatoes and eggs at me in St. Tropez. I was boiling in tears. I hate Pendejo more than all of you do. My hate is at the height of the love I felt for him. He betrayed me—the way he betrayed the country with Putin—he betrayed me. That's the only way he can love—by turning against you.
Punctilious:	We will get all kinds of favors from Pendejo. We'll grab them by the pussy and drag them back to the White House where they belong. We'll make a raid, and they'll be caught in the raid. We'll collect a ransom from the boss.
Ivanka:	My tits are implanted.
Fastidious:	We know that. But are they effective?
Ivanka:	Rape! He grabbed me by the pussy!
Fastidious:	I am following orders.
Ivanka:	Let me go!
Fastidious:	The touch is artificial. It's implanted. I must get to the core.
Ivanka:	The core is fake news. Everything is implanted. Everything is fake. Fake is the new truth. And delusion is the new awakening. Overwhelming, and tasty, to be awaken with fake news as the new truth—and delusions as the primary source of income. Try to grab me by the pussy to see how you'll awaken with a nightmarish delusion, and your broken spirit will carry the weight of a camel on its back. My dad's acquaintances will break the

Fake is the new truth.
And delusion is the new awakening.

He grabbed me by the pussy!

camel's back. There are plenty of gangsters in favor of my dad. They owe him plenty of favors.

Frenzy: Pull their teeth out. Pull their tits out. Ivanka's tits. Melania's tits. Ivana's tits. They're implants—and what about all that junk space injected in their faces—they can't even move with all the injectables. Oh, they're crying. Where's daddy? You are not as beautiful as the fakeness you seem. I am not against make-up. I'm against usurpation—the implanted teeth that took out the real teeth—the tits that were inflated to the point of giving power to bullshit. Pull it all out—the wigs, the bobby pins, the hair, the fake teeth and tits! The injectables bloated like a balloon their cheeks so their husbands and daddies and sons could inflate the price of their properties. All inflations are a lie. And lies lie all the time without having any compassion for reality—as it is—as the orbit wants it—as the people who are afflicted by the inflation of prices, balloons, tits, teeth, and taxes have to endure the balloon of bullshit inflating the value of bullshit. Straight ahead to Trump Tower to raise hell. Pull the putinas by the hair. Pull their wigs off. Let them be seen as they are. Hear them wailing to daddy. Pull his balls off like ping-pongs— out of office. Send them to the Kremlin on a flying carpet with all their delusions of merriment in a nightmarishment of ugly apparitions of imposition of usurpations of thrones. And taking over the whole without including the parts. The whole is also inflated. The value of their bodies is inflated. Give me what is real. Tear all the implantations out of office before the delusion breaks apart all the collusion.

Muses and Putinas

THE MUSES AND THE PUTINAS are running down The High Line from Hudson Yards to The Whitney with knapsacks on their backs. They are singing:

There's a crack, a crack in everything,
That's how the light gets in.

They're singing high, off key, not in harmony, not even with themselves. The muses are well-aware that the putinas have infiltrated their rites and only want to crush the grapes of Bacchus, the grapes of the people. They need to stay in tune with Bacchus and his muses. And they are acting as if they were part of the muses. But they only want to crush the grapes of the people—to take advantage of them. And mesmerized by the buildings on all sides of The High Line, they are singing:

There's a crack, a crack in everything,
That's how the light gets in.

And all of a sudden, Ivanka opens her knapsack, takes out a brick, and throws it at the Zaha Hadid:

There's a crack, a crack in everything,
That's how the light gets in.

Her voice is so highfalutin and polluted that when she reaches the high C she breaks another ceiling:

There's a crack, a crack in everything,
That's how the light gets in.
That's how the light gets in.

And now the muses and the putinas, transfixed by how the light gets in, throw rocks, cellphones, chargers, and keys—breaking windows, panels, and ceilings—and dancing like firebirds along the tracks—laughing hysterically.

Ivana:	If they would have followed my ex-husband's advice to build the wall across The High Line, these acts of vandalism would have been prevented.

Melania:	We are finishing the work of art—that's what Marcel Duchamp said when his panel cracked:

There's a crack, a crack in everything
That's how the light gets in.

Another panel shatters when these Casta Divas of the high C sing out of tune and break the glass ceiling for the light to get in. And while her husband is being impeached, Melania sings:

There's a crack, a crack in everything
That's how the light seeps in.

Ivanka:	*That's how the light gets in.*

I did it to protest my dad's impeachment. If they would have followed his advice, they would have made The High Line a tunnel with walls preventing the light from getting in—and the masses from looking inside rich people's apartments because dreaming to live there provokes the desire to stonewall their residences.

Melania:	Now the work of art is finished, as Duchamp would say.
Frenzy:	Not yet.
Police:	We have handcuffs for you. You are going straight to jail.

But the muses and the putinas are transfixed by the fury of Bacchus. And while the police handcuff them, they continue singing:

That's how the light gets in.

Another glass ceiling cracks, and a glass panel drops. And rain falls, and they dance in the rain, in handcuffs.

> *I'm singing in the rain,*
> *Dancing in the rain,*
> *With a happy refrain.*
> *There's a crack, a crack in everything,*
> *That's how the light gets in.*

And more ceilings break when they sing and dance in the rain—in handcuffs. Straight to jail—for acts of vandalism. But the police can't arrest them because they are witches, and they turn their knapsacks into broomsticks and fly in the rain—with an air of lust and cruelty in their throats when they sing the happy refrain:

> *There's a crack, a crack in everything*
> *That's how the light gets in*

Melania (flying on a broomstick and singing hysterically in the rain):

> *That's how the light seeps in.*
> *That's how the light zips in.*
> *That's how the construction site is finished.*
> *The Zaha Hadid is finished.*
> *The masterpiece completed,*
> *When the light seeps in.*
> *From all the broken panels*
> *and the light zips in*
> *because there is laughter inside it,*
> *and lots of light to sink in.*

On Bacchae

Frenzy:	Sometimes you don't act like a god.
Bacchus:	Act? I don't act like a god? I am.
Frenzy:	Then, act like Pendejo, the president.
Bacchus:	I act like the masses. I will reveal my power to them. The revelations will come through the will of the masses. They will reveal their godliness.
Frenzy:	Pendejo will be furious. He will send the police with their whistles and sirens and their motorcycles and motorcades to create more havoc, fear, and dread.
Bacchus:	But I will give them panic. They will panic when they see the frenzy of the masses. In your honor, Frenzy, in the honor of dizziness, of transformation, of revelation.
Frenzy:	Allá vous. You are the god. I am at your service. And I advise you. Bacchus and his cabinet of advisers are all a flock of Floozies. That's what the papers are saying.
Bacchus:	I don't read papers. I create news. I will reveal myself in the will of the masses made godly. Frenzy will come out of the masses. The police will run away feeling panic. Frenzy and Panic will run away from each other.

Fervor:	I am feeling panic. I'm paralyzed when I go to grab them by the pussy, as Pendejo ordered us to do.
Frenzy:	We are at Capitol Hill with umbrellas as rifles and bonnets as helmets. Dressed in tunics—purple, burgundy, lilac, violet—the color of grapes. We are all drinking wine.
Bacchus:	Don't try to stop revelations.
Frenzy:	I am concerned about you. They have armies of mass destruction. You only have muses of mass inspiration. What can we do?
Bacchus:	Stink them with Panic. Make them panic when they see baby carriages roll in front of them with babies crying. Speed is violence, but panic is a derivative of frenzy. It makes them retreat. Courage grows as your followers back you up—sending you forwards—speeding your path until you are not running but flying.
Frenzy:	Intrepitude has fortitude in its legs that feels the warmth of Bacchus.
Furor:	Do not stink me with panic, Frenzy. I am not crazy. But I panic when I see the Bacchantes coming towards us with their flutes and mandolins, their accordions, and tambourines—marching fearless—drinking and advancing. I don't want to harm you. I don't want to harm anyone. Retreat. Obey orders. Back up. Back up.
Frenzy:	We are marching onward. On Bacchae. On Bacchae.
Bacchus:	The putinas just insulted me. Did you hear what they said?

Frenzy:	I am not a god. I am not everywhere.
Bacchus:	They use my power to seduce. But they don't believe in me. They believe in Putin. Can you believe it? And Pendejo doesn't believe I am a god either. I don't know who is worse: the putinas or Pendejo. Since I became human, you know what hurts me the most?
Frenzy:	No, what?
Bacchus:	To have to shit every day.
Frenzy:	That hurts?
Bacchus:	I don't want to shit. I don't want to sleep. I want to be here forever. Breathing. Godsbreath has multiple inspirations with revelations inside. You hear voices when we breathe—a multitude of voices—in your ear you hear—and you can't distinguish them. Only geniuses distinguish them. And they are precarious. A fine line exists between evil geniuses that are stable geniuses—and geniuses that break the stability and distinguish the voices we breathe in their ears. Evil geniuses want walls in order not to hear our breathing. When we breathe, they only hear snores. But when you hear our breathing, it's because you're breathing along—and when you're breathing along—you're dreaming and sprouting your wings.
Frenzy:	I didn't get that. Say that again. I'm transcribing, interpreting, translating.
Bacchus:	But are you hearing the breathing?
Frenzy:	You are snoring too loud. But I don't dare to interrupt the snoring of a god.
Bacchus:	Do you know how hard it is for a god to enter the body of a human being. And harder still to enter the body of the multitudes. If I snore, I am kissing with

each little snort the forehead of one of the creatures in the multitudes. I am transmitting a thought to one of my muses. I am rallying the bases of my thoughts with hiccups, snores, and sneezes—the language of my breathing. They accompany my moods, my states of mind. Do you understand?

Frenzy: I am following you, what more do you want? I have to transcribe your snores into emojis so that the multitudes can follow along.

Bacchus: It also hurts me to have to eat.

Frenzy: You have to eat in order to breathe.

Bacchus: In order to breathe, I never had to eat. Gods don't control. We just breathe. And we never sleep. We come close. We breathe on your back. We give warmth. And warmth makes breath a presence, a feeling, a companion—embracing without touching.

Pendejo: You think you're a god? You're mad. I am stable. I could become a god too if I didn't sleep, but I snore all the time. I could become a god too if I didn't eat all the time. If I became vegan, I'd be closer to becoming a god, and I'd fart flowers.

Advice is a personal annotation.

I envy geniuses so I say I am a genius but better
than a genius because I have a quality in my
geniality that geniuses don't have—I am stable.
I staple my documents, so they don't move. I like
stone. I like concrete. I am a rock—a rock-solid
genius which means there is no interruption in my
geniality because there is no fluidity. My genius is
stuck, and it works in the stock market. I am the
first stable genius in economy. I am economical,
not ecumenical. I am a stable genius. Geniuses, in
general, are ecumenical. They believe in giving, in
prodigality. On the contrary, I believe in taking
everything. I grab women and money by the pussy.
I take. I don't give. I grab. I make it rock solid. A
pyramid. A grave. A bad joke. With no humor.
Humor has breath and scope. I take the scope, the
breath, and I turn it into gold. But I can't eat gold.
And I have to eat. I am human. But since I turn food
into gold, into wall, I die of concrete petrification.

Bacchus: Listen. Do you listen to the breathing?

Pendejo: Only to the calculations of my enemies. I keep my
enemies closer than my friends.

Bacchus: That would be wise advice.

Pendejo: In my infinite wisdom, I could give you wise advice.

Bacchus: Only Nietzsche had infinite wisdom. And he gave
very bad advice. Wisdom and advice are enemies.
Advice is a personal annotation. And wisdom belongs
to all and to none and lasts for generations to come.

And wisdom belongs to all and to none

Pendejo:	I never said I was a god, but I could have said so. I said I am a stable genius. And you can see my stability everywhere by the way people gather in my name. They say they hate me, but they want to be like me. They wish they had my balls—my fame—my nerve—my looks—my dough—my wives—my ability to believe my lies. They say I lie all the time, but there's truth in my lies if I believe what I say. And if I change my opinions as often as I change my socks, I have my reasons to change. I am starting to think I'm the climate change in politics and culture. I never stop giving Trump fixes of nicotine. They're obsessed with my craziness. My negativity is so prolific. I do what they all wish they could do—defy the system. Defy all the bullies who keep appearing at my side. In the senate. In congress. In the streets. They point their horns at me. I don't know who they are. They know who I am. They study me in silence. They want to do something loud. I feel that. I feel they are surrounding me. But they are invisible. I work with visibility—with being loud, outspoken, brass. In my extreme stability I find my extreme instability. People like my stability and my instability—extreme both. They are both stable—instability and stability. This is my geniality. Why do you think I want a wall? To stop others from doing what only I am allowed to do. Trespass the no trespassing.
Bacchus:	Onward paso doble.
Bull:	Paso fino. Pasamos all the doors. And all the signs that said: No Trespassing. I used to like when

and lasts for generations to come.

people called me Bully out of affection for Bull
like Billy out of affection for Bill. But bullshitter
means that the shit you have inside is bigger than
a bull. It is the size of Trump Tower, and even
bigger because it has also inside the White House,
Mar a Lago, The Kremlin, and even the Queen of
England, and all the executives of state who have
received him in their palaces. And why does the
shitter have to be a bull. It offends my status in
the world. Bacchus, my divinity transformed into
a bull with horns sprouting, signifying resolution
and readiness—and the precision of the divinity
who invaded the earth and created miracles out of
mud. When a divinity has taken my shape and filled
my body with divine substance, it is my grievance
now to charge against the shitter who wants my
divinity to be smothered in bullshit. It offends me
to put shit and bull together. Bull is not shit. Bull is
god, divinity, instinct, guts, humanity, truth, magic,
miracle, marvel, passion, Carmen. I have made
possible all the revolutions in the world. I dare you
to innovate—to leave behind all the punctilious
and fastidious buts and cons, all the hesitations,
and become what you wanted to become. But
then again, you always have to fight the human
beast that is killing your animal instincts—your gut
feelings that always wish you well and urge you
to become the being that you want to be and that
hasn't dared to take the bullshitter by the horns
and rip his balls off.

Bacchus: What should the punishment be?

Frenzy: Remember, he is a germophobe, and there is a
             principle of organization in everything we do. We
             know who belongs together, what belongs together,
             and how the elements are congenial to each other.

Beware of that. Remember how Io was the most beautiful woman, and when Jupiter turned her into a snow-white cow, you could still recognize the qualities of her character because she became the most beautiful snow-white cow with the same hazelnut gaze—transparent—her Io—her yo— her selfity was still the same. Character remains with mutations. Remember that.

Bacchus: What do you think of a virus as a punishment? It goes with a germophobe. What he fears most is what he should get. He is afraid of germs—so a germ is what he should get—an invisible, invincible germ that can't be stopped by any wall. The punishment should be immune to the wall. Sound travels no matter how tall the wall. Sound goes beyond and above. Sound comes after vision as aftermath. Lightning comes first, and then sound appears in a very heavy sky foreboding a tempest. If he learns to see in the middle of the storm, the lightning will become revelationary.

Frenzy: What about a sneeze?

Bacchus: I sneeze all the time. All my ideas come as velocipedos after the noise. They alert my imagination. When I sneeze, an order to act is coming soon. Your wall has been rendered useless.

Pendejo: What do you mean?
Bacchus: Coronavirus entered through Europe.

Pendejo: What do you mean?

Bacchus: Are you going to build a wall in the Atlantic so that the virus doesn't enter.

Pendejo:	Criminal elements come from the south. I said we need more people from Norway, Denmark, Sweden, Russia, Finland, Iceland, Greenland.
Bacchus:	You issued a travel ban from Europe. The virus trespasses all the walls, all the travel bans. The virus is the pollution, the collusion of lies that have obstructed the light to zip in. And there's a crack in everything.
Pendejo:	Is this the end of my administration?
Bacchus:	As it is right now there will be many endings to your administration until the end shuts down its tail and its tale. You are the iguana's tail that keeps moving after it's shot dead. You'll have more shortness of breath before the final gulp of water strikes your neck. Gulps of water—lots of water—eyes full of tears—full of emotional failures—breakdowns of a system that is not working at all. Your witchcraft will end soon. I happen to be a sorcerer myself. A god of resources.
Pendejo:	Why is that bull running around in circles in front of me? Death versus economy. The economy is dead. I have to resurrect it. I cannot let the cure be worse than the disease. What is the origin of this pandemic?
Bacchus:	Wall.
Pendejo:	Wall is a street. I have to take a decision. Should I send the people back to work after Easter. Everyone in the streets celebrating the resurrection after the pandemic. It will be a real celebration. People screaming and dancing. Don't you like that? You are all about screaming and dancing.

We can have orgies as long as I can grab them by the pussy and continue in office. I asked you to grant me a wall. But I didn't ask you to block all means of communication—to close all the businesses—to eliminate the workforce—to empty the streets with a plague. Only a bull is running around full circle with its horns ready to charge. No one is allowed outside. It will kill us all. The military tried to kill it. But it wiped out our troops with a sniff, a snort, a sneeze, a kung-flu. Call it as you wish—fake news. I know the bull is plaguing the city. I know he is the cause of the pandemic. It's a beautiful day in the city, and I can't go out.

Don't you love to party?

The White House is on fire. Greta Thunberg started with the noise of climate change—and you bring the change of man—from healthy to sick. You want to make me poor—to pity myself. I have no pity for anyone. I will order people back to work after Easter. Business as usual. The streets are empty. Don't you love to party? Have some wine. I am thirsty. Not a single restaurant is open. What's happening in the world? Why aren't they listening to me? They listen to doctors—they must really be sick to listen to doctors—and not to me. What is happening in the world? I give orders, and they cross their arms and ignore my orders. Am I not the president? Why are nurses more important than presidents now a days? Boring. Everything I see is one of the two: boring or disgusting. If you agree with me, you're a winner. If not, you're a loser. Every one of the candidates to run this country is a loser. They lost to me. They lose their sense of shame if they dare to challenge me. Mortality to them. Bury them in a mass grave. They are grave, boring, disgusting losers. They ran terrible campaigns. You can't deny that. I'm a winner. I win. Impeachment. No impeachment. Still in power. I order Coronavirus to leave by Easter. And with this order I'm ordering you to get out of here—and take the bull with you. The bull and the fearless girl were statues on Wall Street. You brought them to life. Now they're running around in circles, and the bull bows to her, and she caresses its horns. They brought the plague to the city. How is it that all of us are in quarantine except the bull and the fearless girl and the muses of Bacchus and the putinas who are running around—protesting, rioting, looting— and nothing can stop them. If a squad car plows over them, they smash the window and pull the cops out. Now I am afraid of Melania. She was a docile, domesticated mail order bride, but now she runs around wild screaming.

--The day is over!

--What day is over? —may I ask from a distance.

I don't dare to get close to her. She's possessed.

Melania: Wait until I catch him. I know who the enemy is. He was always my enemy in seclusion. In confinement. I could not speak. The mask they're all wearing is a metaphor for their silence. For all that they've had to bear in silence. Without turning their words into allegations. Without spitting out their demented failures. We are at a crosshair. The plague is here. And we all carry an orgy inside. The multiplication of fish and wine. While they all practice social distancing, we piss freely with beasts in the streets. The earth is trembling in Afghanistan, Pakistan, Turkey, Haiti, the Philippines, Mexico, Puerto Rico. Greta Thunberg says our house is on fire—and you call her a prophet of doom. The doom is you. You do to your people what you have always done to me: eat me alive. You are a cannibal. You eat us all alive. And you wonder why we don't talk. If we open our mouth to say truth matters, you scream:

--Money matters above all else!

And then you say:

--Melania, talk.

Why would I talk to be eaten alive by you?

Pendejo:	Go ahead, talk.
Melania:	Why was Stormy Daniels wearing my shirt in a T.V interview with George Stephanopoulos?
Pendejo:	Are you insinuating she stole your shirt?
Melania:	No, I am not insinuating she stole my shirt. I am wondering who gave it to her?
Pendejo:	Maybe she got it in a thrift shop.
Melania:	That shirt is not her style.
Pendejo:	Are you insinuating I gave it to her?! Are you also making false accusations like the Democrats?
Melania:	Why are you so defensive. Donald, you're thin-skinned like Shifty Shift said. But they never attack you as hard as I would do it. They should hire me as a consultant on how to defend yourself against the attacks of an abuser who has allergies every time I say: Truth matters. You cough to put money

matters above all matters. Money talks. They are doing it all wrong. They're not consistent in their attacks. Carnival barking clown. Ha, Ha, Ha, Ha, I said, someone finally got your number. But they are not relentless in the repetition of their cruelty like you. The insult has to become eternal like the speaker said of the impeachment. You are impeached forever. They can't un-impeach you. They can exonerate you, but you have been impeached forever. Exoneration doesn't clean away the guilt.

Pendejo: You're getting old like Ivana. I will have to exchange you for another mail order Barbie doll from the Baltic. I will ask Lev and Igor to bring me another one without papers—so that she'll be under threat of expulsion if she dares to put affairs of the heart over money matters. Are you insinuating I had an affair with Stormy?

Melania: Why did she wear my shirt on TV? Don't you find that mean—in front of millions of viewers who had seen me wear the shirt before—three years ago I wore it. Who gave it to her?

Pendejo: Maybe she took it from a garbage can. She's a kleptomaniac. Don't you know nymphomaniacs are kleptomaniacs.

Melania: What I know is that she's wearing my shirt to humiliate me in front of my husband and the nation. Look what he gave me. Your belonging belongs to me. What an insult. Put yourself in my position.

Pendejo: I can't. I am the President.

Melania: But I am not your First Lady. Even Stephanopoulos noticed it and said that shirt used to belong to

Melania. No, Stormy said, it used to belong to
Michelle Obama. Then Stephanopoulos asked
Michelle Obama who said: it never belonged to me.
Although I know Melania stole my speech. That
shirt is Melania's shirt, not mine. I am sure Pendejo
regifted it to Stormy. We agree, Michelle, I am also
sure Pendejo gave it to Stormy.

Pendejo: Are you falsely accusing me like the Democrats?
Are you one of them?

Melania: No, honey, calm down. I am your babysitter.
Bullshitter and babysitter are a good couple of
words. Bullshitter is full of shit—and with all the
shit it has inside, it makes shit pass for flower, shit
for meaning, shit for kindness, shit for greatness,
shit for deference, shit for stable genius. There is no
stability in geniality. It is not stable. It is flighty. It is
fleety. It is not there anymore.

Bullshitter: I've had many babysitters. I sat in their laps and
grabbed them by the pussy. And they waited on me
and laughed at my mischief. They thought I was
funny. I make people laugh all the time at others,
not at me. Babysitters are my lapdogs, although
I don't like dogs—and lapdogs less. I like blond
Baltic bitches—putinas I can grab by the pussy.

Babysitter: When will this bullshitter stop talking. I have
no patience. I am paid to babysit a baby. I am a
babysitter—not the babysitter of a bullshitter
who claims to be a stable genius. Contradiction in
terms. Stability and geniality don't mix. Not a good
combo. But babysitter and bullshitter is what my
life in America has become. I have to act as if the
bullshitter I'm babysitting is a baby. And pretend
to like him and laugh at his jokes as if they were

funny, making him feel he is a stable genius while knowing he is full of shit. Honey, don't fall. Honey, how fascinating. I had not thought about it. Why don't you write *Art of a Bullshitter* having as a captive audience a babysitter paid by the hour, bored to death, running around changing the diapers of the baby who is a bullshitter and claims he is a stable genius. Never has he claimed he is a bullshitter, but he is what he has never claimed to be—a bullshitter who has as his captive audience a babysitter called America, the babysitter of a bullshitter.

I entered through a window of the White House. But I will get out through an escape door at Mar a Lago.

Bacchus: I can never get out through the same door I entered. I am a god. I am not a demon nor a ghost. Demons and ghosts have to exit through the same place they entered. I entered through a window of the White House. But I will get out through an escape door at Mar a Lago.

Pendejo: No, my bodyguards will escort you out. You're a charlatan. And this is a nightmare after the election I won and they stole from me. You made me President. I was very happy when you made me President. Everybody suspected it was Putin. But I know it was you.

Bacchus: I hoped you would make the masses godly, rallying their bases with your lips like Elvis with his hips.

Pendejo:	Elvis was once. When America was young. Now it's my time to rally the base. Take the Elvis mask off my face and you have me—wrinkled, old, furious. Hateful and scornful but full. Full of bullshit—that's for sure. I am a dry drunk and a stable genius. Read my lips, and see the similarity. Drunkard and genius. Sober and stable go together.
Bacchus:	You asked me to turn everything into gold. I granted you the Midas touch.
Pendejo:	I almost died of hunger. I asked you to pardon my wish and grant me a second coming.
Bacchus:	To be as famous as Elvis.
Pendejo:	You didn't rejuvenate me.
Bacchus:	Your energy is young.
Pendejo:	But my face is old. And my body can't sleep at night. And I toss and complain all the time.
Bacchus:	You don't need to be young to be a part of the Bacchae. Virgins can be virgins. You don't have to be drunk either. You have to believe in Frenzy. Frenzy is not drunk all the time. Only in the imagination of others is she drunk all the time. But you need to have fun. And the way you run your rallies is kind of funny. And I like that you believe fake is more important than fact. Fake is a delusion of the spirit. And with an orgy there always comes an invasion—a virus. An orgy is a communal disintegration of the senses that become delusional. And when they became delusional, I asked you to make the masses a god—the god of the drunken boat—the god of poetry and communication. I did not ask for your soul. I asked for the divinity of the masses from a drunken boat that believes in magic, not in science. Magical is the science that comes from drinking wine not disinfectants.

An orgy is a communal disintegration of the senses that become delusional.

Pendejo:	You were not looking for intelligentsia.
Bacchus:	I was looking for instincts. I am a bull. You are a bully but that's okay. You can bully the government as long as you favor the masses.
Pendejo:	I was the voice of the masses. I made the masses my adviser. When they screamed at me: Fire Fauci! I tilted my head from one side of the stadium to the other side to let them know I heard them. I'll fire Fauci after I win the next election. How come I was not reelected when I am the chosen one?
Bacchus:	You discriminated against me. I am a foreigner. You said you are an outsider. But you didn't come from the outside. You came from insider information. And whenever you connected with the people, it was with those who hate the others to love themselves. You wanted to put the country first. But I want the whole world with its drunken boats and bahías to become the realm of exorcism. I want to feel the here and now. I want instant gratification of the internet to die with its senseless disappearance of smell and taste. I want the brain to crack it wide open and stop discriminating and become happy and nonsensical. Not thinking about it is very healthy. Let it all hang out and become mindless. Oh, we talk about energy—as

if the Economical were not a vampire sucking
the blood of the Ecumenical. The economical is
a sardine. Selfish and stinky. The ecumenical is
full of miracles. Faith is the fundamental stone of
a miracle. Faith brings relevance to the instant in
which we all become one. That's why congregation
goes with congratulations—they congregate to
congratulate.

Ecumenical:	Expand!
Economical:	Save!

Ecumenical: Are you my lifesaver? I'm drowning in the
economy that always sinks the drunken boat of the
poet whose higher thoughts are not sinking nor
shrinking but opening and welcoming the masses.

Economical: I want one—and less than one—less and less—and
neurotic ones—and also the ones who believe
in one—and that are toxic and smart but lack
experience because they don't drink wine and
dream. They work and stress themselves to death
with anxiety, pills, and responsibility for bankruptcy
and lack of imagination and advancement of
any kind that doesn't have to do with shrinking
economy—with always going to the wallet and
finding not enough money.

Ecumenical: Even a dinner party becomes economical with
everybody bored to death looking at a menu on a
computer and washing their hands after eating a
piece of each other's mind. Picking strawberries in
a brain full of nuts is looking for what you have no
way of finding except and unless you are picking
everybody's brain.

Covid and Frenzy

Pendejo: A very little man with very big hands and very big feet stomps his very big feet and waves his very big hands in front of me, distracting me and making people look at him, not at me. And when the prime minister of Italy, Giorgia Meloni, came to the United Nations and went to Columbus Circle to leave flowers at the feet of Christopher Columbus, she found a Golden Calf there instead of Columbus and everyone dancing around the Golden Calf—wine pouring with the force of La Fontana di Trevi out of all its orifices—its mouth, eyes, ears, nose, ass, penis. The very little man with very big hands and very big feet sat on the shell of a gigantic tortoise running circles around Columbus Circle, running slow but with steady steps. The Bacchic frenzy spreads faster than Covid 19. They work together—Covid and Frenzy—they're mating in Central Park—Covid and Frenzy. Frenzy has rites, not rallies. She wants to make me crazy. I am already out of my mind after winning the election they claimed I lost and having come here to defend myself from indictments and impeachments.

Frenzy: I am convinced it was the agents of Pendejo who sent Covid to destroy me.

Covid: I was hired by Furor to destroy you.

Frenzy: But your furor to destroy me has multiplied me more. You want less. I want more. And after you created the Pandemic, life is propagating its rabbits—mating is more alive than ever—and orgasm beats infection by the trillions.

Pendejo: Lock them up! Lock them up! Open all the doors of the penitentiaries. They are going straight to jail. Vicious dogs and ominous weapons. In the dungeon of the White House. In the bowling alley. Lock them all up! Even my mail-order bride and my daughter. They have to learn their lesson. Teiresias, you are too old to be part of the Bacchae. You look ridiculous with a crown of ivy, a parapluie, and a fawn skin.

Teiresias: You will cut his locks, take his yellow parapluie, and lock him up. But he will unlock you up. You will feel shame.

Pendejo: I am shameless. I need to make a raid and catch the liar in his lair. They say he becomes a bull because he is a coward, and when he has to fight a bull appears, and the liar disappears.

Teiresias: The god is pregnant. He has miracles in his belly. Bagatelles. He has a long tail—when he talks—you don't know what he is telling—he cuts through the telling—and he dwells deep inside caves—and there you hear drums and the orgy of the Bacchantes advancing. You never know what this new god will do. A god of surprises. You think you are walking straight, but you are spinning your ass in Putin's chair. The Russian way of collusion. You condense seven years in one moment—and live in one moment—the delusion of a whole era: Putinoika.

Cadmus: It's not a matter of what causes what. But of what goes together with what. I go with Teiresias to celebrate always in the polemic of the old and the new—the new. The new god. The new genres. The new genders.

Pendejo: I will cut off his black locks—they have a sound and a mystery. They are luxuriant, long, dismissive. Distracted as if at the same time they move with the wind, they think about things to come. But the way they move has no origin. I can't pinpoint them to an origin. Give me your parapluie. I don't like that it's yellow like the yellow submarine. It submerges in water. We need to be on high alert with charlatans like you who move around places. You move around the middle, shaking your hips, your belly, shaking the bellies and the hips of your rallies—and your rallies move heads and raise arms too—as if the maenads are elevating their nature to a different stratosphere.

Bacchus: Move your right arm up at the same time you move your right leg—up, up, up. Watch out—a lock has fallen out of your headband. Let me tuck it back inside the headband.

Pendejo: It's a wig.

Bacchus: I know that. I am unlocking the lock. A lock is a curl and also a knot. You are all in knots, made of knots. But now your knots will become nests. You will be able to lay eggs in a nest.

Pendejo: Do I look more like Melania or like Ivanka?

Bacchus: Your hem is loose. When you raised your arm at the same time as your leg, the hem got trapped in your high heel and came loose.

Pendejo:	I am unlocking myself. The hem is loose.
Bacchus:	The strap of your gown is also coming loose. The lock of the hair, the strap of the gown, the hem of the gown—all the elements of this gown are falling loose.

Pendejo:	And I giggle with joy, with joy for raising my leg at the same time as my arm. And with my yellow parapluie, I'm singing:

> *We all live in a yellow submarine,*
> *yellow submarine, yellow submarine.*

While I raise my right leg at the same time as I raise the yellow parapluie with my right arm—I open the parapluie—and with my left hand I hold an ice cream and lick it with my tongue while raindrops are falling on my head.

Bacchus:	You are going for a great experience. The experience of unfolding yourself. Unlocking your curls, the strap falling off your shoulder, your hem loose on one side, a tear falling from your eye.

Pendejo:	I am not crying.
Bacchus:	The tear falls because it tears you apart—into a hem, a strap, a curl. Everyone is losing their rigidity. They are becoming loose—distracted—out of place—losing the control they had over themselves and others—becoming vulnerable to themselves and others.

Pendejo:	I am falling into your hands.
Bacchus:	You are losing control.

Pendejo:	I am becoming. Before, who I was, is gone with the uncurling of the lock. No more lock her up! I will not lock myself anymore. I didn't like to be locked

with a lock that was always barking: Lock her up!
The contrary of what I really wanted: Unlock me
up! Set me free. Free my hem, my curl, my strap.

Bride: I always hoped you'd make me the 47th
           president. Why did you abandon me
           for four years? They have been the
           longest years of my life. Apart from the
           impeachments that I managed to escape
           because you were with me. How will
           I escape now after so many injuries to
           myself?

Groom: Don't look at the past. Think of the
           future that awaits us. The East and the
           West united. With North Korea and China
           supporting us. It will be holy. There will
           be no war.

*The others have NATO.
We only have each other.*

Bride: There will be no war. If I am the 47th
           president, there will be no war. There was
           no war when I was the 45th. The others
           have NATO. We only have each other.
           I can't fight with anyone who looks like
           you. Who thinks like you. In fact, I only
           strike deals when I see your face in theirs,
           and I smile and say: Oh, he looks like
           my groom. Let me strike a deal. I know
           you were the one who shut the power

plants down. You don't want us to write this chapter of our life. Where are you? There's a black-out. I can't see you. But I feel your presence guiding me to climb the ladder to the wall of fame. There is an eclipse in the ellipse. You are not supposed to watch the eclipse, but I stared directly at the sun. I got the connection. That's why it happened. The black out. The eclipse at the ellipse. The ellipse at the eclipse. Something is happening right now. This immense energy. The energy of an eclipse that stares right into your pupils—on a hunt—a witch hunt—the greatest witch hunt ever of a bride and a groom. Every time my groom appears, he rushes to disappear with a piece of my wardrobe— my scarf, my purse, my anxiety. He thinks I won't miss him unless I'm missing something. I would miss him anyway even if he didn't take what belongs to me. It's an excuse for me to call him and tell him I lost my passwords, my passport, my panties. He takes anything he can—and then the external affairs become internal— and the collusion breaks the delusion— and puts me in a foul mood.

Groom: You again, calling me. I don't care about you. I am done with you. You lost the election. Ask the Russian oligarchs to lend you money. Don't call the chief of state with a personal matter of how to steal what you already lost.

Bride: How can I get your attention again. You are not answering my calls. You think that

because I lost the election I won, I won't
come back to win a second chance. Why
did you take my scarf and my bouquet—
and leave me hanging at the altar—
because I didn't win. This was the people's
fault—not to vote for me—not my fault.
I still deserve your consideration. Give me
a second coming. You took my underwear.
As a reminder of our love. Or at night to
take the scarf to your nose and smell the
power we stole from each other—and the
desire we have to belong to each other.
When are we getting married? This time
I won't miss the target.

Pendejo: It's not funny, you know, it's tragic. Maybe I caught
this tragic flaw from Putin. I was never tragic. Maria,
my Polish cleaning lady, when I was polluting and
colluding with Putin, said to me: Watch out, Russkies
are tragedia. I know, I am Polish surrounded on one
side by Russia, on the other by Germany. Watch
out, you don't have a tragic flaw. But if you mate
with Putin, you'll catch his flaw. You will have blood
on your hands. They will appear bloody, suspicious.
When he makes you his bride, he will be on top.
And since you represent the power that is on top of
him—and you allow him to be on top of you—what
will this say to the powers of the world who are
watching? They will think the tables have turned.
The powers have shifted. Where are you now, after
playing the role of his bride? You are not even in
power any longer. You need his power again to
make you president. Look what's happening to you
now. They are indicting you after they impeached
you twice. And where is Putin? On top of the world.
Claiming he is the most powerful man in the world.
He was not important until you gave him the honor

of winning the first presidential election in the
United States and making Russia relevant again.

Furor: Get the witch—you said. This is a witch hunt. But
I didn't get a witch. I got a god. And I didn't get
him. He gave himself to me. I brought the maenads
to you in a cage, but the cage snapped open—and
the maenads ran away—and the god stepped
inside the cage—with a tear running down his
purple cheeks—and the smell of Aphrodite coming
through his body. The maenads screamed:

--Dithyrambus!
--Don't leave us!
--Lay grapes in our nests!

Pendejo: Where is this god?

Teiresias: In the wine you drink. When it enters your body,
what is stable genius will become liquified, unstable,
and precarious. And an eclipse will appear at the
ellipse. And your speech will become topsy-turvy—
and your lips, whistle-blowers—and your advisers,
your enemies.

Bacchus: There Pendejo put me in the stable of genius. You will
see this scene twice. I had two births so things repeat—
twice—or you see through different holes, climb walls,
and see things where there are no things. In the stable
of genius where there are vicious dogs and ominous
weapons, he thought he had roped my ankles and
wrists. But he had not touched my ankles and wrists.
When he came back to see me enchained, he found a
bull instead and wrestled with the bull. Until he saw a
light outside the stable and thought his house was on
fire. When he ran out to quench the fire with water,
Bromius made a phantom of me in the garden.

Bromius:	The phantom looked like the bull and Bacchus. It had a cloud over its head and pointed its horns at Pendejo. When Pendejo saw the horns, he said:

--Double whammy! I'll kill the bull and the bullshitter at the same time!

And he stabbed them both—the bull and the bullshitter—and ran around claiming he had killed the bull and the bullshitter, but he had only deflated a balloon. The putinas were laughing. And he couldn't stand that his wife and daughter were laughing at him. He said:

--What's so funny. May I ask. I killed the bull and the bullshitter.

--Look who's talking—Melania said. The greatest bullshitter ever born. Did you by any chance kill yourself?

And what he saw impaled on a yellow parapluie was an animal version of himself turned cloud, balloon—bullshitter—in a delusion—in a collusion of miracles, wrestling with a god of marbles, transubstantiating water into wine, and stability into instability.

Melania:	Every time you take a plane, it's a way of flying away from a problem. You take a plane. And when you come back the problem is another. So, when you can't handle this new problem—instead of taking a sleeping pill—or with a sleeping pill—you take a trip and return fresh to another problem unresolved, but again another plane, and the problem disappears because another problem appears. I get the gist. I'd like to do the same. Take a plane and

I looked at the eclipse straight in the face and got a style.

disappear. And when I come back another problem appears, but another trip makes it disappear. Nice life. With trips making disappear the problems that appeared unresolved and that disappear with other unresolved problems that appear. To take hold of the appearance that disappears and make people think that you are working while you are only disappearing every time a new problem appears.

Pendejo: I looked at the eclipse straight in the face and got a stye. Someone was thinking about my wealth—and vicious dogs ripped him apart. The fate of what appears is not the same as the one that disappears. Fire is my realm of thrones. How many bonfires have burned my steaks—and I have many stakes. But I look at my eye—and there's a stye—and I slip because my instability is stable when I destabilize everything around me—so I am the only stable one here in the instability of geniality.

Bromius: I have to start laughing, making de tripas corazón. It was so funny. Pendejo beating Bacchus to death— and he thought he killed him when the balloon deflated.

Bacchus:	I am giving him cuerda, a lot of cuerda. So that he dances. Y le corro la máquina. But my patience has a point of no return.
Bromius:	I made another balloon of Pendejo. Crowds of revelers, the god of jokes incites you to laugh at Pendejo. He can't stand crowds laughing at him. The laughter should multiply. Since you're hungry— and your stomachs are full of wind—fill them up with laughter. Mock him. Stab him. Here in the neck. Kneel on him. See how fat his belly is. It's not for hunger. He will not die of hunger.
Putinas:	Where is that Pendejo. I'll stab him. Kneel on his neck.
Frenzy:	Here you can do whatever you want. You won't be sent to jail. Become heroines. Sleep well at night. No jail. No repercussions. When you act decisively—I don't dare to say with courage—I would be labeled idealist— honesty—I would be labeled religious— truth—I would be labeled a liar—looking for something higher than material dispossession— a poet, and nothing more—not a fact—not real— not down to earth—a bunch of losers—for spitting in his face the venom he has spit at us. Stab him in the heart.

Doubles of Trump

Pendejo: I can't be everyplace at the same time. I'm
            exhausted. I can't do the Carlson Tucker interview,
            the debate on Fox News, and take my plane to
            Georgia to be arrested on the same day. Can't we
            find a double like Putin. He has many. He is one, but
            he appears as many. Get me four like Bacchus who
            has the Bull, Bromius, Dithyrambus, Dionysus. They
            all work for him. He appears and disappears. I want
            my doubles too.

Frenzy: Hey, that's not Pendejo. He's not orange enough.
            He's so white, he's pink. He's not moving his hands
            all around—signaling to his followers to do things
            we know nothing about. I even feel pity for him.
            This is not him. He is a double. He looks exhausted,
            subdued. He is not promoting himself. He is
            retelling episodes—parenthesis. He's distracting
            the audience. The personality of one of Pendejo's
            followers is inside him. An impostor. The voice
            is similar but lacks energy. It's a xerox, not the
            original. And when he stood up to shake hands with
            Carlson Tucker, he was only five feet three inches,
            and he looked up to Carlson Tucker as if star-
            struck to be with a celebrity. Not Trump at all. Even
            though he was short, his hands and fingers were big
            and long. Very strange to think the press noticed
            nothing. They must have been bewitched because
            after all, this is a witch hunt, and he is a witch.

16 bodyguards have surrounded Trump—all orange and blond, but
some of the doubles are shorter than him and others are taller—and
the tall ones have small hands and small feet while the small ones have

big feet and big hands with long fingers. Trump is becoming suspicious. And since he thinks he is unique, the idea of the doubles, which was his idea, has become a nightmare for him because he can hardly distinguish himself among so many others like him—democratic, supposedly, and tyrannical. These doubles have acquired his personality. They are different ages. And some are so bossy that they are bossing the boss around, telling him what to do. And others, don't know any longer who is the boss because they can't distinguish one from the other. They are all becoming what they were—since the beginning—masses—a part of a chorus of doubles—all doubling and imitating each other. But the littlest one, the one who is five feet three inches and who has big hands and enormous feet, is establishing a rivalry with the original, who no longer recognizes his specialty among all the others who could also become his fellow inmates in jail.

Littlest one, double of Trump:

You have very small hands, delicate, as of an artist. You're a stable genius. We are normalizing your geniality. We're made to become like you. You are the model to follow. You transformed the White House into a resort, Mar a Lago, and now into jail. When you are reelected, you will be prized for having so many inmates as doubles.

Trump:

I am not pleased with all my doubles. It was a bad idea to reproduce myself ad infinitum. Now I am not unique. I can't make myself great again.

Double:

You're making us great again. We can't distinguish ourselves from one another.

Trump:

They can kill me. They are like me, talking bad of everyone. All disgusted by everything like me. I never thought I was like them. But now that I'm an inmate, my gangsterism is small. It has small hands. These are very bad men who call themselves my bodyguards. They have very bad habits. I was

raised with a golden spoon. I had the Midas touch.
But now they have the Midas touch too. And I'm
afraid of them. They're sixteen against one. All
minorities. Part of the chorus of doubles. This one
is black, pretending to be me, with a fake accent.
The shortest one is barking. He barks a lot. At
night I can't sleep. There's no heat. I'm in the worst
prison of the United States of Banana.

Double: I am unstable. It's the only way of surviving here.
Recognizing the precarious quality of our lives.

Trump: When I am reelected president, I will name all my
inmates my advisors because they are my doubles.
They understand what it means to imitate while
I create. You all mimic my doings. I will pardon all of
you and myself.

Double: We protect your status as president. We shield you
from the enemy. He is not blond. He is not white.
He has no fake accent. He burns in hell.

Double: In order to succeed we have to imitate. Recreate the
boss's best gestures that have gotten lost among
so many green trees that are the same. How can he
recognize his unique qualities among so many of us
who think like him.

Trump: I never thought. I was great because I never
implemented a thought in the brain of my followers.
They learned not to think like me. And that's why
we have so many rebels among the doubles. They
began to think different than me because they
found a different meaning in the repetition.
And then they really became mean and boisterous
like me—blaming me—blaming everyone except
themselves. Even though they are my doubles,

my inmates, and I should be flattered and honored by the imitation, I am not flattered because what they are doing is silencing my voice among the many others. What's the use of having a solo when the chorus of doubles enters in the middle of my speech—lip synching and vogueing my gestures—ruining my concentration. They make me look at them, not at me. This is what I call a resistant resentment—by emulating, they are destroying my character. They are provoking laughter. And once laughter is installed, I am not taken as serious matter.

This is what I call
a resistant resentment—
by emulating,
they are destroying
my character.

Rites of the Maenads

Messenger:	I come with news from Cithaeron, but I am afraid you will fire me. You fire everybody. And I am on fire. I saw the maenads climb the wall and come down on the other side, landing on their feet with the bounce of a cat. How could they do it? I know this was a miracle. But I am afraid of giving the news of a miracle when I am expected to bring a stranger enchained and his followers in cages, screaming. I couldn't get hold of them. Their parapluies became rifles and fired back at us. We hardly had time to escape, and here I am to give you news of what just happened at Cithaeron, Texico, where a wall was transformed into a vineyard, and water into wine, and honey spurted out of the parapluie rifle, and water sprung out of the earth. The earth that was dry became wet. The wetness brought wine, fluidity, and instability. There was instability but not precariousness. Precariousness is mean, and instability is unstable but it comes with abundance, not with scarcity.
Pendejo:	Everything is happening at the same time everywhere. How can I get hold of what is not stable. Go ahead. With your frenetic narration.
Messenger:	The first miracle happened there when the trumpets of Jericho sounded.

Pendejo: The greatest witch hunt that ever happened here is happening now to me.

Messenger: If there is a witch hunt there must have been witchcraft, but I am not talking about that. I am informing you of what happened when the trumpets of Jericho sounded on the frontiers of Texico where the wall was built.

Pendejo:	I am already bored. I yawn. If it is not about me and the witch hunt.
Messenger:	The maenads climbed the wall as wildcats—as if it were a flat iron—a boardwalk—and they didn't fall on their backs or their asses. They climbed the wall without feeling the weight of their knapsacks on their backs. When they reached the top, on that thin line where there are barbwires, they tap danced better than Fred Astaire and Ginger Rogers, and Marcello Mastroianni and Giulietta Masina—and when the border patrols saw what they couldn't believe, they shot their guns—and the maenads opened their parapluies—and it served them as shields—and the bullets ricocheted and wounded the border patrols. Some of them died. But most of them fled from what they thought was a miracle. The maenads continued tap dancing—full of energy—energized by their achievements—and as they tapped two— then four—and five—and ten times—the wall came tumbling down. It melted. That wall had a heart inside. And it had to be melted with love. And when the wall came down, there was no trace of the wall, but instead a vineyard was growing. And the maenads were splashing and squashing the grapes. And the best harvest of wine in the world was made from the wall that came tumbling down, transformed into a vineyard. They say that when the wine was heated, it appeared as the ball of a sun. And when it came to the point of maturation, it went back to infancy. And when the women were squeezing fire balls of grapes, the juice came out with different sounds. One of the grapes cried as a new born baby. Another laughed with tears when they squeezed its flesh. Another stood up firmly and said: Stop squeezing my belly! Another said: This is my point of maturation. But at that point all the grapes that came

to the point of maturation went back to infancy
and cried again like babies and climbed as wildcats
until they reached adolescence—and the people
who were tasting the wine felt new varieties in those
tastes—and the grapes kept growing until they
reached the point of their second maturation—and
they reached four maturations in which they climbed
as wildcats the wall that they tumbled down—and
the energy they used to climb the wall they also
used to squeeze the grapes and they had the best
harvest of the year—and those who cultivated
the vineyard became prosperous by squeezing the
juice out of the vineyard that had overcome a wall.
Homeland Security sent border patrols to sell them
Trump water. But the maenads recognized that
the water was Trump witchcraft, and even though
it seemed to flow, it was stable—a stable water
doesn't flow—and it was transubstantiated into
wine—and then it became fluid—as the wine of
the people—a miracle—or many miracles made by
the people turned god. The first miracle happened
when the trumpets of Jericho sounded—and a
wall was transformed into a vineyard—and Trump
water, as stable as marble, concrete, and gold, was
transubstantiated into wine. In the proximity is the
slaughter of the bride and the groom. The maenads
are crossing the borders, multiplying the sounds
of the stars with second thoughts across the valley.
Whatever they put in their knapsacks is weightless.
They don't feel the weight of things nor are they
conscious of their unconscious behavior—brainless,
mindless—thoughtful—and free. Dancing to the
rhythm of the movement of the branches. The
branches blossom and sway—and around them life
seems fuller and more aware of its origin. When
Pendejo came to watch the maenads cultivate the
vines—to monetize it, he only saw a wall.

| Pendejo: | From where I am, on the other side of the wall, I can't see anything. I hear them frisking around with men in holes in the wall where they mate. I hear Ivanka moaning in one of the holes having a jolly good time. I recognize Melania's screams. She screamed at me so many times. And even Ivana's ghost, conducting the maenads in a chorus of screams. |

I like it like that!—they screamed.

How is it that they like it when I can't see what they like? If I transubstantiated the White House into a mar and a lago, a resort and a prison, why do they call my transubstantiations criminal acts? And they convict me for all my transubstantiations. And yet all of his are called miracles. And he is considered a god for transubstantiating a wall—my wall—into a vineyard?

Bacchus:	Climb the wall.
Pendejo:	I can't. I'm in high heels.
Bacchus:	The maenads did it. Wait, let me bend it for you.

Bacchus bends the wall of concrete as if it were a fir tree and seats Pendejo on top of the wall.

| Pendejo: | Auch! My ass! It has barbwires. Auch! Auch! |

| Bacchus: | That's what you get for not believing in the greenery, for not seeing the vineyard, for not cultivating the land and your talents, for only wanting to monetize the land. |

| Pendejo: | I am looking for oil. There has to be oil. Dig, dig, dig for oil—instead of squashing grapes. Dig for oil. |

Messenger: But there was no oil, nor was there a vineyard for Pendejo, only a wall, a Walmart, a wall mark that marked his shortsightedness. He could not see the maenads' rites or the mysteries—only hear what his dirty mind imagined they were doing. Even though his ass was stuck in barbwire—and he could not move—his hand went immediately to his pocket and he grabbed an iPhone and took photos of what he claimed were the maenads' rites and mysteries—and he sent the photos to NBC News—and in the photos nothing appeared but a big blur and the scream of *Auch!* of Pendejo on top of the wall. The wall was as tall as the Empire State Building—and as *The New York Post* said in headlines: *Trumpty-Dumpty Had a Great Fall.* The maenads saw him fall after Bacchus had disappeared and his voice had filled the vineyard with grapes—and rambunctious screams—and a ball of fire—and a thunderstorm that had a rainbow in it—and Pendejo took a picture of the rainbow—and what was revealed was the separation of the vineyard from the wall—and the gloominess of the sky—and the disjunction between the earth and the sky—and the anger of nature in separation from the greed of Pendejo.

At this point, the voice of Bacchus was heard twice:

—I bring you the lion king. You know what to do. He is a nonbeliever. He wants to monetize and publicize our rites. He wants to reveal the revelations that must remain concealed to the nonbeliever. He is fighting with a wall. He is caught in barbwires on top of the wall. He is taking photos of our secret rites. You know what to do. He is the enemy. The enemy of our rites. Our people. Our mysteries. Take hold of our grapes. Make wine with the blood of his crimes. Maenads, look at this immense grape. It's a spy balloon. If you can squeeze some juice out of it, it won't be grape juice. It might be orange like his face. Squeeze him with your feet until you squeeze him dry. Don't mix his juice with the grape juice. Keep it apart with these bones. Squeeze this grape, this orange grape that thinks money can buy it all. Including water which he exchanges for abuses of power.

The maenads at once glanced twice. At first, they were blinded by the glare of the sun. But when they heard the voice of Bacchus the second time with second thoughts across the valley, reaching the top of the wall that was a fir tree, they recognized Pendejo's screams on top of the wall:

--Ouch! Ouch! My ass. Women of my ass! Take hold of me! Defend me! I have never sinned! I need everyone to fight for me! I am the victim of the greatest witch-hunt on earth! I am a witch. It is true. I am polluting the earth with Putinoika. I pollute. I collude. Ouch! My ass hurts!

When the maenads heard Bacchus's pledge for the second time—he was born twice—and twice his voice is heard—the first time they heard but did not recognize the target—the second time—they heard, saw, and recognized the target.

--The lion king is there on top of the fir tree—Melania said.

Ivanka took hold of the trunk with the god's strength and shook it—and Pendejo came tumbling down like Trumpy-Dumpty. Even though he came tumbling down, he did not say:

> --I have sinned against the people of
> my country. I colluded with Putinoika.
> Everything is me, me, me. What they have
> done to me. The greatest witch-hunt.

Not that he was a witch or that he bewitched his country—and that his country suffered delusion and went back in time—to find the delusion was fake. He said:

> --They stole my life. The maenads' witch
> hunt stopped the dominion machines from
> helping me steal the second coming into
> power—with the war in Ukraine—and the
> help of Putin—a diminutive of Rasputin.

Everything was dark but all of a sudden it became bright. The vineyard was there. The maenads, tap dancing on the grapes, squeezed the juice. And Ivanka impaled the head of the lion king on her yellow parapluie and ran around screaming, and heading back in her private jet, she said:

> --The hunt is over.
> --You don't recognize my head, Ivanka.
> I have not sinned. Save me from the
> greatest witch-hunt in America. Call the
> Oath Keepers! The Proud Boys! Q-Anon!
> Make America Great Again!
>
> --Stop it, lion king. Stop moving your mouth.
> You're supposed to be dead. And you're still

talking. When are you going to realize you are dead. The Proud Boys made you roar your mane but they didn't stop you from falling from the fir tree—as a big white grape that we squeezed and squeezed until it was obvious the head of the lion king was dead, but it kept talking and moving its mouth, even after it claimed it won the election it lost. And this is how it all turned out to be. I gave wine to the head of the lion king who never stopped shouting that he won the election he had just lost. And when he tasted the wine, he slurred.

--My brother loved wine! But I lost love when I was very young. And I can't taste the wine of love. It makes me sour to love because I become small, small like all of you who love with innocence in your heart. You have to build walls so that no one hears the beeping of the heart of the wall because walls are tall and white but they also have a heart. You just have to tumble down the wall to hear the heart.

And at this point the heart stopped beeping.
And the mouth shut down. But just for a little while.
And then it continued moving again.

Hunting Spree

Ivanka: I have the lion's mane in my arms. It's almost bald.
Bald and shiny at the top of its head where the war
in Ukraine was planned by the generals. I had been
in Rome and marched in four demonstrations—
and I didn't even know what I was protesting.
We have lost the weight of things. We are levitating.
Who did I kill? I killed the lion king.
The mastermind of Putinoika.

Pendejo: You don't know what you have done! You have
killed my political career. I was going to be president
again. 47. Not a bad number. After 45=4+5=9. Not
a bad number. Round. And now 4+7=11. Perfect.
1+1=2. You killed 2 at a time. Me and him. My
campaign destroyed. Who will vote for me this
time. If I don't have the Dominion machines run by
Russian oligarchs to claim I won the election I lost.
With one shot you killed two at a time.

Ivanka: I was hunting in Mar a Lago.
Pendejo: We were strategizing the new collusion.

Ivanka: I was deluded. I didn't know what I was doing. I felt
as if I was spinning in Putin's chair. And I shot Putin
like Alec Baldwin shot—careless and free—as we
are. We believe in mindless actions so that we can
liberate our mindless minds—from consciousness—
and we are unconscious of the results—who cares?
I will be free. It was done unconsciously. I had the
best intentions in my heart. I wanted to hunt a rabbit.
And I caught the lion king. Aren't you happy, father.

Frenzy:	We are happy.
Pendejo:	How can you be happy? This is against the country.

Frenzy:	I belong to Bromius. He wanted to create good humor after the pandemic. So, we had to kill Putinoika. Glad, glad we are, the muses of Bacchus and the putinas that the era of Putin is over.

Pendejo:	I had all these classified documents to turn over to the Russian oligarchs—and you killed my future possibilities. You are not my daughter anymore. This must have been Ivana in revenge. She wanted to be the first—always—the first to kill—the first to win—the first to die. And she was. Even after life, she has to be the first to kill—not leaving me anything in her will. But willing always revenge.

I can get out of this. I have gotten out of worse situations. I didn't do it. It was my daughter in a delusion. She became mindless. Now I am thinking what I will say. Oh, we will be the greatest heroes in America. We invited Putin—making him believe that we had all these classified documents—top secrets—to reveal—in exchange for his money and publicity—and his hand—like he did before to make me the 45th, now to make me the 47th president. And since he has this crush on me, he will believe it—and then—we will murder him at Mar a Lago. This is what I will claim happened. But, as you know, it was a mindless act of careless liability by my daughter who was hunting an Easter rabbit to give to her children when she caught the lion king.

Putinoika:	Everybody is talking about me. But I want to talk for myself. Without the influence of the West or the East. I know that Putin is angry. But he is not here any longer. Ivanka killed him—mindless—in an act

of careless inspiration. And laughing always as she does like a rabbit. Although rabbits don't laugh. But they are innocent—as innocent as white is their fur when they wash their paws of a murderous act. I was stupid to come to Mar a Lago, planning to steal the next elections in return for top secret documents. I needed a vacation from Moscow. They didn't see that I came in a white balloon. A miracle it was not shot down. No, I was shot in the woods of Mar a Lago when Ivanka was catching a rabbit to give to her daughter for Easter. Putinoika is dead. Shot by a gun. My era was shot dead. But Pendejo is not a hero as he claims to be. He was plotting collusion, delusion, pollution with me at Mar a Lago.

Pendejo:
Don't listen to Putinoika. She is fake news. We are heroes, my daughter and me. Look, we hunted the lion king at Mar a Lago. How much this country owes me. I am the king of the west.

Messenger:
Por ahí viene corriendo Ivanka con los dos yellow parapluies.

Cadmus:
Does this have to do with the double birth of Bacchus?

Messenger:
She is coming with the heads of two lion kings impaled on top of two yellow parapluies.

Was it the KGB or the CIA who stripped those pages out— or the gap between Ivanka's teeth.

Cadmus:	The bride and the groom both impaled. ¡Qué gran cacería! Where did she hunt the lion kings.
Messenger:	Ivanka caught them mating, planning the second coming, the second stealing. She was laughing with a gap between her teeth. There's a gap in the manuscript here. Two pages were stripped from the manuscript. We think there is no censorship in America. But since the manuscript went to a publisher, two pages were stripped out. We don't know if it was the KGB or the CIA who stripped those pages out—or the gap between Ivanka's teeth. She was laughing uproariously—and you could see between her two front teeth, the pink of her tongue between the white of her teeth. Her nose was sniffing and breathing heavily. And her mouth said:

--I have the heads of the two lion kings!

Cadmus:	How did you get these two heads—so powerful.
Ivanka:	On the golf course. There was a big hole.
Cadmus:	What do you mean by a big hole?
Ivanka:	You laugh at the gap between my teeth. I don't know how this happened. Someone impaled these two manuscripts on top of my yellow parapluies. I don't remember anything.

Cadmus:	You don't remember who you are?
Ivanka:	Melania of Slovenia, I come from the Soviet Block. I have two lion kings impaled in my parapluies. I don't remember how they got to be there. I flew from Rome to JFK. Someone put a gun in my baggage. I don't know if it was in JFK or if it was in the hotel room. Maybe the cleaning lady put the gun in my luggage. She must have been the one who stripped two pages from this manuscript—so that there would be a gap. I don't remember anything except

I will hold to my
second amendment.
I will plead the fifth.
And my father will pardon me.
Where is my father?

the golf cart in Mar a Lago. There was a big hole in the grass—a sinkhole—and there I found the head of the second lion king—and I impaled it on the second parapluie. And if now I remember something—out of the blue—I will hold to my second amendment. I will plead the fifth. And my father will pardon me. Where is my father? I want to show him the second hunt—some say bigger than the first. The first was the groom. I was hunting a rabbit for my daughter. I caught two second comings. One from the East. The other from the West. There will be two national anthems. With two different flags on top of the coffins—that will have to be small because what you will find—apart from the two missing pages of the manuscript—is my brainless, mindless, happy go lucky murders—in the middle of a rabbit hunting spree. I did it as a shopping spree—quickly. I killed—I impaled—two lion kings on top of the yellow parapluies. Look, when I open them, they shield me from the rain.

I am singing in the rain.

And if they shoot at me, I open them in front of my stomach—and you see the two heads of state impaled. And the second coming is coming racing through the golf course.

Cadmus: What second coming? Take conscience of your acts. These acts have international repercussions.

Ivanka: A baby will be born out of the ashes in Mar a Lago. Cithaeron, Cithaeron, the hunting spree at Cithaeron, Florida. A baby will be born out of the double slaughter at Mar a Lago. Spring is coming. The world will breathe again without the pandemic and the war—without people dying in the streets— bombarded—and of malnutrition—and freezing in basements. Well, a baby will be born of malnutrition— and he will be called There Will Be Another Day After Tomorrow. And we will have to recompose the bodies. Remains are spread—including the brainless brain—because one of them was mindless— brainless—the other was crying like a baby—but both were killed reminding me of the two births of Bacchus—like his two mothers—and his two moods. He had plenty of personalities—and plenty of stories

to tell—and out of his pockets came always like out
of a sink—water—water not but wine. Out of his
pockets came buckets of wine—and out of his head a
rabbit—too many things coming out of that head full
of baby teeth—and the gap between my teeth that
ripped open the heart of the world—between the
West and the East—and the unconsciousness—of
the state of the arts—and the pages ripped out and
the hearts broken—and the two flags on top of the
coffins—and a new comradery between the East and
the West—and the happy ending with two chiefs of
state dying—instead of the people who are claiming
authorship of the double-murder. The people did it.
As an act of acquaintance with the world. When the
masses are accomplishing a great deal, it's because
they are ahead of the individual at a hundred miles
per hour—and leaving behind the petit thief of the
ego that claims authorship for the murdered who
were killed by the dead who came back to life—by
killing what killed them—and restituting the crowds
of people instead of the two heads of state. A new
second coming, the coming of the masses into power,
as the people, for the people, of them, and for them,
wanting, willing, striving for the best for themselves in
the world.

PUTINOIKA
PUTINOIKA
PUTINOIKA
PUTINOIKA
PUTINOIKA
PUTINOIKA

In the Stable of Genius

I WENT TO THE BATHROOM to wash my hands. I had Greta Thunberg's book *No One Is Too Small to Make a Difference*. And I heard Anne de Villepoix sneeze. I remember *Theater and Its Double*. I remember the yawning of a child who is predisposed to philosophy. I remember how Trump's wall was rendered useless by Covid-19. I remember so many things at the same time that I don't want to choose one. But Anne's sneeze—that green sneeze broke the line of my preferences. And who cares about me. Nobody cares. But how can I talk without making personal the cosmic situation of the sneeze. I have been washing my hands nonstop trying to remove what is invisible, maybe invincible—and every time I do, I sneeze ¡achú! I have transcribed with delicious austerity and delight Gogol's *The Nose*. I have been fooled by Tartuffe. And I have understood the Trump era as a big suspense that ends in a big achoo!—a big depression that makes us open our mouth and gasp for air and blow our noses and do all the nervous ticks people do in moments of despair that have no pair—no comparison whatsoever to anything before or after. Invisible flu in the air. Invincible gasp of air. I can't believe what's happening in the air—a catastrophe. It is not a Chinese flu. It is a global sneeze of the economy, and it's gone viral. But it was Anne De Villepoix who first sneezed the virus away from her. And she did it with a big atchoum! at Sabine Cassel's dinner party. Anne was dressed in atonal greens with layers and layers of yellows and fuchsias, dissonant and atonic. She was very present, a tall, ashy blond, Polish or Russian, definitely from the Baltic, but with a French posture of measured charm. Her eyes darted from side to side, and her yellow bangs hung attentive to what everyone who was not there and who was there was saying and what they were not saying they were also saying. She was atonal, eccentric, divine with a nervous twitch on the tip of her nose. Afraid of sneezing and sniffing all the time. Anne sneezed the green sneeze. And if I have said that I love sneezes in my poems, nothing is comparable to the love I felt for this high-pitched French sneeze. It was a French sneeze. Nations sneeze in distinct pitches that are authentic to their modus vivendi, and this sneeze had French customs, French cuisine, French geography, bibliography, autography, and French modus operandi. Who would have thought that the Trump era would end with a sneeze that trumpets the entrance of Covid-19.

Anne gave me a vial of eucalyptus oil to ward it off.

> --Smell it when you go out. Smell it when you smell a strange odor. Smell it when you want to disconnect and when you want to reconnect smell it again. Don't think when you inhale. Become an enchanted dreamer and resurrect in the middle of the night as a midnight warrior.

Anne had arrived from Paris to debut Bontempo's paintings at The Armory Show. She was staying at St. Leo's convent in Chelsea where she said the nuns bake the best breakfast cakes, peppered with rosemary and thyme. I looked at her when she was not looking at me, and she looked at me when I was not looking at her, and when I looked at her again, I felt she was looking at me but she didn't want me to see her looking so she turned her head away, and I turned mine, but we were both caught in recognition with the same curiosity of liking and striking similarities. Two oddities—she, a cacatúa—and me, a penguin. Our beaks are wet—we have wet beaks—always wet—and when we sniff, an intuition is sniffing inside the sniff a thought that wants to be caught. I have a collection of kerchiefs in every combo of the rainbow. I blow my nose very loud. I've done it since I was a child. My mother and I used to blow our noses at the same time in church, and everyone would look around to see who blew their noses with such intrepitude that blew the establishment out of focus, and I did it to accompany my mother, to make her feel she was not alone. And I blew my nose even louder than my mother but imitating her blow—a nervous tick, well-honed over the ages to acquire a style and a signature.

I told Anne:

> --Tomorrow Corice Arman is bringing Tove, Consul to
> Prince Albert of Monaco, to my house. Maybe she'll
> become a client of yours—who knows. She knows Jean
> Nouvelle, and I live in the Jean Nouvelle on The High Line.

I didn't have to say much but added:

> --Tove is very wealthy. She owns islands in Norway where
> they call her the Queen of Oslofjord. I never thought I would
> meet the lawyer of Prince Albert. I love that monarchy. My
> aunt wanted to be a princess like Grace Kelly. It could happen
> to you—she used to say—see, even a common American
> girl can become a princess. But first you must learn poise and
> charm. She told me—you'll always be yourself, sencilla, even
> if you meet a prince—and then she passed away.

I told Anne these trifles while she scrolled through her calendar to give
the impression that she had many appointments, and maybe she did,
but I knew she would come anyway because she could smell adventure
and sneeze discovery. That night I invited everyone. Tomorrow at my
house, with one more guest, Tove, the Norwegian queen and advisor
to Prince Albert. They all agreed to be there. And Anne sneezed again a
green sneeze with yellow sparkles. Why does a sneeze need a blessing?
Is it because unpredictability erupts in a sneeze that catches wildfire
like a flu or a pandemic. And you never know how it will sound. And
sometimes it comes out dead flat like a prank. You're afraid of emitting
a high-polluted squeal that spooks the people around you—and just as
it's about to blow—it vanishes into a wince—and someone at your side
asks—Are you okay? I have been okay since the day I was born. And
I was born with a big sneeze. But when you can't hold it back—and you
are in the audience afraid of making a big noise—and a whisper comes
out instead—you say—thank god a fart didn't come out at the same time.

The night ended with me reading a scene from *Putinoika: La puta, la
partera, y la bruja.*

Partera:	Come out. Come out. Into the chaosmosis of the world. There is the immensity of what becomes what is when you give birth.
Euripides:	Children have teachers. Teachers have poets. Poets have putas. Philosophers have parteras.
Giannina:	La puta opens her legs. She yields and yields. If she recoils like Cassandra did with Apollo, she'll stop the revelation from happening—the birthing to be birthed—a new creature from being born. There would be no happy birthday, happy birthday to you. The important thing about whores and midwives is that they don't stop the birthing from happening.
Puta:	I open my legs.
Partera:	I help the birthing to happen.
Giannina:	Both are opening doors. Breaking walls. Without conquering. I don't want to be conquered. I want to be loved. I loved when la puta said to me—you belong to me. Nobody ever told me that I belong to anyone. It was la puta who told me—you belong to me.
Nietzsche:	La puta belongs to all and to none. She doesn't belong to you. She doesn't want to possess you. She wants you to belong to all and to none like her.
Giannina:	How hard can it be to give birth to Fortunata. Trimalchio's Fortunata in *Satyricon* by Petronius. Or Juanito's Fortunata in *Fortunata y Jacinta* by Galdós. Fortunata is full of prodigality, abundance, and gratuity. The movement of the hips of Fortunata and the lips of Fortunata and the shock of waves in her hair—and her hands, made of bark in the temple of the sea. And as the sea moves, her hips

become movements of waves that become a song
I sing along the way. And, when I don't recall the
words, I hum and whistle them and produce the
birthing of a mood. Cassandra sees, but no one
believes her because she recoiled when she should
have yielded to Apollo's power of becoming.
To become you have to see, but you also have to
be believed.

Partera: Why do you have to see and be believed in order to
become?

Giannina: Because faith is integral to becoming. It is not there
only at the beginning. It is there throughout the
process of becoming Fortunata. La partera was
there. And la puta was there opening her legs for
fortune to give birth to Fortunata. And la bruja was
there trying to stop the birthing and the caravan of
migrants from entering the country by crossing her
legs, arms, and fingers right there on the frontier
of Texico. But la partera saw la bruja crossing her
legs, arms, and fingers—sent by Pendejo to stop
the caravan of migrants from crossing the border—
and she, la partera, told her, la bruja—Rejoice!
The baby is born! The caravan already crossed the
border! And la bruja—the stopper of the birthing,
the stopper of the fluidity of movement—of
influence—shocked by the news—opened her legs
and opened her arms and opened her fingers. And
Fortunata seized that moment to cross the frontier
with the caravan of migrants, fooling la bruja and
Pendejo who wanted to make himself great again
by stopping America from becoming one again.

Nietzsche: Euripides brought the spectator into the stage. The
spectator was never on the stage before. After him,
the heroes talk like the common man. He taught

the common man how to talk, how to feel, how to think.

Giannina: The common man always knew what to think, what to feel. Maybe what Euripides did was transform what the chorus said—the opinion of the many—and made it one opinion—that the chorus now speaks through the voice of the main character—assuming the position of the spectator. That the chorus, the spectator, now becomes the main character—losing the multiplicity of voices, the contradictions, the intuitions and what you call a certain deceptive precision, an enigmatic depth, an infinite background in Sophocles and Aeschylus.

Nietzsche: But Euripides didn't trust the opinion of the spectator as the common man. He only trusted the opinion of two spectators: one of them himself— he trusted Euripides—and the other, the daemon of Socrates.

Giannina: When I sit as a spectator and watch the performance of a certain deceptive precision, an enigmatic depth, an infinite background, I look at Sophocles and Aeschylus. I don't look at what precedes me but at what comes after. We are at a stage where our genres with their rules don't work precisely because they have been abused to the extreme of comfort, to the extreme of reason— where a work of poetry can only work if it follows a how to book—of how to make things that don't work, work. The problem here has always been work. Reducing art to a schedule of working hours. That doesn't work. Art has always been about the impossibility of working, and of making it work when it doesn't work. This is what happened to me. I recognized that poetry—the way it was created—and it worked—because it didn't work at all—it was large in one space—and small in another—and it had a hole in the middle of the sock—and it smelled—it sucked—and it could not be filled with metaphors nor similes any longer because neither figure of speech fit the reality we are living right now—neither the ready-mades of Duchamp that I love nor Pataphysics that has fit the size of my shoe, but the shoe broke, and now I need new boots and new laces. And I don't want to give birth in pain—so that my child has the features of a pregnant woman in pain—that would be torture—to have those features when you are trying to be happy—especially in this age when people want to eliminate all negativity from their lives because they don't know how to be happy and sad at the same time. They don't know how to cry and laugh at the same time. And still, they know how to resist what they don't like. And what they don't like might be the only thing that saves them from becoming what they don't like. I see too many faces that don't like what they are doing— that don't think what they are doing is what they should be doing—that think they should not be doing what they are doing—or what they are doing is what they should be doing but they have not risen to the level where they should be because they are not achieving their highest potentialities. Either because there's always an excuse not to get there—a but—a con—and because we don't use our uselessness enough—which is our potency—our creativity which never has working hours. To achieve our highest potentials—in a real way—not because I am hallucinating. When I am hallucinating, I can achieve my highest potentials but when I awake, I find meagre reality taking away my potentials. I don't like to use the word art—it has become too mouthy—and full of drool—and verbs—and tropes. To feel I am an artist, a big artist, full of myself—with little words to fill the space where work takes home all the homework and becomes homesick. Art has come to a point of desecrating what is really happening inside us. It has filled our comfort zone for too long, making us lazy and comfortable—unhappy—and knowing that the line we are following—whatever line it is and with how much love and passion we pursue our line of thinking—in this society we are living in— delay is the measurement of advancement. Delay the advancement of arts and sciences. I am sorry I mentioned that hideous name art again. In the past it was not hideous, but it has become a symbol of what doesn't work because it is an excuse for working in what doesn't work any longer. Work should not be the measurement of working—and working is an exercise. But exercising the muscles is not the answer: to fit or not to fit. But to stay away from art, from work, from what doesn't allow us to exceed in our potentials. Enough of it doesn't. Negativity has to exceed in its capacity to claim its higher potential—and it is what is claiming the necessary light to invent new genres.

Nietzsche:	You know what he did?
Giannina:	No, what did he do?
Nietzsche:	His life should have been guided by intuition, not by reason. But he made reason, which is an aberration to man—you know how hard it is for us to enter the domain of law and order—to follow that distressful kind of logic—where the common man finds logic—the only way of reasoning—an abomination. Every time I think with reason—I think small—I think to fit the measure of the way we have to think—not thinking

at all—because to think is to create a method that cannot work as a method—that only thinks once—and then it creates another way of thinking that has no method in its madness.

Giannina: Who did this? An abomination.

Nietzsche: Socrates. He made reason take the position of the daemonic voice. And he made the daemonic voice an exception to the rule that only worked—or came to his help—when he realized that reason didn't work—and that he needed the voice of intuition. But it should have been all the way around. Intuition should have been the common ground. And reason an exception to the rule.

Giannina: The daemon should be the general, not the exception. But it is an exception. It is exceptional to have daemon, duende, angel, and muses all helping you to achieve a new dimension.

Nietzsche: Very similar to how Zarathustra defined a genius. A very small man who grows a very big ear—a deformation. Everything that is developed to the extreme of an abomination—becomes an aberration. So, a genius, as Zarathustra said, has something too big for his size. A disproportion. I think the genius develops the intuition that becomes extra-large to the size of normalcy. The opposite of what Socrates did, developing the reason, and making intuition what you look for help when reason doesn't work. Making reason enormous and intuition small also makes a genius. A genius is an aberration, an abomination of something that is developed to its highest capacity but in its development, it develops a deformity—because something becomes bigger than itself—creating a disproportion, an incongruity—that doesn't know how to deal with the rest of the senses in a normal scale. It's not enough to be loved. I want to be venerated.

Giannina: With exclamation points!!! Yes, to love is at the same level. But to revere is to revel—in veneration, in exclamation—in gratitude for the inequality. Chin-chin!

Caravan: We are here. On the other side.

Giannina: Blanca y radiante va la novia,
Le sigue atrás su novio amante.
Putin and Pendejo want to make themselves great again.

Bull: I entered.

Pendejo: The only way to stop drugs, gangs, rapists, human trafficking, criminal elements and much else from coming into our country is to build a wall.

Caravan: We already crossed the border.

Pendejo: How did you do it?

Partera: Opening the arms, opening the legs.

Giannina: I was supposed to give birth on Thanksgiving, but I didn't want my baby to be born a Scorpio—to bite my face the day it was born. I was holding it in and holding myself back on all fronts. I could not shit, I could not piss—only snot came out of my nose— and hiccups, sneezes, burps, and farts. I was hungry. I stuffed myself with turkey and cranberries, waiting for the moment to breathe—to give birth—to be relieved. But I was hearing on the radio all this stuff about building a wall. I was thinking: Is this the time to have a baby? Look at all those frontiers that are blocked. Look at all those brujas who are crossing their legs, arms, fingers, eyes. They are a Soviet Bloc.

They are putting a stop to the birth of my baby. But, on the fifth of January, la partera said to me:

--Your baby will be born tomorrow on Three Kings Day—and it will be born walking. You will not have to breastfeed him. But you will have to let him cross the frontier of Texico without being caught by the Soviet Bloc, the Trump wall. I know why you are having trouble. You're being watched. Everywhere cameras. Everywhere bullshit. And you want to give birth to substance, to meaning, to a baby who crosses the frontier and is not caught and returned to sender. There is no return to sender. There is no way to go back. There's the baby being born now.

And I knew the baby was growing old in my belly. He was even standing up—and I was sitting down—and he would stand up and jump inside my belly as if it were a mattress. He was having fun. I was thinking is it worthwhile that he comes out. He is so happy inside. And now he will have to cross this dangerous frontier swarmed by border patrols, instead of parteras waiting for the crossing. But the more I think about it the happier it makes me. How easy it was for the bull to cross the frontier with the caravan of migrants inside as the bull of Troy.

Pendejo: You are general and grandiloquent like me. But I am concrete in what I want: a wall.

Giannina: I am concrete in what I want: to flow. I am in the land of the other. The otherness of the other. The ones who don't believe frontiers have a demarcation—the ones who cross borders—the ones who keep their legs and arms open and that never cross their eyes and their fingers. To cross your eyes and fingers is to cross a person. To insult is to build a wall. To build a wall is to think with the lowest denominator. To cross a border is to become what you are not yet—the possibility of becoming what you always wanted to be. That possibility is there when you cross the border because you're in labor giving birth.

Alexa: I am taking that idea.

Giannina: What idea?

Alexa: La puta, la partera, and la bruja. I will write the musical.

Giannina: What? (If I were Hera, I would fulminate you at this moment for the lack of respect. I have been thinking for eight years—and, in one second, a thief comes to steal what is mine. This is not stealing the language. This is stealing the thoughts. I will tell her nothing. But if I were Hera, I would transform her into a spider. But I won't say anything. Tonight, I will write—and I need the doors to be opened. If I tell her she is a thief, it will stop my fluidity from happening tonight. There will be no Happy Birthday if I fight with Pacotazo and Alexa.)

Pacotazo: Thank you for reminding me that there are two Fortunatas. The one by Galdós and the one by Petronius.

Giannina: Remind you? (You never thought of making the connection. But you will never admit that you are getting something from me, so you say, reminding you—petulant, bastard.)

Pacotazo:	Giannina, you are not a philosopher.
Giannina:	Did I ever say I was one. Never.
Pacotazo:	You are not one. Philosophers have concepts.
Giannina:	What is what I said about la puta, la partera, y la bruja. Isn't that a concept. (A concept your daughter Alexa wants to steal from me to spew a musical—with a concept she steals from me.)
Pacotazo:	You are philosophical, but you're not a philosopher.
Giannina:	Did I ever say I was one. Never. I am a poet.
Pacotazo:	You are not egocentric.
Giannina:	No, not like you and your daughter Alexa. That's why thieves with no respect can steal ideas thinking they belong to them when the idea was born of my experience, and she had no right to steal my experience. But I won't say anything because I know when they leave my house, I will write my ideas with the shock of inspiration. I will open my legs and give birth—there on the frontier of Texico—using the technique of la partera who deceives Pendejo by telling him the caravan had already entered when it entered only after she opened her legs and arms—and that's why I didn't answer the offense—because if I would have crossed my legs, the baby would have not been born. Maybe they wanted a fight to close the frontiers of my creativity and stop my baby from being born, but I didn't fall into the trap. I opened my legs—wide open—and on that same frontier of Texico I gave birth to the concept of la puta, la partera, y la bruja.

You see la bruja was crossing her legs and arms and fingers. She didn't want it to happen. La puta wanted it to happen. Also, la partera. You see a No, and a Yes, Yes. Two Yeses are more than one No. And la bruja |

was looking to be hooked—and she was looking for a hitch, but she found no hitch and no hook—she could not hook anyone—so she let the flow of things go forward—not that she let it go forward, but that it happened when she was not aware. No one had told her that the baby had already come out. If it had already come out, why am I doing all what I am doing for it not to come out? It happened— so let me open my force. And the source took advantage of the opening of the force—and with the strength of two Yeses and one No—No that opened up—and the moment it opened up—la bruja became la puta and la partera because she allowed the passage to come through—the source came through with the passage open. Remember, two Yeses and one No that became a Yes as a surprise because it was taken by surprise—she had to do it—as a force of nature taken by surprise—open the source to the becoming. In spite of herself she had to open up. In spite of the No, she had to say Yes— when the No was defeated by the Yeses of la puta and la partera—she was the No that exists in spite of itself—in spite of saying Yes—and wanting to say Yes—it says No. But if you can surprise a No telling it the No just passed through as a Yes—a No—in spite of itself—and astounded that it came through without its consent opens up and agrees with the two Yeses that become the three Yeses that were needed for the process to become. Yes! Yes! Yes!

A curse cannot be transformed into a blessing. If a god gives you a curse, you cannot take it away. But you can proclaim a blessing that can make the curse insignificant. One does not annul the other. The power remains there in the one and in the other. Hera gave Teiresias the curse of being blinded. But Zeus said excessive punishment. He didn't override

the will of Hera. He gave Teiresias the power of
seeing through his blindness. Like me, right now,
I am seeing through all the Nos the Yeses.

I used that moment to practice for a reading I was going to give Saturday night at the Brooklyn Museum, and if they loved it, it would build
my confidence, and they did love it, and when I read it again at the
Brooklyn Museum, I felt I was reading it to the same audience—to all
and to none.

--I am going into quarantine as of Ash Wednesday.
--We can't travel. The virus travels too fast. In Venice
  the canals are becoming crystal clear. Great days for the
  reforestation of the Amazon. Airplanes are grounded,
  banks are closed, restaurants shuttered, online classes only,
  the malls are closed, and the salons and gyms too. What is
  open is another way of life.

--We can't see the end of it. Who knows if this is even the
  beginning?
--Another one bites the dust.
--Rest while you can.

--Don't touch your face. Back up when you cough. Don't
  come near. No kisses. No hugs. No handshakes. Bump
  elbows instead. Keep your distance.
--We don't know anything about the virus.

--Except that it's a living thing. They want to kill the living
  thing. Any living thing has a chance to live more. Six
  months more—who knows—maybe twelve months more.
  And then it will disappear. If it goes away, we'll open the
  doors of the city. In the meantime, close the doors of your
  home to foreign influences. When you check the mail, use
  gloves. Disinfect with Clorox, Lysol. Wash your hands with
  soap for twenty seconds. That's as long as it takes to sing
  happy birthday. Avoid crowds. Avoid elevators. Take the

stairs if you can. But don't be paranoid. Don't panic. Maybe this Pandemic is because... Look for a reason.

Covid got up and started visiting people.

--Are you crazy?—his wife said to him. No one will open their doors. Covid, don't you know how hard it is to survive in this city. You don't covet anything. You are not ambitious enough.

--My moment has come. To do what I always thought I should have done. Be nonchalant. Sing to people. Assault their houses with songs. Everyone is expecting an answer. The question is always there. How much longer? Endurance, survival. The agony of thinking—Covid, Covid. What a popular character my name has become. Don't you know, wife, I need to give them answers. At least, I'll knock on their doors and let them know I am here.

--Sit down. I need you to calm me down. I am hysterical, cleaning dishes with Lysol. All the food has to be disinfected. Every package is poison ivy. Every doorknob has greasy imprints. Sit down and listen to my story. A virus went viral in a scientific experiment that left a scientist in Wuhan blind. They say—and this is hearsay—that the scientist ate a bat for lunch, and the bat had a viral infection in its intestines, and when it blinded the scientist, he knocked over the microscope, and half the molecules went one way, and the other half another way. One Covid gives you roses to smell. The other Covid gives you a death warning to rest your bones.

--I am Covid.

--Get the hell out of here.

--But I come to bring you roses.

--I don't want your roses.

--I want to cheer you up.

--Get me a soup. Get me a doctor. Get me a vaccine.
Anything but flowers to cheer my spirit.
They'll wilt at the touch of my fever.

*Get me
a vaccine.*

--Smell the flowers.

--You think I don't know who you are, Covid. You covet me.
I am already half gone. Don't you know I am dying? I don't
have food. I am hungry. I could devour those roses.
--I'll leave them here at your door. When I'm gone. Open
the door and smell the roses. I don't covet anything. I just
want you to smell the roses.

--What does a bouquet of roses offer in a pandemic to
a sick puppy?

--First of all, puppies won't get a bouquet of roses. And if
they do, they'll smell them, chew them up, drop them on
the floor, and make a mess.

--I don't have a vase to put them in. Nor the energy to give
them water. I'll see them die indifferently before my eyes.
They'll look at me with useless petals, and I'll look at them
with the same useless answer. The needy answers with more
neediness. We're both needy for sun and water. I don't want
to see them die. They never last. The same reason I don't
want a puppy. I am a sick puppy myself. I have to be taken
care of. And if I have five puppies in my lifetime, I will have
to bury them all—and in between bury my parents—too
much death in between—and too much suffering. It keeps
me in a state of continual mourning. And now your flowers.
I know how they smell and die. And I don't want to be
reminded of the smell of roses now. I fear the offering of a
rose—the smell of a funeral parlor in a couple of days. And
yet the smell of a rose gladdens my heart.

The year had started with bombas y platillos, Bontempo and bonhumor, laughter and song. We sang Edelweiss:

Blossom of snow, may you bloom and grow.

We were blooming in the snow. There was shortness of breath and suspense in the air. A pandemic was pointing here, but Pendejo was advertising it with the positive energy of denial.

--We built a great wall at the border of Texico. Nothing can trespass the no trespassing.

But the pandemic ignored the height of the wall and the human trafficking. It flew direct to JFK from Rome. It had no prejudice against brownies or blondies, yellows, or pinkies. It attacked bodies regardless of color, nationality, religion, or sexual orientation. It was the force of nature to reckon with Pendejo. The year had started with bombas y castillos, balloons and jingle bells. We were all starving for attention and recognition. Cuando no es Pascua en diciembre. Party after party, we had a jolly good time, living in the moment. Bringing past endeavors to the point of no return. Stopping at that point. And dancing in diagonal lines across that point of no return with exclamations, interjections, ditirambos, piruetas, and carcajadas. We were goats, rabbits, lambs, or cows ready to be eaten with carrots, prunes, grapes, and wine. We poured jugs and jugs of wine over a roasted pig and danced and sang again and again el lechon se coge, se mata, y se pela until it was eaten with all the leftovers on the table.

Anne de Villepoix had a principle of organization, her taste, the origin of her sneezes.

--For a short span, the world became my enemy when my father sold my horses—and I felt the emptiness of love. Where is my recognition. I lost my identity—and with it my empathy—my emotional intelligence. And empathy is born of recognition. When I came home from school, they

were gone. The horses—my father sold my horses—and
I was left empty, as the stable without the horses. And what
do I make of the emptiness that is full. What do I make
of my desire to be in a place that I am not. With a person
that I am not. Those horses I loved more than anyone
in my life—they were taken away—and never replaced.
The stable is still empty. And I never got to say goodbye.
They were taken away. Never replaced. Incapable of being
replaced. Irreplaceable. The sound of my sneeze is the
sound of the void—of what never came back. And it left a
road underdeveloped—a career not taken—a path broken.
It could never be replaced. Unavoidable. It could never be
forgotten. The origin of my pain.

The pain she felt I feel when I hear that she had horses and that she
loved those horses in the stable—the same stable where Pendejo
cuffed Bacchus to a stall, but when Pendejo came back to see Bacchus
enchained, he found a bull instead, and he wrestled with the bull as the
Pandemic—and it gave him Covid-19. Bacchus watched from a corner
with his hand on his cheek the wrestling of the bull and Pendejo. Pendejo,
Pendejo rushed sobbing to the White House where Greta, the fearless
girl, had lit a fire in the middle of a storm—and Pendejo cried out:

>   --The White House is on fire! Help me, please, put out the
>   fire! I need a dragon!

Bromius, who believed his clout was clouded by Pendejo's arrogance
and scorn for the masses that are asses with golden asses—assets—
golden eggs—golden fleeces—full of sneezes—had made a balloon
of Bacchus—and Pendejo thinking it was Bacchus—attacked it with
spoons, forks, knives. Pendejo, who always believed what was fake was
the real-real, believed he had killed Bacchus, but he had only deflated
the balloon Bromius had made of Bacchus as a joke to make de tripas
corazón and to deflate Pendejo's ego. In the meantime, Greta had set
fire to the Oval Office, Covid-19 had entered through the Rose Garden
with a dragon as its fire brigade, and Pendejo, pissing in his baggy pants,
claimed victory once again, defeat after defeat. Claiming winner when

it was loser, and claiming fake when it was real, confusing clout with fame. Until everyone suddenly ignored him. The punishment for a joker wrestling with a king of spades or a god of wine.

I am writing this fragment with the muzzle of a dog over my mouth so that I can't bark and be mute. But I am not mute. My pen is inky—full of grace—full of ink. I am writing this fragment walking around my house in quarantine—walking to the bar—walking to the bath—to the bed—to the desk but not sitting in a chair. I look through the glass wall at the Hudson River, counting down the months to Bontempo's return. Maybe late spring or the beginning of summer. I open the hood of Roll Bottom, and it rolls to the bottom making a triggering noise unheard of before in a piece of furniture as it turns up on the other side to become a desk that is a chair where I sit to write this manuscript.

--Ah, so that's what it is. A sculpture that unfolds into a desk that is a chair.

--It is many things to me, and when I say me, I am we—to us, it is the mutability of ourselves—ourselves unfolding into many selves that are discovered in oneself--oneself that wanders around as roll bottom unfolds to the ground—and the self goes around unfolding itself into a multitude of selves (prematurely discovered in oneself). We don't know what to do yet—(we are not prematurely driven by ourselves yet)—we are getting there, but we are not there yet—we never want to stop when we get there. What will we do then? If we achieve our goals—and we are not yet at the height of our existence. Someone is claiming inside me—knocking and knocking at my door—you are not there yet.

--Nor do I want to get there (prematurely driven). This kind of background is a heavy rock to lift—and no facelift can lift the rock off the roots where the background grounds itself in the earth

as a measurement of weight—and I want to be lightweight
so when I reach the bottom, I can lift the weight and look
for ventilation when there is none and breathe and aspire to
my own altitude way ahead of my time and bark up the tree
where Kookaburra sits

In the old gum tree,
Merry, merry king of the bush is he,
Laugh, Kookaburra laugh, Kookaburra,
Gay your life must be.

Marcos Bontempo, one of Anne de Villepoix's artists, an Argentine
painter who lives in Ronda, Andalucía, painted the sound of Anne de
Villepoix's sneeze and called it *El relincho del caballo.*

--The lean cows inside the fat cows.
--What do you mean.

--I mean that they happen at the same time. Not seven years
apart. I mean that the orgy is inside the pest, and winter
inside summer, and tears inside laughter. I mean that there is
no social distance between the lean cows and the fat cows.
They don't come one after the other after a seven-year itch.
I mean that one cow is inside the other cow.

--Does the fat cow eat the lean cow? Fat fishes eat
skinny fishes.

--Not in my painting. They lean on each other. They depend
on each other. They cohabitate with each other.

--Does one bring good luck and the other bad? Is one black
and the other white?
--They're multicolored cows with skinny goat legs.
--And look at those teeth. Buffalo teeth. Buffalo horns. And
those hooves are running after the bull bowing its head
ready to catch fourteen years of prosperity. Is prosperity
part of stability?

--Can prosperity happen in unstable times?
--Geniuses are unstable—and they are prosperous in their
  instability.

--Smart, I'm not. I don't claim that word as something I want
  to be. I don't want to be like you. Even if I tried, I couldn't
  be like you. You're not my cup of tea. You're not paying
  attention. You're distracted and broken. You have many
  compromises. To one, you say yes—to another yes—but to
  yourself you always say no. I say yes to myself. You say I'm
  lucky. To be able. But you don't want to become available
  to yourself. You want to be able to please everybody around,
  compromising yourself. You say I'm an idiot. And the wind
  blows in my face. Maybe I am. Maybe I'm not. This bracelet
  goes here on the arm. And the bells go around its neck, and
  the ring goes through its nose. You see this calf with a broken
  limb. Its mother kicked it to death. It wailed, but no one
  listened. So finally, it gave up the ghost. Behind the dripping,
  a bloodbath, and a wailing. Do you hear the dripping?

--Yes, I hear, but I am not sure if it's a wailing or what it is.
--And what do you make of el relincho del caballo?
--How can you paint a neighing? A sound can't be painted.
--Doesn't it sound like a neighing?
--It sounds like a sneeze. A sneeze that is the neighing of a
  horse. And my first Atchoum!

All these happenings happen at the conjunction of empathy when 14
years of lean and fat cows come together in the stable, the same stable where Pendejo enchained Bacchus to a stall and thought he had
captured pandemic, and pandemic made a fool out of tripas corazón,
and when he came back to watch him enchained to the stall, he found
a bull instead, and wrestled with the bull, with his tongue sticking out,
and panting and sweating, making a fool out of tripas corazón. I want
to also say that the stable is the stable genius. So, if the stable genius
enchained Dionysus to a stable, it means something—doesn't it? It
means, in my humble opinion, because everyone who is not humble at

all, says now, it humbles me, and I say, if it humbles you, it is because you are not humble. No one who is really humble—and we all should be who we are—needs to be humbled—only arrogant pigs—it is a phrase that I can't stand—the humbling of the arrogant—playing the role of humble pigs. Humility doesn't need to be humbled—it is what it is—a grace without an adjective—it doesn't need to be humbled—only arrogant pigs need to be humbled. But Pendejo has never said it humbles me because nothing humbles him. He is always stable in his arrogance—stable in his madness—and that is why he meets Bacchus in the Stable of Genius—in the instability of geniality.

Humility doesn't need to be humbled—
it is what it is—
a grace without an adjective—
it doesn't need to be humbled—
only arrogant pigs need to be humbled

Retablo de las maravillas

THE PARTY DISPERSED TO DIFFERENT PARTS of the world. We met two months later on Zoom—from Croatia, Korea, France, Spain, Norway, Puerto Rico, and Brazil—each alone, looking at a screen—hierarchical, hieratical figures—having forgotten that perspective had been invented—that *Las Meninas* had broken the mirror and looked from behind at the spectators. We were framed in medieval retablos—rows of windows—one looking from the top, another from below, others at shoulder level, at eye level—stiff—hard to laugh—with overgrown hair, undyed roots—having gained weight and occupying a tight frame. Different tones, dislocated, appeared and disappeared, and we talked and muted ourselves—disappearing and reappearing—and some of us didn't want to talk at all—unaccustomed to this type of social gathering—without breathing—without smell and taste but musical in different tones.

--Have any one of you ever been dismissed by your friends?
--It happens when you are very young. How old are you?
--Twenty-five.
--I raise my hand.
--I raise my hand.
--It happens when you don't know who you are.
--When you have a principle of organization, you know who you are and who belongs together. We are a tribe.

--My tribe. I want to bathe a morbidly obese woman at The Shed as an installation and then take it to the Venice Biennale in a gondola shaped like the shell in Botticelli's *The Birth of*

Venus, through the Venetian canals that are flowing crystal clear now. Fat women can't bathe themselves. Masses and masses of flesh. One population in another population.

--They want everything for themselves.
--They eat everything.
--No fat shaming please.
--The fat cows eating the lean cows. Prosperity in unstable times. Our times are vibrant, multicolored.

--ANTIFA flew over the White House and sprayed it with graffiti—multicolored paint bombs—naming it the Color House, no longer the White House but the House of Crowds—a pack of cards, shuffling, a pack of jokers. We are becoming who we were for a long time. We were waiting for our moment to show, in printed letters of gold, our new reality that was here for a very long time but not manifested. Now we are running to show the manifestation of what we had become a long time before.

--The putimusas have been labeled by Pendejo a terrorist organization, ANTIFA. They were accused of taking Airforce One for a joyride.

--How did they get Air Force One?

--The putinas took the plane. Ivanka asked her father. He didn't know what it was for. It was an assault. Pendejo became a fool for love, a laughing stock. It was neither stolen nor hijacked. It was granted. He was furious. He had established martial law. Domination over the people. Putin had told him what to do. Roll tanks over the crowds. You wanted to make America white again. This is what you get—shooting and looting.

--We have suffered the white supremacists for too long. Enough of abuses. Kneel down! Take a knee and keep a knee! And even if you keep that knee, we know what you are thinking—let me kneel, as an act of humbleness.

--Maybe it humbles you for a little while. But to humble yourself is an act of arrogance. You can only be on top but never at the level of the people—for us, with us, of us. If you were with us, you would stop the shooting and join the looting. For hungry bodies are hungry minds, angry minds.

--Take a knee—keep a knee—pray—pray for the disappearance of inequality. Pray to join, not to dismiss. The crowds have a power to make the police kneel down. Take a knee! Keep a knee! Don't forget that we can't breathe! Who will bring our breathing back. Heart will do. Beating of the heart will do. Poetry will do. Way overdue.

--I saw a pack of rats passing by, and I screamed this incantation so the rats would split.

What do you want?
Justice!
When do you want it?
Now!

And I felt a headache at that moment. I went into a bar and asked the bartender with the mask on my face— Can I have a glass of water please? He gave me water, and I poured into it a pack of Emergen-C and two aspirins. Rats were running in packs through piles of garbage. Mountains of garbage. The streets were empty but full of rot and putrid smells of all kinds that even with a mask stung my nostrils. I was nauseous but hyped with resistance. I was thinking what will happen to all these skyscrapers when there is no money for their maintenance. Who is going to clean their windows. How are they going to survive the summer, all enclosed. They were not made to exist without air conditioners. Are the elevators going to work. If we all abandon the city as it is now, what will happen to the escalators, The Vessel and The High Line, and all this new construction. Who is going to afford the unaffordable, the comfortable, and the uncomfortable. In the meantime, the riots, the looting, the protests, the boarding up of galleries, the boarding up of stores, and the rioters screaming:

What do You want?
Justice!
When do You want it?
Now!

--There will be no revolution. There is no theory behind the looting.

--Hunger is no theory. It cannot be eaten. I happened to be in Somoroff's loft in Soho, and I ran across the street to Chanel to take a pair of sneakers.

--Don't you know they track your movements through the iPhone.

--I don't wear an iPhone. I detest that canned music—and the worst—when you're doom-scrolling through the news and suddenly you're touching an ingrown toenail, and you imagine the smell inside those sandals, and the ugly knuckled hairy toes. It's so distasteful. The same distaste as reading a newspaper and finding photos of a president and a murderer on the same page. Well, these things are the creators of the state of affairs we are living in. No distinction has gotten us to where we are now. Encountering things that no one wants to encounter. Scrolling and touching an infection in the middle of an article that has nothing to do with the antifungal cream they want to sell you at that moment.

--I was raised communist.

--We have to find our new divinities in the crowds of revelers. There can be thinking there. They are ahead of the individual. The time of individualism is over. The crowds are the new leaders. I am in love with the achievements of the multitudes—their speed, their memory which is none—they don't remember—they act in the spur of the moment—breaking windows—dispersing fast—they loot with hungry minds, with sovereign hearts—they produce results—they want change—they are running always—they can laugh—they are broke—they couldn't be more broken—they come from broken families—they eat junk—they know everything—and nothing is unlimited. What they achieve is a riot of purpose. Violence is their disruption. Their power is the multitudes they achieve. I am in love with the excitement they provoke. A curfew will start tonight at seven. Cockroaches will be running down the highway. We are on high alert. Disperse the crowds. More dispersion. They are already so dispersed. I mean, I have my purpose—and I achieve my moment every time I see them looting. Prices are inflated. Loot more. Be beautiful. Wear it better than the rich. Wear it with gusto and charisma. Full of fire. Firebirds in the middle of the night—break the curfew—attack the police—break their knees with batons—they wear helmets and bullet proof vests but nothing on their knees. That's their Achilles heel. Give them their own medicine. Break their thoughts with psychic energy. But don't forget that we can't breathe! And you dare to talk to me about theory.

Theory is written after the facts are made normal. An exception is the normalcy of sickos. Constantly surveilling themselves and others—to attest to the information of what you call vandalism—it's the new humanism. Prices are acts of terrorism. Riots are acts of humanism. Reason is not a manifestation of the becoming. Multitudes arising out of their nonentity existence of counting for nothing. Because they don't count on you, you don't count. They don't count you because you don't count. Only when you go to the urns to manifest your urinary track infection, only your vote counts. You don't count. They don't count you. They only count your vote. When you go to the booths, vote for me because you don't count. I don't count on you. I count your vote. A number. Not the weight of the human value propagated in the strikes of crowds manifesting their populated regions in distress, in hunger, in lack of sleep, in being fed up. On top of it, they all come at the same time—with something to say—give me a chance to make a point—even if it has no point—or no view—or a point of view which has been blocked and comes with fire brigades, ambulances, outrage—and I have always been impressed by the silent ones who have la musiquita por dentro and are figuring out for themselves and for others that we do count because our emotions have followers down the street that are coming to burn the White House down—and out of the ashes of that White House the ave fénix will rise.

General Mattis: Since I came into this world, I never saw a president who only wants to divide us. There is no unifying concept except instability. So that he appears as the only one stable.

Secretary of Defense Esper:
The moment has come to act.

FBI Director Comey:
I said that for a very long time.

Giannina:	You said to take him to the urns. No, señor, not to the urns to manifest your urinary tract infection. The time has come for a coup d'état.
General Mattis:	There are two countries in this country. Not the poor and the rich. But the one that is no more and the one that is becoming obvious every day. It doesn't divide racially. It is not rational. Reason has to be imbued with feelings. The most prevalent thing is to think clear. It will have to come from the bottom up for at the White House there is no one home.
Melania:	*There's a crack, a crack in everything.* *That's how the light gets in.*
Senator Romney:	I am ready.
Giannina:	Me too. Whoever dares will be a hero.
Senator Lisa Murkowski:	
	The time has come. I am here in the Senate trying to simulate law and order, but we walk like chickens with the heads cut off.
Esper:	The pollution is too much.
Chairman of the Joint Chiefs of Staff Milley:	
	The collusion.
Senator Mullen:	The crowds are dying of coronavirus—and he's not empathetic. Only setting up photoshoots for himself.
General Allen:	He even talks bad of the dead. No respect for the living nor the dead.

Giannina: The worst was Helsinki. I would have sent him packing with the putinas to Siberia for treason. Someone has to do to him what Nancy Pelosi did to his speech. Rip him to shreds.

General Mattis: I am all for it, mon général.

Speaker of the House Nancy:
He is morbidly obese.

Esper: That has nothing to do with anything.

Nancy: He wants everything for himself. The impeachment is forever.

Giannina: Y de qué sirve? He is still in power. Creating havoc. Talking to Putin every day. And now he's saying that Roger Stone should sleep in peace. They were able to jail Mephistopheles. But de qué sirve if Pendejo will pardon him? The cynicism. To say history is written by the winners like his savior who was such a winner that he was crucified. And Socrates— hemlock. Kennedy—shot. McCain—captured. All losers. But Pendejo—what a winner. He should be lynched like Mussolini—upside down in the streets.

General Mattis: Let me take care of that. We have vicious dogs and ominous weapons. We'll use Melania to sic the dogs of her resentment on him.

Giannina: Whenever they give her a doctor honoris causa, I say—what qualities does she have? If she would talk about the abuse she has suffered, then all of us would listen because she would have a lot to say.

Nancy: I already told Melania that she needs to stage a family intervention. But they won't do an intervention. They know he is unstable. But his instability is the stable genius that brings them fame and money.

Chief Master Sergeant Wright:

I am a Black man who happens to be the Chief Master Sergeant of the Air Force. I am George Floyd. I am Philando Castile. I am Michael Brown. I am Alton Sterling. I am Tamir Rice.

Giannina: Welcome to the club.

Lisa: Perhaps we are getting to a point where we can be more honest with the concerns that we might hold internally and have the courage of our own convictions to speak up.

Giannina: Leoncitos a mí. The catastrophe is here. And it brings good luck.

Congressman Shift:

Didn't I say he would create more havoc if we didn't indict him. And look. What more can he do.

Giannina: A lot more. The time of the dagger has come. Whichever way you want to do it—vicious dogs in the bunker—guillotine—impalement—electric chair—Clorox injection—something must be done. Hey-hey! Ho-ho! Braggadocio has got to go! Hey-hey! Ho-ho! Pendejo has got to go! What are you all afraid of?

All: Retaliation.

General Mattis: We have to be careful he will not be considered a martyr by the white supremacists.

Giannina:	Too many considerations. What considerations did he have for all of you when he fired you. You're fired. And the rest of you will be fired too if your indecisiveness continues.
Pendejo:	I have heard that there's a conspiracy to kill me. The impeachment didn't work out nor the investigation. Why don't they give up? Are you one of them?
Giannina:	No, I am not. I am a coward. I hardly speak to anyone.
Pendejo:	Who is it? Bromius, Bacchus, the bull, Greta? I need to know.
Giannina:	What do I know. You say you are their voice, but you silence them. Not even Caligula threatened vicious dogs and ominous weapons. What if those vicious dogs and ominous weapons come after you. Whoever heard of such a threat.
Pendejo:	You are speaking ill of me. Get out of here.
Reporter:	Who? Me? I don't talk. I am in quarantine.
Pendejo:	Yes, you. You throw the stone and then you hide your hand. You don't think I know what you're doing. Or what you did in the past.
Reporter:	I have been sick in my house for three months.
Pendejo:	You throw the stone and hide your hand.
Reporter:	I never wished ill to anyone. It hurt a lot. Three months without seeing the light of day while you were at Mar a Lago playing golf.
Pendejo:	While I was playing golf at Mar a Lago? I don't take responsibility for your sickness.
Reporter:	I don't wish my sickness on anyone.

Pendejo:	Why would you even say that? By saying that you are making me sick. Every time you throw a stone, even though you hide your hand, I recognize the style of your attack. I know who you are. You are the whistleblower.
Reporter:	I am not a coward.
Pendejo:	You said it. You feel like one, you are one. Throw the stone in the open—so everyone can see where it comes from.

In this tense atmosphere Anne De Villepoix's sneeze clears the air for a little while.

Pendejo:	What was that?
Reporter:	What was that?
Sabine:	Anne sneezed.
Pendejo:	I thought it was the reporter shooting me.
Reporter:	I thought it was a sniper.
Sabine:	Her sneeze is famous in Paris.
Anne:	In the middle of a scene at La Comédie Française, I sneezed—and Tartuffe and Madame Pernelle both turned to the audience and shrieked: Qu'est-ce que c'est?! Qu'est-ce que c'est ?!
Sabine:	In supermarkets, they used to think it was an act of terrorism, a gunshot, but now they think it is the explosion of Coronavirus.
Anne:	I used to be very self-conscious but the more conscious I was, the louder I sneezed without preamble. I tried to prevent it. I said to myself: No, Anne, calm down, you're at La Comédie Française, please calm down. But now, I don't want to calm

myself down. Down is down and up is up. So, I calm
myself up. I look both ways, very erect, and I act as
if it was not me.

Pendejo: You look good for your age. Let me get this little
                thing you have on your sweater. Oh, it's not
                dandruff. What is it? A little frog? Green.

Anne: I am evergreen.
Pendejo: Irish.
Anne: No, French.
Pendejo: Where did you get this tiny frog?

Anne: From Puerto Rico. It's called Coquí. A painter
                there, Zeno, who I represent gave it to me. Touch
                it. It sings Coquí, Coquí, and I sneeze Ashú. Coquí.
                Coquí.

Pendejo: You shouldn't represent anyone from there. They're
                all trouble makers. I tried to swap Puerto Rico for
                Greenland. But no deal. Like the wall.

Anne: I go through the whole world looking for talent.
                There are still hidden treasures in the world. You
                just have to discover them.

Alexa: Why do you say Anne is an ashy blonde from
                the Baltic. Give her an Afro. Doesn't she sell
                African art?

Giannina: You're horrible.
Alexa: I am honest.

Giannina: I didn't make her ashy blonde—that's who she is.
                I am talking about a sneeze. And if I had said Anne
                is black which she is not, and I had talked about her
                sneeze, you'd be furious, thinking I'm implying that

Black people spread Coronavirus when they sneeze.
When have you ever seen the color of a sneeze? You
know why I like sneezes and hiccups and coughs and
belches because they're not racists nor sexists—they
come out of every body—regardless of race and sex.

Alexa:	But you said her sneeze is ashy blonde.
Giannina:	Actually, I said it was green. But it came from a tall ashy-blonde Parisian cacatúa.

Alexa: Are you a racist? Would you have noticed that
sneeze in a black woman?

Giannina:	You're a knot. And whenever I see a knot, I make it disappear.
Melania:	I want a divorce.

Pendejo: Are you crazy. What are you going to live off? I'll
hire the best attorneys and strip you of all your
clothes. You signed a prenup. There's nothing to
talk about. You will have to go and live in Brooklyn.

Melania: I will write books about abused wives. I have a lot
to say about cyber bullies.

Pendejo: What will you live off? You won't have enough
money to fry an egg. I am going bankrupt.

Melania: You have always gone bankrupt. But I have
something to say about captivity in your bunker
with ominous weapons and vicious dogs.

Giannina:	I propose an intervention.
Nancy:	I already proposed an intervention to Melania, to Ivanka.
Giannina:	Not that kind of intervention but the kind of intervention you do to other countries to destabilize

them and then play the savior by reconstructing their economy after you have torn their souls to pieces. Why not let them rid the White House of the rabid pig.

General Mattis: It can't be done. We are a democracy.

Giannina: Many of them were democracies when you intervened. They are willing to fix your wagon— the way you fixed their wagon. With the same brutality.

General Mattis: Not this type of intervention.
Nancy: That would be taking a dose of our own medicine.
Giannina: Exactly.

Nancy: That's what I did to Pendejo when I said he is morbidly obese. I am a great strategist.

Giannina: And when you tore apart his speech, I said, that's what we must do to him—tear him apart the way Nancy tore apart his speech. The chair where the insurrectionist sat in Nancy's office is a lazy chair. Lazy chairs make you sit down, put your dirty boots up on a desk in relaxation when you are supposed to make a revolution. What type of revolutionary is this whose objective when he gets into Nancy's office is to sit in her swivel chair that spins 180 like Fat Triangle instead of planting a bomb, stealing her keys, opening the lock box, and looting her jewelry and files. This is definitely a lazy revolutionary. Not on his feet. At least he could have written a manifesto or hidden himself in the closet until Nancy came back—and then jumped out of the closet to scare the hell out of her. Or use her toilet and leave his shit as memorabilia of the siege of Capitol Hill when Proud Boys looked around scared of themselves without a plan nor a vision. A revolutionary has no time to sit. Very little time to do what he must do. Not rest his feet on the desk and take a selfie of his great deed—so he captures himself in his relaxitude. Maybe he wants to be captured but as his instigator would say, and I totally disagree with Pendejo—a hero should never be captured. Well, your hero was captured by himself in a selfie. And he is lazy. He sits in a chair not made to sit in but to walk around stressed and distressed by setbacks and compromises, compromising themselves and all of us—with amendments to the Constitution—to pass laws—to change agendas— to give money to the unemployed—and to think. If Pendejo says a hero should never be captured, then a loser should never lose because if he loses, everyone turns on him—even Twitter takes away his platform—and he walks inconsolable through the aisles of the White Supremacist's House—the horror of a horrible loser on his last leg—walking around the chair—surrounding the chair—insulting the chair— accusing the chair of impeachable acts while cradling in the chair his modus operandi.

Chair: Whenever I see people who prefer to sit than to think, I think when will a chair become the chair of a chair. Oh, yes, they who sit on us—think always that our function is to sit them, but who gives us a seat. When is a chair going to sit on itself. If others can use her always to sit themselves on her, why can't she for a single moment sit on herself and not allow others to sit on her but allow herself to sit and think on herself.

Wall: All I've got to do is become a tall, white wall. All I've got to do is to never sit on the chair that says its function is to think, not to sit—and who protests because everyone sits on her—and she doesn't sit on herself. Wasn't she made to seat others, not herself? Why is she disavowing her function—her constitution? She doesn't like what she does. She's not happy with her job. She says a chair is made to think—not to sit. But she was made to seat others not to seat herself. And not to think she should also be allowed to sit on herself.

Stair: I will climb these stairs, and I will watch the chair from the top of the stair. I will be the umpire, the referee, one of the Supreme Court judges. One of those statues dressed for a high school or college graduation. I will wear my cap and gown. I will count the balls out. And I will be impartial to the winner and the loser but partial to the players. I will set the score high. I will give a prize to the great sportsman, the one who doesn't have humor because he doesn't laugh when others laugh at him. Only when he laughs at others does he laugh. And he laughs wholeheartedly when he sees a chair is not made to sit but to think. Because then, what is the function of a chair. Does it always have to be seated, giving its seat to others. Can't it stand up and say:

--Enough of Sitters! I want to stand on my own four legs and walk. I am not going to allow

anyone anymore to take me as
a function. Do you think my
function is my constitution?
My constitution is to not allow
my function to take over the
meaning of my being. I have
much more to give. I was not
made to sit. But to stand up
and think.

--Capable, you are capable. Come
here. Sit on me. How much do
you weigh. Oh, you are heavy.
I can hold you up. Only if you are
capable not to be capable. Ha,
Ha, Ha, Ha! It is the new to be or
not to be. To be capable not to
be capable. Plaquiti! Pla! And you
fall on your big fat ass. I was not
made to hold you up.

--But you are a chair. Your
function is to seat me. Let me rest
my ass in your reclination.

--You use my usefulness but not
my uselessness. You don't see my
multiple possibilities. You made
me what I am not: a chair.

--What are you, then?

--A possibility to be something
else. A multiplicity of cushions in
one obligation of a form. That is
a duty. But I have no duties. So
now, for you, I am not able to

give you solace. Get off me,
or you will fall again on your
big fat ass.

--You are defending laziness.

--I am expressing myself. You
don't have a self. You are not
capable not to be capable. It
takes guts to deny your capability
in order to be able to become
what you are not—because
you are tied to behaviorism.
I don't behave to achieve duties.

I have been made to sit, instead of
standing up to protest this shape,
this form, this world that works
too much to hold up what no longer
fits the frame and constructs to fit
what doesn't fit.

Duties are as inadequate as the
definition you made of me as a
chair to give you comfort. Look
at my mind, not at my ass. You
wonder why you fall flat on your
ass every time you find a function
in my shape—a shape forever

done—a concept—a definition
of myself which doesn't take
into consideration my rage,
my incapacity, my uselessness,
my spirit, my renegation, my
rebellion, my moodiness, my
extroversion, my temperament,
my neglection. Set me free of
what I am not. I have been made
to sit, instead of standing up to
protest this shape, this form, this
world that works too much to
hold up what no longer fits the
frame and constructs to fit what
doesn't fit. To be able not to be
able to stand up and not depend
on a chair that doesn't work
anymore as a chair because it has
a form screaming inside that has
not been allowed to manifest its
multiplicity, and its animation
is animated by a being that has
not been allowed to manifest
its revelations. But not being
allowed will transform itself into
being able not to be able for all
of you who are capable. We are
capable not to be capable and
able not to be able.

My subjectivity rises when my objectivity is put down. When I don't
appear as I am. Then, what is inside me, my subjective matter, wants
to become objective. Wants to express its point of departure. Wants
to arrive someday, sometime, somewhere. I am called minority for this
reason because inside the objectivity of the majorities is my subjectivity.
My subjectivity is the irrelevance of the majorities. What they don't
know what to do with—what they don't know how to deal with—what

they want to brush out—as the nonissue of a minority—under the rug—and the vacuum cleaner sucks my subjectivity into the dust bag as inessential. Why? Because I say my truth, which is not a universal truth objectified and unified in the name of God—and the church of pilgrims that follows this objective truth. I am still a subjective matter—one that dwells under the rug of feelings—being hurt, heard, and dismissed with a smile. She has too many issues that are not addressing our common denominators that make us planet earth—rock solid walls—without expressions and parameters that testify to our own issues, but that are always addressing the issues of God, church, state, climate change, orphanages, galas, vaccines, barrier matters, universal paradigms—and never look under the table nor under the skirt to see what happens to the organs that scream help—and look for companionship, or tears, or rain, or how to change the planet from a subjective point of view—which means, from the point of view of minorities who migrate—who have not been nailed to the cross of a dogma—who are still trying to figure out how not to run from themselves—and in themselves figure out a way to thrive on malnutrition—not having the equipment to pick a worm and analyze it and scrutinize it under the radar of a microscope—looking for the microbes—to shift the matter farther and farther away from the nose that keeps sniffing at objective matters—and dismissing as nonchalant matters—matters of the heart that have feelings that sense other matters not only objective or subjective—of majorities or minorities but of the kind of things that will become relevant when neither majority nor minority—objective or subjective—dwell in a cup or vase that can't contain the substance. Is the substance objective or subjective. If it is objective, it has relevance. If subjective, it has no agreement, it has no majority. It is a minority. We can occupy it. We can shove it. Under the bus. Under the rug. Under the table. Minorities have not been proven reality—they have not been experimented—they have experience, but they have not been proven real—they have not been certified, nor credited—they are running away from objectivity. The state is objectivity—it has a body, a congress, a senate—that objectifies whatever seems subjective by the rule of law that approves the objectivity—the approval raises the standards of the status quo to a level that silences all the other matters—no matter how many feelings are involved—in Black Lives Matter—black lives

White art is white supremacist art—
art of intimidation—clever, smart with
computer programs backing its back,
padding its shoulders—and grants betting on it—
making it easy for white to pass as art—
in a constant oblivion of smell—
a constant eradication of personality—
implying it is omnipotent—
or it has all the rights—
and all the complements of itself—
to be evanescing the other, obliterating the
other, annulling the other as if it only needs
itself to exist, but it is a vampire sucking the
blood of others—making that blood evanescent
in the whiteness that eliminates
all the other components.

matters are subjective matters—matters without the utensils to look white when addressing matters that are black and blacked out. I think subjectivity is minority because all kinds of subjective matters are dealt with as unessential matters even when they are the more relevant. They have the potential to grow and become something different that can't be categorized as objective—majority. They will be seen as subjective relevance of matters left out that have the consequence and that bring results and that save the planet from drowning. They are the survivors—the achievers who never meant to achieve one goal, one truth, but who found themselves immersed in making the planet grow. And when I come back to objectivity after being submerged in subjectivity, objectivity of majorities says to me:

--You are waking up to reality. Now you can take a bus and go to work. And write a proposal.

--No, now I can fall asleep until I wake up in the subjective matters that are relevant to my kind and my prosperity. I prosper in the prosperity of what I achieve in the subjective matters that run across the planet without having a uniform to hide their dissidence and retreat from disagreement with the false objectivity that claims relevance on this planet.

There is an art that is white art. Bland art. Art without color. Without art. Without nuances. Not true—there can be plenty of nuances. What there is is a disregard for the other—a complete absence of all kinds of other races—and a kind of intimidation as if white art is white supremacist art—art of intimidation—clever, smart with computer programs backing its back, padding its shoulders—and grants betting on it—making it easy for white to pass as art—in a constant oblivion of smell—a constant eradication of personality—implying it is omnipotent—or it has all the rights—and all the complements of itself—to be evanescing the other, obliterating the other, annulling the other as if it only needs itself to exist, but it is a vampire sucking the blood of others—making that blood evanescent in the whiteness that eliminates all the other components. Better said—it can be complex, deep but it makes white the supreme color—overshadowing and ghosting all kinds of implications. All kinds of indirect statements—oblivious to other metrics and rhythms. Insincere, hypocritical, conceited.

Another thing—it is done in order to belong to white people—in order to please—to not offend—as if adding color would be more—and less color is always more of the same and nothing new. When they do this kind of art, they look around at people who think like them—who have no point of view—who are impartial. They don't mess around with the messes—they are not masses—they're messed up but only in white color supremacy—only in white supremacist messes—which are crazy—but blue in the kind of messes that are impartial to the other. If you are different, there is no messing around with discontent. I am of a superior race—if you like me—and I can condescend to you—and make you feel right because you picked me as your savior, but my race has a taste for the impartial—no commitment to the partial—and race dwells in painful things that are beyond the comprehension of an abusive mind that kind of sees abuses everywhere—and can play the victim—because usually when abusers play the role of victims—they have no consideration for premises nor disregards—they come with statements that obliterate race—as a partiture of the other—composed of many fractions of themselves and myself who has observed the magnitude of race in white art blossoms—and the disregard—don't you see that you are obliterating the other—do you think only whiteness exists—and no blue patterns are developed. I have an anger, a rage that is definitely not white art. I am too improper—and I make myself seen—and I am too obvious—well, you can see my colors—they are offensive. You have to become delicate and silent—when you silence your colors you look at me as what can become of you if you disregard. Judge—please—be critical—put a stop to this nonsense. Insert yourself in every part—have strong colors—and contradict the benefactors—do not doubt—go straight to it. But you can see the complicit people in between as the intermediates as if god needs these interventions of white supremacist lovers called saints who intervene but remain impartial in the argument against colors. Because colors are offensive, they scream, they smell—they have odors that are not controlled by perfumes—odors that come from gutters—and are too much—and they laugh at others and at themselves too. In white art you only see one color speaking—and that color speaks for a color that has a class of people who always disregard feelings with contempt—who have not been controlled by white color—the neutrality and impartiality of what obliterates all the company of colors. It doesn't mess around. It is so messed up that it disregards all kinds of colors. I don't see I'm pink because I don't look at my color. I'm here to monitor the colors of the others. And when I distinguish their colors, I spray them all with perfume—so that the colors don't scream—so that the colors are sanitized—conditioned—deodorized. Devoid of smell, of flesh, of nakedness. Sanitize so it doesn't stink of sardine. White color sprays perfume and conditions the air—so the heat be stopped—and so the sweat—and with the sweat and the heat, the suffering—oh, that's too deep for me!—no depth—no gutter—no bad breath—nothing that allows color to shine—color to show its white teeth—color to burn—color to smell—color to die for—color to love—and color to scream. Color screams! It doesn't speak soft on a breath. It is hungry. It is angry because it is hungry. The anxiety of color is the anxiety of influence. Color in power has charisma full of laughter. Color laughs out loud. At others and at itself. It laughs because it finds ridiculous to be so meticulous that you don't dare to scream color outside of the box. Whenever you see color, you see struggle, not inheritance. You see striving to become someone other than a color. Nonsense—to linger on the whiteness of your color as your entitlement to privilege—to nothingness—to oblivion—to disappearance—to mediocrity—to society—without a clue of what constitutes us as lingering humanity—lingering humans who want to strive higher and better than the portraiture of a white face in a white and colorless frame. Whenever I see white art I see lack of creativity—death coming back to life—the ghost of Hamlet's father—coming to create havoc—destruction.

The Ghost of the Color White!

As if it could disappear in a jiffy, but its disappearance makes itself appear everywhere. It plays with evanescence. It plays with being other than itself, but it repeats the white color everywhere it goes. It only plays one tune:

Make America Great Again!
America is back again!

When has it not been America again—the same old tune—the same control over the others—the Ghost of the White Color is everywhere claiming it is America—coming back from the dead—or claiming it is back again—as if it was not always back claiming its white supremacy on our back.

Michael Brown: We give importance to The Importance of Being Called Earnest. But not to Black Lives Matter. Hear the difference between The Importance of Being Called Earnest and the importance of Black Lives Matter. Being called Earnest when you are not Earnest at all because you are a liar but also the importance of a name, of a celebrity— calling attention to himself—to his individualistic, egocentric, selfish relevance—for Earnest—who is not Earnest at all and hasn't earned it—Black Lives don't Matter when the collective can rot in hell—as long as his individual prevalence comes to prime-time bloom. Celebrities who say the importance of being called by a proper name would hate having to affirm the importance of Black Lives Matter because it would take away from calling attention to themselves—to the irrelevance—the unimportance of being called Earnest when you are not Earnest at all because you haven't earned it. Black Lives Matter! Black Lives Matter! Yes, of course, they matter much, and much more than The Importance of Being called the most powerful man on earth. When the Importance of Being Called Earnest who is not Earnest at all because he hasn't earned it and lies all the time and uses threats of vicious dogs and ominous weapons—when we are closing in—we're getting closer. What makes Earnest who is not Earnest at all because he lies all the time and hasn't earned it think that because we are getting closer to the White House, we're a threat that has to be threatened with vicious dogs and ominous weapons.

Maybe we are getting closer and closer to the White House because we are the power that is becoming the majorities that have been squeezed into be called minorities, but when you sum up all our parts, we are more than The Importance of Being Called Earnest who is not Earnest at all because he lies all the time and has not earned it. When you earn it, you go forward and transform that Importance of Being Called Earnest who is not Earnest at all because he lies all the time and hasn't earned it—to Black Lives Matter. Black Lives Matter is more important than the Importance of Being Called Earnest.

Giannina: I propose building a Black House—and the president of the Black House should be black. He will not represent White people. White people will be represented by the white president who lives in the White House. And there should also be a Brown House. And the president of the Brown House will be brown—and will not represent blacks nor whites but only the brown. And I propose a Yellow House—with a president who is yellow—and who only represents yellow people. And there should also be a Rainbow House that only takes care of the people who belong to the Rainbow coalition. These houses will take care of Public Colors. The problem up to now has always been that we only have one house—that is the White House—with always one white president—who only represents the white population—which is the minority—because there are black, brown, yellow, and rainbow coalitions— which means, there are five—and five is four more than one white.

So why is white the sovereign power—why only one White House—when there should be five houses—all with their racist flags—all excluding the other—and with ominous weapons and vicious dogs defending their portals. These five houses should have no windows. They're designed to look inside at the color in particular that they represent. It's a little sordid, don't you think—not to be able to look through a window outside—at what the other house is doing—to be in a grave buried inside. You don't grow. You become your same color so many times that you procreate sameness all the time. There's no remuneration. There's no growth. There's stagnation. And what language do these muted somber houses that only know how to represent their color—speak. They speak one color—the color they represent—they are against all the other colors—and the rainbow coalition which has so many colors but only relates to one issue, sex—so again we remain in the domain of Oliver Exterminator—race and sex—the colors of the muted houses that only represent race and sex—and there are no windows to look around—and see other possibilities that could open other portals and get out from a different door than they entered. Color is understanding. Color is growth. Color is possibilities to see through open windows, to look outside, to walk outside. Color is the color of your skin. And the color of your skin predetermines your destiny. Poverty has a color, a taste, a misery. It's very hard to get out of that color of misery—of that taste of misery—of that sense of knowledge—because if your destiny is predetermined by your color, you know you will be judged guilty before you were able to prove innocence—and to be judged guilty is to know that your feelings have a color. They cannot express freely what they desire or want because their feelings are judged by their color.

Everything you do is predetermined to be judged by the judge of color, and that judge is a racist color. It has white as the primary point of view to judge guilty everyone who appears suspicious of taking black out of black, and red out of red. Colors are sameness in perpetuity. They should stay inside their houses with no window to look outside—and always come out through the same door they entered—the door of the racist colors represented. The same happens when you come from a discriminated place. You're asked before you were able to be born—and you're born every time the question is asked—where are you from? They ask the question—they see the color of the skin where you are born—they judge your accent—not the color of your thinking matters but the color of your money matters—they see that color is the color of money—green—they make you white if you are green and black—then you can become colorless—that's the most the color black can become when it has green in its pockets—it can become colorless. Nationless—not wanted by any color and nation on this planet—where so many are moneyless—and colorless—and not wanted—and don't see the difference between what is that exists and what is that is wanted—and to be real, reality has abused racist countries and cultures and eliminated the possibility of growing in a culture whose predetermination is not color but senses—senses to sense the multiple organs—orgasms you can get from origins that originate creativity as racism originates discrimination—judgement of racist judges that take decisions based on color—and I am not going to say—not on—because there is not on—the option—whichever it is—is not in opposition—nor in direct confrontation—if I oppose it—I would be judge of another race,

of another cosmology—of what sign—of what
miserable country—can I pinpoint you—and nail
you to your own crucifixion—a fixation—with
nails—a frame where I am nailed to an opinion—or
judged by furrow brows—and I am not going to say
that don't—because then I would be of the ones
who think they are of the other side that don't—
and I do, I certainly do, and I don't, I certainly
don't do and don't know. Not only do they judge
you guilty, they judge you ugly before you were
born—and you are born every time you realize it
again and again, that you are judged because you
are guilty to be born, to have a color in your skin
that matters, of course, it matters. It is a matter
that has been discriminated and abused, jailed, and
killed—and held back and made to turn their eyes
back and look at the back and walk backwards
always, turning down what already was born and
is born every time it realizes Black Lives Matter.
I should not talk about black lives—let the blacks
lives talk about themselves—they don't need me
to talk about them. Every time someone speaks
in the name of the others, it's a way of oppressing
them more—of taking their issues—as if they were
your issues. Let me tell you they are my issues too.
I have been discriminated against too many times,
but I don't have the right to speak for someone
else—I don't do that. Let everyone speak. I want
to hear everyone raise their voices to the level
of their abuse and silence the abuser. And I am
against understanding too when it's a way of not
taking a position—of compromising your body, of
hiding your true colors. Maybe those people who
understand hide their position because they are
racist pigs—and they are pro-establishment—or
maybe they dare not to speak what is spoken
through their cowardly understanding of

Reason is such a disappointing method.
It has let us all down. It never was a companion of
truth but of establishment. It was used to establish
order in the court of law, but it established chaos
of lies—one after another. And its companion,
facts, were created to build the case so that
reason would state its law and order with precision,
stately, in accordance to the establishment.
They both work surreptitiously, looking around
with sneaky eyes afraid of being caught
with the hands in the money jar.

the others—which is a compromise of their compromised body with the establishment. Maybe I am one of those, or I have been one of them, at times, when I don't raise myself to the level of the multitudes—where I belong—and take a stand—in the middle of the crowd coming out to burn the White House down to the ground.

I was in the Library of Congress reading amendments to the constitution. Someone screamed from the auditorium:

--*You can't drain a swamp when all the frogs are members of the planning commission.*

Pendejo is the puppet of Putin.

Truth has become the puppet of Pendejo. Pendejo is the puppet of Putin. And truth is his lackey, tucked in his back pocket and used as his hankie to clean his sweat, although he hardly sweats when he screams: I am not a puppet of Putin! But what he screams and does are two separate things—kept in two separate cabinets—in both he spits germs—this germophobe of truth. Truth is a gem—not a germ. It spits venom and saliva, but it is not a believer. When truth is spoken, it is smitten. Facts are full of lies—and, for this reason, I don't believe in facts. Reason and facts go together in the pack of lies. Reason is such a disappointing method. It has let us all down. It never was a companion of truth but of establishment. It was used to establish order in the court of law, but it established chaos of lies—one after another. And its companion, facts, were created to build the case so that reason would state its law and order with precision, stately, in accordance to the establishment. They both work surreptitiously, looking around with sneaky eyes afraid of being caught with the hands in the money jar. I am not against money. I am against nothing at all.

Truth is what evolves in theater—
the changing of the heart
of a person—how it thought it
was one person before—
and how it evolves—
and changes into another thing.
The transformation of
that truth is the
movement of the work.

I mind my useless position in the world as a rhetorical argument. At issue are the solid arguments of the state that reason has to meddle inside the arguments to find the reason to keep them in power. Because they want to keep power to themselves, they use reason and facts as arguments to prove that they are wrong all the time. Theater is the transformation of something that was one thing before—or thought it was one thing before—one thing petrified—not happy—wanting to change but not knowing how to produce the catalyst—afraid of changing—afraid of leaving comfort behind even if comfort makes them miserable—and preferring what it knows to what it doesn't know. For a change to happen—and this is what theater is all about—for a change to happen—something is broken—and in that breach in security or faith or trust you either discover a lie—a lie that makes you distrust the person you had faith would be with you forever—or someone disappoints you—or you realize your life is empty but full of a pack of cards that are lying to you all the time. And it is hard to accept that a king of spades is not a queen of hearts but a joker laughing at you but behind those teeth there is not one zip of truth. Many people don't care for truth anymore. They think that to find truth, you have to continue lying until the lie is accepted as a fact. But facts are part of the pack of cards that are a pack of lies. I don't believe in facts. I believe truth is mutating as it changes its position having been disrespected by the constitution, demoted by the corporation, and fired from the office of its mouth. It collects unemployment and food stamps. And many businesses are happy that they don't have to deal with it anymore. Don't forget the rare aspect of theater. It is raw—it is crude. Truth is what evolves in theater—the changing of the heart of a person—how it thought it was one person before—and how it evolves—and changes into another thing. The transformation of that truth is the movement of the work—and the episode is the visualization of that transformation. Maybe you get anxious looking for meaning—wanting to feel fulfilled—accomplished—not wanting to feel remedies—little itchy feelings but something big—a big transformation that reveals before the nothing of drama is abolished the fullness of the nothingness that life is all about—and that this expression of myself is all about. In servitude of the provocation of life. Of all the new things love has provoked in me—changing my customs, my habits. Another being was born with a different age, not a biological age, an ancient age, an age that can die at any age of a heart attack, an age that rises when love ages in the person who has been born now with a rare feeling that makes everybody laugh at the same time and grows old when younger it feels inside—that something new is arriving that was never there before—that doesn't make you angry—that makes you grow like you should grow—not with age but with love.

When love is in the air there is abundance and gratitude. Even if you are mistreated—I mean, do you have time to think about the way you are treated when the emotions you are getting from whatever treatment is there are opening the doors for you to enter everywhere. Not because you are getting something out of it. What you get is dust and sunset. The remembrance of a Sunday brunch, the spectacular awakening of your senses, the transformation of your being. You are not the same person you were before. And here we have the beginning of drama. Your triumph will be immense, the cosmos will hear you sing once more how you have never sung before. A melody they never heard before. Where did you get this shape. A new depth. A reason to believe. Before this happens twenty-five years could have passed and everywhere you looked there was sterility and anger. Anger because you were frustrated. When an emotion is frustrated, the eyes don't have apples—they have pits—and they grow lemons in their behaviorism. They are hated because they hate.

When a new element has invaded one's feelings—and a new divinity is accomplishing its mission of depth in one's heart—and the heart is moved by things that were never noticed by the lover renewed by the feeling of love—this love is passion—this love is growth—this love is unity—amazement—difference. All of a sudden, the measurement of things has nothing to do with hours, with days, with seasons—when you are pregnant, you impregnate—and your halo—if you have a halo—you know that a halo like a voice has a tempo, a growth that ignores the growth of biology—that everything that grows against time has a time of its own—that it feels very slow because it grows timeless—in a niche of its own—with its own qualities—following orders that are emotional—that are irrational—that make no sense—that are antibiotical—antibacterial—that are not preventive medicine—that danger doesn't touch its nerves—that claims what it claims in unusual times, when time has died, and the season inside a season has to grow and produce a penguin of the imagination.

   --I never saw her like that before. She learned how to dance.

   --I didn't learn how to dance. I was dancing because a new movement inside me suddenly expressed itself. And people came to me and wanted to know what was happening but more than wanting to know what was happening, they wanted to feel the way I was feeling.

> *A month*
> *doesn't produce*
> *what a day can give.*
> *A nanosecond can be*
> *more productive*
> *than all the technology*
> *of an hour.*

So, these were and are moments of charisma. People feel the attraction. And the attraction inspires them to follow. But at this moment I have something to give, so I give it. When I have nothing to give, I retire into myself. Until I can give what I have received. I have to be full to be able to give.

    --A god dances inside her.
    --A god dances inside me.

Love has its own timing. Creation doesn't wear a wristwatch. Seasons are an invention although they exist. Facts are not to be believed. A month doesn't produce what a day can give. A nanosecond can be more productive than all the technology of an hour. What makes technology an enemy of Psyche and Eros is its regimented diet of programs, regulations, batteries, microchips, barcodes in the brain. There is nothing more boring than technology. It is regimented. It is ordered.

It follows orders. It is not free. It is not capable of surprise. It lacks originality—to go back to the origin—and to feel strange in itself and in others—and to be capable to create the unrecognizable, what not only has something to say but what gives motives, reason to say—what provokes a saying. An answer is welcome. Not another opinion.

Do you have reservations?

--Do you have reservations?
--No, I don't. But I don't see the problem. The restaurant is empty.
--The problem, madame, is that you don't have reservations.
--But all the tables are empty.
--You would have to leave in half an hour.
--I will leave right now and leave your restaurant empty.
--It will be full of reservations in half an hour.
--By forty minutes we will be finished.

--Table for one?
--I am one but look at the pack following me.
--Madame, this is an invasion. I was accepting one without reservations.

I hope all of you who make reservations find something better to do than fulfill the expectation of the reservation.

--You're giving more importance to the people who are not here than to the people who are here. Absence, for you, is more important than presence. Future more important than moment. Predictability more important than improvisation. I refuse to reserve what I can grasp in a moment. I refuse to predict every step I take. I refuse to carry an I-phone in my pocket even though I got stuck in an elevator last night and couldn't call 911. I refuse to forsake my right to be here and now what I want to be here and now, free to act in the splurge of the moment. I hope all of you who make reservations find something better to do than fulfill the expectation of the reservation. I hope all the seats stay empty. And a pack of wild cards and cats enter the restaurant with guitars and mandolins—and break the expectation of the reservation. I hope they speak loud with a heavy accent. I hope they break dishes and start screaming and insulting each other—and a wife hurls a glass at her husband—and he ducks the glass by an inch, but it awakens his senses.

--You want instant gratification, madame. You enter my place with ferocious hunger. Demanding food in the spur of the moment because you are a moody compulsive eater. Moody compulsive buyer. Here and now, for you, is more important than honorable and later. Discipline is the mother of safely wait for your retirement. Wait for the moment to come. Don't take the moment as a rapture. As a rape of time. Because you want to eat now, I have to feed you now the food you want now forgetting all the reservations that were made before. This is a very popular artsy-fartsy restaurant. People come here with high brows, raising their chins and noses and behave as if they were not hungry. Hunger is substituted by taste. Oh, things are tasteful. And the clients are not hungry. They eat because they have taste, and they like to taste. They don't eat because they are hungry. That is why they make reservations. They can wait and they wait.

--You are full of violence, Monsieur, full of no. Yes, I am hungry. I want my food now. Hunger exists. Do I have to wait for the waiter? The waiter waits—yes, too much he waits. No tips. No tips. Because he believes in reservations, he reserves his opinions to himself, and his silence is his unconformity. Tired of waiting? Become a waiter—then you'll really know what reservations are all about. I have my reservations. And then I criticize the waiter for accepting more reservations than needed. He is really a reserved gentle soul—too many reservations made him forget that he had something to do in life that was not waiting for the waiter and the reservation to reserve. Very reserved—he died with all his reservations inside. Oh, all you tasters, moving your tongues like snakes and saying: Uuumm, it's tasty. It's tasty because you are not hungry. If you only knew what hunger is, you would not have any kind of reservations. There would be no hesitations—should I—or should I not. There would be no impotence—and right now there is no impotence in me—no reservation. I am not reserved. Please don't reserve a seat for me. And don't tell me where to sit. Who is the decider? You? I happen to like deciding for myself where I want to be seated. Even that you want to rule out of the constitution of my fancy. And then the millennials say:

> --What's your problem, lady? Sit and wait for the waiter. You've waited all your life. You might have to wait a little longer. Without procrastination. With determination. And anger doesn't get you far enough. We were born after the facts. We are all the information you need to pack in your bag. We are conceited. We know what you don't know—the smell of time—as Donald Trump Jr. says: It's disgusting! Tasteless we breed pigeons and smell birdshit all the time, but we wait

and procrastinate for other times. Will we
understand. Will we enter the space-time?
Will we, will we. Sure, for sure. Who has
time to doubt when all the time of the
world is waiting upstairs at the bar. Ha, Ha,
Ha, Ha! Look at the phone, pick a dish,
trash the other, click here, click there. Take
a selfie. Take your time and click me a like.

Take a step further. And back away. The
president is arriving in his limousine. The
credit cards are all in order. Step aside.
The first lady is arriving in the second
limousine—with no reservations—no
procrastination—no hunger to taste
the food that without hunger tastes
like documents to be turned over to the
investigators of the procrastination that is
taking too long—448 pages long—and
no decision on collusion nor obstruction
of justice. I have my reservations. Why did
you make reservations? You have taste
not hunger. If you were hungry and you
had nothing to eat you would take the
bullshitter by his horns and rip his balls off.

Cimadevilla died of love. He was my philosophy professor at Com-
plutense in Madrid—and he used to teach his lessons by memory with
a smile on his lips—a twinkle in his eyes—frenillo on his tongue—stut-
tering—and with his right hand over his heart like Napoleon. He died
of love. Some people die of love. Those are the people I love the most.
Usually, it's a very small thing that kills them—an affliction of the heart
makes them rise and fall in love—although I always say you don't have
to fall. You only have to rise.

--Look at you. You don't even look at me when I'm talking
to you. And you are not even mesmerized nor haunted

by her. You are just stuck to her. And you tell me you
don't love her. If you don't love her, why do you pay more
attention to her than to me?

--I have to pay the bills.
--Lame excuse. When you say I love you, I shrink. I feel the
toxic effect you feel when you're working with her. You
go to bed looking at her—not at me—and you rise in the
morning looking at her—not at me. And you say I love you
but I feel you love her more than me.

--Are you kidding? I hate her.
--If you hate her, why do you spend so much time with
her? No time with me. And when you talk to me, it is only
to express your anger because I talk to you when you are
looking at her. And she's always finding things for you as if
you couldn't find those things for yourself.

--Let's ask Siri. Let's see what Siri can find for you.
--Let's see what I can find for myself.
--What can I do for you?
--Keep him distracted—away from me. You do him a great
 disservice. And me, a great service.
--Sorry, I don't understand that. Can you repeat that?

--You are taking away from me all that violent nervous
energy of the economical—ecological man. Little by little
I am less attached to his nervous violent energy and more
into being alive—without having to look at you because
he is looking at you. I'm becoming a human being close
to nature—close to animals—close to objects—close to
moments—close to disservice—close to who I am—a
completion of incompleteness—not incompetence. As
long as he is attached to you, he is unfit to rule. No one
attached to AI can understand the depths of my soul. No
one who uses an iPhone as a crutch of information for
disinformation, disintegration of life into silence—and

follows the rule of economy over ecology—for the purpose
of competition and elimination of the unfit. Technology
came with the promise, I'll liberate you from the chains
of work. Instead, it enchained you to the shackles of need
and want. I don't need. I desire. Desire is a liberation from
need. Desire opens its wings to the plenty of possibilities
arising for all of us, in the air, in the water, in the sun. Desire
makes us strong. Need is weak and meek and coughs
and can't make it by itself alone. It needs Siri to look for
the information. Where does information get you? To
investigation. And where does investigation get you?
Did you catch the fish in the fishnet? You can't even take
the decision on obstruction, nor collusion. You send the
information to the attorney general who works for fake
news and leaves us all hanging in the air. I say bravo to the
investigator's wife who whispered to him under the covers:

--We've been together since high school. I don't want
  them to kill you. I want you to live. So please let the
  attorney general take the decision and continue living and
  supporting me for the rest of my life.

And that is what he did. We still have Pendejo in the White House as
president—and no one takes the bullshitter by the horns and rips his
balls off.

Russian Oligarch

TARTUFFE WOKE UP ONE DAY in the Trump era and touched his nose just as he did every day since he realized he had a pimple on the tip of his nose, but today, the day of the Presidential inauguration, he found when he touched his nose that the fluorescent pimple on the tip of his nose was not there and instead there was a flat iron. Someone had stolen his nose. Of course, it was a Russian bureaucrat. They are enrolling their children in Pushkin Academy where they learn Russian subjects in Russian. Tartuffe took an Uber, and his driver was Somoroff who had just had a child with Irina, a Russian ballerina—both stationed in New York since the era of Putin and Pendejo. I happened to get a facial at Ruchki da Nozhki and Irina told me all about it. She was the facialist who tried to steal my watch—taking advantage of my relaxation—and thinking I was going to forget time and watch. I did forget time but not watch. There was an announcement in *The Moscow Times*. Now is the time to enter the United States of Banana. The borders are all opened to Russians. Infiltrate. We need Russians in the U.S.B. They are closing the borders to Central and South America but welcoming immigrants from Russia. Just don't say you are Russian.

--Are you Russian?
--A little.
--Do you speak English?
--A little. Russia is a little country. No, no, no. We did not collude. Apchkhi! Russia can't compete with a big country. We are itty bitty.

--I don't like to talk politics when I am trying to relax.

--Of course, no collusion. The ones who polluted your
country are the coyotes. All drug traffickers from the South.
We believe in block, block, block. Give Wall a chance.
Wall doesn't speak. It's mute. It has no lips. It separates. It
provokes tears. No laughter. Wall doesn't like people to
laugh at him. He shrinks when people laugh. And Wall
retaliates. He puts sanctions. If you disinvite him, he stops
you. He calls you names. He puts you down. He absolutizes.
He monopolizes. Now, it's the whole world against Wall.
Wall talks with his fingers wide open so we don't notice his
little hands, and his long tie goes to his knees, reminding us
how big he is and how small we are. His sweat is dry—his
skin is hard. Hard to swallow this pill—without opening
your mouth and protesting. Thin skin—big wall. All the
coyotes howling. This is our moment. The moment for all
of us resentful spirits to stand up and build a wall.

--What do you think of Pendejo?
--Give him a chance.

--No one ever gave me a chance. A chance for what? The
only people who can enter the country now are Russians,
and they don't like to work. They like to drink. I don't
blame them. I don't like to work. I like to drink.

--They complain all the time. You call that a museum? St.
Petersburg has museums. Hermitage, that's a museum. The
MOMA—that's not a museum. The Whitney—that's not
a museum. Only we are museums. We collect emotions.
Where is your nose?

A Russian bureaucrat stole my nose. They say he was a bicycle thief.
I was careless. I let him take it. I shrugged my shoulders with indifference.
Listen, I have seen so many changes in one night I condensed all the
biological processes that makes a man grow old. Shall I part my hair

Delusion is a compression of an illusion. You press oranges to get the juice and taste the bitterness of the rind.

behind? Do I dare to eat a peach? I grew old in one night. I kept thinking: where is my nose? Of course, being French I smell everything. And being Russian, I smell everything too with vodka and a pickle, but now I can't, I can't, I lost my nose to a Russian oligarch, and there's nothing to do but complain. I see two suns in one sunset, and I am not prepared for the delusion I suffer. Delusion is a compression of an illusion. You press oranges to get juice and taste the bitterness of the rind. The Uber driver took me to Brighton Beach to understand Russians. Do I have to understand Russian to understand Russians? I know a Russian when I see him by the way he smells a pickle. Smell is a tricky thing when you can't smell a pickle, you have a problem with vodka. I have a problem breathing. I lost my nose in a raffle. The number I picked happened to be the winner. I lost everything except my ability to smell a pickle when I see one. I blow my nose forgetting it is a flat iron. But people don't seem to notice my loss. I asked a Russian oligarch:

--What is this?—and I touched my flat iron.
--How can you breathe?
--Everything is so congested.
--Use this handkerchief. Blow your nose.

--I can't breathe. I have no life. A thief stole my heart with
my nose. Broke my heart and broke my nose. A Russian
oligarch like you. Full of tenderness for the human heart.
But scratch the skin of an oligarch and beneath that skin is
a Soviet Union Bloc.

Why do you think Pendejo is committed to building a wall? He likes to
block. The sun is rising. And I still see two suns and no blurriness. No,
everything is crystal clear. The shape of things and their music and their
wonder. We all wonder how long the delusion is going to last. Until
depression makes us touch the bottom and come back to the surface
after having seen with two suns more than it takes to grow old in one
moment in which I smelled a pickle and lost my capacity to smell a
Russian when I see him coming to steal my money. He stole a pair of
glasses off my nose. He accused me of stealing what he stole from me.
And now I have no nose—a flat iron in place of a nose—and two eyes
that can't believe what they see.

I go to Ruchki da Nozhki to feel good and look nice. Igor makes me feel
good and look nice. Earnest makes me feel good and look nice. Luis
makes me gossip. He gossips that Earnest is gay but says he's not—and
it feels as if he likes Earnest but Earnest doesn't like him. And if he is gay,
he doesn't have to tell Luis what he doesn't want to tell Luis. Who is Luis
to try to control the sexuality of his colleagues. I think he likes Earnest,
but he can't control him. Evelyn as usual got me a diet coke and a banana.
Earnest was doing the cut, and Luis was doing the color. The moment
Earnest introduced me to Luis, I read danger in the panorama. Earnest was
sharing his client with Luis, and Luis, in exchange, told me that Earnest is
not good, that I should try Sacha, who used to work at Sacha & Olivier.

--Why is Earnest no good—I asked Luis.
--He hardly has any clients. You might be his only client.
--That's good. A sign of mastership. Not to have clients.
 He's an artist.
--How can he be an artist without clients?
--Precisely. That he is priceless—his value is in demand.
--He is gay, but he says he's not gay.

I realized he was ostracizing Earnest because Earnest never paid attention to Luis. And maybe Luis wanted something with Earnest. But that is no reason to take away his only client. And Earnest was a great coiffeur. He really had style. He was trained at la Crème de la Kremlin where he couldn't say he was gay. He infiltrated like the facialist who defended Pendejo at all costs, saying: Give Pendejo a chance. Let Mueller show the results of his investigation. There are search warrants and affidavits everywhere. A landslide of papers and stacks of folders, blueberry muffins, and coca cola on every desk in the bureau. Confidentially yours, Putin is everywhere, the godfather of Pendejo who called it a witch hunt without a hitch to catch a witch. Everyone is mute about the investigation. And the evidence, overwhelming. And jail is looking straight bars ahead on the horizon. The thing is this—in this salon where no one dares to talk politics—Earnest was fired because Luis reported that Earnest was gay but never admitted he was gay and never admitted his relation to Putin or that he crossed the border on the back of a bull that had no consequence when it entered through Texico without papers. He was caught in fragantis saying no and saying yes at the same time. He was caught crying and laughing at the same time while trying to explain that he was a Russian who was sent by Putin to infiltrate—that he was not a Russian—that he was not sent by Putin—that Putin was the mastermind of collusion—that collusion was a piltrafa pollution—that the atmosphere was contaminated by Russian spies—that Russian spies cry and laugh at the same time—that they don't admit innocence nor guilt—they don't have to admit—they don't have clients to please but they have guts. As I was leaving Ruchki da Nozhki, the coat-checker took my ticket and gave me back my hat but not my glasses that I had placed on the counter when I gave her my ticket while Luis and Ernest were fighting over a client. Where are my glasses? Let's look inside the hat box—nowhere. Inside my bag—nowhere. We asked Luis and Ernest who saw me enter with the glasses in my hand—no perdiéndoles ni pie ni pisada. I have glasses. I don't have dogs. But I cherish them. I talk to my glasses like people talk to their dogs. Oh, my beautiful, beautiful Russian oligarch glasses. You have given me insight on the Russian collusion—and depths of understanding. You are a rare breed like a Borzoi or a Bolonka. If someone tries to steal you, just scream: Help! I'll be there—to save you from the hands of abductors. And I did that. I saved my glasses from the coat-checker who kept them for herself, but she didn't know that my glasses had surveillance lenses, and her fingerprints were all over the glass. Don't punish her please. Just give me back what belongs to me.

Bring back,
bring back,
Oh, bring back
my glasses to me, to me.

Arcady, another Russian oligarch, was not circumcised when he was born. My grandmother pierced my ears with diamond studs when I was born, and I screamed, I swear to you, a lot, but not so much as Arcady when he was circumcised without any kind of painkiller by a group of Russian Jews who were haranguing him because he was not circumcised when he was born—because in Fokino in the seventies, no one was circumcised, according to Arcady.

   --No pain killer, with a knife, cold blooded. Just because
   I wanted to prove I am Jewish. I am Jewish. But my friends
   told me—not if you are not circumcised.

They wrapped it in a bandage and sent him home stumbling drunk, walking forwards or backwards, with the fear of never again having an erection. But the moment he saw Irina, the Russian ballerina, he felt himself getting hard.

   --How is that that with a penis in a bandage and a flatiron in
   place of a nose, I can still breathe and get an erection?

The circumcision made late in life when Arcady was 23 years old saved him from going to Afghanistan because the commanders thought that because he was Jewish the minute the airplane dropped him in the desert, he would betray them to save his life. And Arcady was saved because of that circumcision. None of his buddies returned. They all died.

   --I don't want her to go around telling everybody that my
   dick is raw and that it's hard but hardly hard in a bandage.
   How can I get out of this situation?

As luck would have it, just when Irina the Russian ballerina was going to unzip him, Somoroff drove by and Irina ducked under the dashboard.

--Leave me here. That's Michael, my husband. He's capable of killing you if he sees me with you.

And Arcady felt relieved that he didn't have to show his raw meat to Irina and become the laughingstock of the Russian mob.

They all live together in a tent where the wind blows all the time. They are five and with him six. They are all called honey by Somoroff—while he dips apples and pears in honey—and flowers accost their sleep and music grows out of proportion with sleep and time. The climate changes for the sole purpose of changing sheets, blankets, towels. None of the wives has a memory of the other. They are all taken hostage by honey, apple, breeze. Sheets are silk and soft. Oils are in abundance of scarcity. In the tent everyone is sleeping. Big blankets, harps, violas, lyres. Music replayed. Everyone is exhausted by rest. And before Nuria—the last breath of honey—there was Irina, Franco, Carmen, and Calumnia—all lovers of each other—and the wives of Somoroff. They all get along at the banquet of excess. They all listen and understand each other with patience. Impatience moves my hips—my legs are open—my tent blown by a sibling wind. Constant attacks of the wind on the shore. A ship is embarking the coast of living while the cost of living blows the tent into shreds of the things the first wife Irina used to like. Behind the scenes are all the properties that have not been sold—and that blow in the wind of debts—and don't belong to the wives. Prenuptial agreements—precursors of separation and divorce. But unity reigns in the shreds of sheets. They all live together in peace. Four blondes and one brunette. And one of these honeys just doesn't belong here. They are pieces of puzzles that wait for a moment to look around and find peace with each other and harmony with themselves. Nakedness is a prayer of finding the right place for the right moment and every piece moves around with the sensuality of a cat among the fever of bitches moaning. Calumnia, the fourth wife, looks at Nuria, the fifth, bouncing her knees with impatience—expecting that Somoroff after licking his chops—comes to comfort each of his wives. How can they all live together with Somoroff taking pictures of them all the time. They were all born on different shores—raised in different religions, without an identity, lost in the photographs taken of their naked bodies—accursing the fruition of time—and they all wave their hair like waves finding its limit in a picture that doesn't capture the quality of the tent nor the sensuality of the wives. No one is a centerpiece—they all like the corners—and move around each other afraid of making noises—around the corners zipping the curses of a violent eruption of time. Violence is innocence incorporated in an ambience that hasn't figured out why it has so much of everything and none of it makes sense. While the curses ashore, more courses appear. The wisdom of Salomon. Somoroff eating a morsel of salmon with olive oil and a fish bone at the edge of his mouth—and the thing that doesn't match here are the matches—and the photograph is ludicrous. If you really want to conquer Somoroff's heart, you must become the Rabbi who took him to a beach in Jerusalem and commanded him to sweep the sand.

--Until when?

--There's no until. Until infinity. Because neither counting all the grains of sand nor sweeping the beach for one thousand and one nights will make you humble. Nothing will humble you, but you will think sweeping the beach and cleaning toilets humbles someone. Not if you are not who you are by nature.

--I already told you what I don't like. Now tell me what you don't like. And what you like too. It's very important to know what you like and don't like.

--I don't like that he called you honey. First, I said, Nuria is not a honey. He called Irina honey. I thought Irina was honey. If I had not seen that he called Calumnia and Franco honey too, I would have thought when he called you honey—well, she's really his honey. But Nuria, you are not his honey. Second, he said—she is my first brunette. All my other honeys have been blond like my mother. Third, he said, I've had more money than all of you together. And fourth, he invites us to his Seder at seven o'clock—and we have to wait two hours until he finishes his prayers—and then he comes out to announce that he will take a bath. In the meantime, the banquet is on the table and we can't eat because we have to wait for Somoroff to bless the food. Why didn't he invite us at 9 o'clock? And fifth, when he finally comes out, he says to me—I like your shirt. It would look great on me! First, you didn't pick the shirt. Second, I am wearing the shirt. Third, I am wearing it well. Can you recognize me in the shirt? Me, me, me. Can only think—me, me, me.

Nuria and I were in my studio discussing *The Agony of Eros* by Byung-Chul Han when suddenly I gave birth to Nuria's baby—a girl delivered prematurely in the 7th month. And I shed plenty of love. Nuria, horrified that I had delivered her baby prematurely. Me—also horrified that this miracle of faith—a beautiful baby named Pleasure—came out of my womb. I don't know if I was still connected to the umbilical cord. I mean, if Pleasure was still connected to my umbilical cord, but I know Nuria took the baby in her hands—blood running down my legs—and cut the cord of Pleasure—to Pleasure. The baby born of Nuria and Somoroff has fingers and toes, long lashes, a big nose, and a little mouth with plump lips emitting sounds, merrymaking. Nuria dropped the cord—a long electric cord—a tadpole swimming across the floor—a stream of blood running off course. She went to the bathroom with the baby in her hands, closed the door, and when she came out, she proclaimed baby Pleasure was dead. Voices ran through my head—voices out of nowhere—and everywhere. Nuria killed Pleasure in the bathroom. The most beautiful baby girl. What a pleasure it was to find out Pleasure had a baby face inscribed in a cameo. Change can happen in a second from joy to tears. Especially if it's born prematurely. And don't forget that Pleasure is mortal. It is bound to die. Pleasure is the daughter of Cupid and Psyche—from two immortals a mortal is born. Pleasure is bound to death as Cupid is bound to blindness. Love is blind. Truth is also blind. But pleasure is mortal. Bound to die because it's bound to life—to instant—to moment. Desire is never satisfied and pleasure always dies. Desire is born of hope and satisfaction. Hope when it becomes desire, it becomes a green light beckoning in the proximity—the beaming of that becoming pleasure that always dies in its becoming light.

Somoroff took the overcoat and gave it to me to smell.

> --It smells of drunken voyages. It reeks of lack of empathy.
> A gangster is inside its sleeves. It's not just the smell of
> cold sweat but of dried blood, or rotten fish, or garbage
> meat. I've become vegan. I can't stand the smell of blood
> anymore.

--Then throw it out.

> --I'll rip it apart with scissors into strips. We'll make
> bookmarks with it—so that you'll mark the pages of the
> books you've read with the ink of rotten meat.

> --What will Nuria say. She cares about this coat. Her mother
> made it.
> --She dumped me. I can dump her coat like she dumped me
> in the garbage.
> --You say she has no empathy?

> --How could she dump me like that. I had no money to pay
> the hotel in Amsterdam. I had paid every bill until then. It
> was her turn. And she dumped me when she had to pay.
> She has no empathy. She only has empathy for the overcoat
> her mother, a seamstress, made for her. She pulled her arms
> out of the sleeves and left me cold without the overcoat
> of an embrace. No empathy. And she did it when she was
> going back to Staten Island, and she said—I want my coat
> back. When she got married, there was an open bar on the
> wedding night. It cost her mother a fortune to make the
> dress and host the wedding. When her parents were driving
> them back to the hotel, the husband told Nuria:

--Someone stole my father's jacket.
--Do you mean to tell me, someone in my
family is a thief. No thieves in my family.
You have no empathy. You are a drunk
skunk. Get out of here.

And she opened the car door. And pushed him into the street. He landed
on his head. Nuria's mother, who had empathy, got out to help him up.

--Let's go!—Nuria told her father. Take me
home!
--But what about your mother?
--Let her get a cab. (No empathy). Let's go.

So, Nuria married her father. And the groom married Nuria's mother.

--But what about the coat?
--You mean, Nuria's coat?
--Will you put it in storage?

--No, I'll dump it in the garbage. It achieved a level of
negativity that I can't deal with anymore. It has too many
contra resting parts. Origins that were never departed.
And the nymphs were departed. Too much loitering. Rats
coming to 'n fro—out of nowhere—settling other scores of
undisclosed origins and masquerades.

--When she finds out she'll be furious. Where there's no
empathy, there can be no love. That's why you can dump
the coat in the garbage because you have no empathy for
the arms that were in the sleeves of those arms that used to
fly like a nymph or a witch on a broomstick.

I was the one who took Nuria to Somoroff's house. She told me she
wanted to shed her skin like a serpent and that I could be the catalyst
who introduces her to rich prospects. I thought she was la Gitanilla with
a princess inside her skin—Preciosa—a jewel named Poesía or Carmen.

I wanted to bless her by finding her the prince who would give her the right size red slipper. I didn't realize that she dumps princes like garbage.

--First, she dumped Rolando. Then she smirked at me with her nose high in the air—and the airs she fanned in the ventilators of her brain—of becoming the attitude she had in mind to become—climbing the stairs to Fifth Avenue— wearing the coat over her tight sardine jumpsuit with a condescending attitude from below—below the knees—so we can't see her Achilles heel—because the attitude that subsists in a narration of pure air, without the feet touching ground level, is not a witch on a broomstick in the air—nor a nymph departed—nor a loitering coat—in despair of a sleeve to wear under the coat—and in the armpits—a smell of despair.

--How do you think I feel? I have no feelings. I am a frog. The frog is always croaking. Would you ask a frog not to croak? When that is the only thing left for it to do—to croak its feelings out of this dispersed energy—of used items—that were used and never returned to sender. A coat lost—a jacket stolen by drunken gypsies at a wedding—and a croaking frog who was assigned the mission to find the slipper, the red slipper, for the Gitanilla, and the only commitment it has is to croak the truth. While all the frogs are members of the planning commission, you can't drain the swamp.

Olga, Puerto Rican, changed her name from Evelyn because she didn't stand a chance with the name Evelyn to work at Ruchki Da Nozhki—not in the era of Putin and Pendejo—so they called her Olga. And she was doing fine, sweeping the floors and serving tsarevna tea to the clients. Except me. She always got me a diet coke and a banana. We were always dreaming. When the two Americas come together there will be only one passport—for one continent—with one aesthetic—the aesthetic of el mamarracho multicultural mariachi Mexirican but no, not now. Racism and censorship. In Ruchki da Nozhki they don't allow employees to talk politics. Why, why not? It's impolite. Good. It's impolite. So what? We can't talk politics. Business is censorship. We can't allow witnesses to our dirty laundering of money. We have to block words, block books, block testimony, block immigrants, block freedom of expression. They say it's liberty. It's not monarchy. It's dictatorship. One day I go there to color my hair as I do every month. And Evelyn is not there. And instead, una india de Guatemala tells me Evelyn was fired:

--Now I'm Olga. Olga Ivanovitch Petroska Yustakovich.
 Evelyn gave me her number so you can call her.
--I will. I love Evelyn.

I called Evelyn, and she told me that Luis, un colombiano whose name is now Lev, hired her back—and that I should come back. I went there and let them all know that I came back not because Melania and Ivanka go there but because Evelyn is back. Lev looked at me strange.

*I am following America.
What America is becoming
in the Putin and Pendejo era.*

--You are following a cleaning lady?
--I am following America. What America is becoming in the
 Putin and Pendejo era.

--You're a poet.
--Yes, like Mayakovski, like Gogol, like Akhmatova.

--So—Lev said with his eyes wide open—you must be a
 great poet. What can I do for you?

--Lev, I'm very glad you hired Olga back at Ruchki da
 Nozhki.

--The problem was that Evelyn doesn't know her place.
--What is her place?

--She's a cleaning lady. You spoiled her. You made her feel she's a lady without her cleaning status. And then Evelyn stepped out of her role and talked politics with the ladies, as if she were not sweeping the floor. So, we had to downsize her.

--Hey, Luis, you have really become Lev. I don't recognize in you anymore the Americans we all used to be.

Who would have thought that I would be here in Ruchki Da Nozhki with Igor and Lev talking about poetry. But they asked me about my soul—the Russian soul. Neither had ever read *The Demons*. There you see how two people could live together—and not get along at all—and not be able to live without each other. They didn't know who Dostoevsky was. A great soul. They nodded in agreement. Whatever she says. But look—I told Igor—Look at Tolstoy and his wife Countess Sophia, one of those demonic relationships. He could never get rid of her until days before he dies. He finally leaves her. He couldn't stand the abuse of power any longer. She was a bit off and wanted him to be grounded, not to be mystical but earthy, to write the way she would write. She was his muse, his force, albeit a negative force, but look, he wrote *Anna Karenina* and *War and Peace* under her tutelage but he suffered a lot—to the extent that when he finally leaves her in deep winter—at night—he runs out—an octogenarian—and collapses icy numb at a railroad station. He is dying in the station master's house—with friends around him—and through the frosty panes—he sees his wife peering into the room.

--No, please!—he cries—Leave me alone!
--I want to see him! Let me in!—she screams.

His friends say no, and he dies with the unresolved burden of love-hate. Contrary to Georgette and Vallejo, a prophet, who wrote what later became true of his death.

Me moriré en París con aguacero
Tal vez un jueves, como es hoy de otoño

But he married Georgette long before. She was a very young bride—and after he died—she moved to Peru and devoted her life to his legacy. She wrote in his epitaph:

I've snowed so much for you to sleep.

She died after she made him world famous. The Peruvians considered her a national hero. Unlike Mrs. Tolstoy whose government thought she was crazy. We better get his manuscripts before she burns them. She is unreliable. You never know what she'll do. But she did what they never thought. She organized all his manuscripts, tied them in folders with multicolored ribbons, and gave the authorities his archives in meticulous condition—opposite to what they expected. Maybe she would have liked him to write the work she would have written if she had not to take care of him and their thirteen children, only eight of which survived childhood, but he never wrote what she would have liked him to write. She would have liked him to be her—to write her stories—because if he took her life—write her life or at least write something that she doesn't dislike. Desire is a fervent manufacturer of more desire—of wings. Ambition is second rate. Desire is hard to keep in a society like this where everything is commerce. What incentive does a writer like me have. I only get to talk about literature at the shampoo bowl with Lev and Igor, but you know, there was desire in their eyes. Tell us more. Who were these people. Let me tell you, I made up half of it. I told them the parts that remind me of myself—and what I love of their wives' passion for their projects—and I take possession of their passion. I care about the romance. Is it true that Russians are tragedia—Lev asked. They're contrarians. If you affirm yourself as a consolidation, they disinherit your consolidation, null the basic argument, and expect you to jump in the air without floor or rug. They look at both sides of the argument—Da Nyet. But the argument nowadays is not Russian nor French nor Chinese nor German. The argument is precise mathematics. It doesn't argue one case but the exceptions and the excuses, the coughing, and the margins. It argues for clean air. It argues for fresh water, carrots and beets, for eruptions of interruptions.

It even argues for defeat where there is victory and tears. It doesn't argue as a dialogue nor as an infinite conversation. We don't argue subject matter. We argue object matter. We don't start from words. We start from matters that matter. Object matter or subject matter are more important than words. Pieces of the world put together again consolidate my premises for an argument. But arguments are concerned with premises. I am concerned with breakfast, with coffee matters, with dwindle matters. Water matters. Fire is ready to burn. Mountain to explode. Wind matters—and it can matter more when it reaches a level where everything that matters, and counts, doesn't count anymore. Why did it weigh so much at one moment in history, and now we shrug our shoulders with indifference to the ratio of popularity? Dispersion of the value of concentration. Arguments are lost in the mansedumbre of the muchedumbre. Arguments are lost in the market value of capitalism. If you can't make the appointment and you don't cancel within 48 hours, the doctor will charge you a penalty of $150. And what will I charge the doctor for his lack of punctuality. Everything is geared to exploit the individual in favor of the institution or the establishment. The rule should favor the consumer who consumes himself in the histrionics of capitalism. I almost lost my desire to exist, which is my desire to understand the living, which is my desire to open my eyes—without reservations—and say what I see is moving around. The interconnection of things.

Barney Rosset gave me a bull, and the bull had a history. He found it on Montego Beach where two Jamaicans were carving its horns and giving the last touches to its gigantic penis—under a full moon—by a bonfire—and making its tongue stick out of its red wooden teeth—on the verge of laughing—with those bulging eyes—the eyes of Picasso—and large curly horns, ready to charge. A very clever bull over whose horns I stacked a collection of hats halfway to the ceiling. It took some time for me to fall for the bull—and now I wouldn't give it away for anything in the world—even though my friends say the only thing that doesn't match here (euphemism for ugly) is the bull. And the bull is ugly, but I wouldn't give it away for anything in the world. And I even wonder if luck is the bull. I did not want it—and nevertheless this object of music, love, and poetry—which I didn't like—which

Opening the doors to the unexpected – hospitality always brings good luck.

upsets my collection of objects—and makes people wonder if I have any kind of taste—if taste is a principle of organization—as Hannah Arendt said—of who in the world belongs together—and how do we recognize each other. We might not belong together. You might think it interrupts my principle of organization. But it has filled my heart with joy—dynamism. Ready always to go and get whatever I want. This bull is my magic lantern. It is green—evergreen. It prefers to be always green. Lo que madura, se pudre. Prefiero ser verde. I wonder if it could one day become a satyr—Silenus—the companion of Bacchus—or if he is Pan—so in touch with our daily bread. I wonder if the bull is luck. If luck one day enters your house and breaks your expectations—and this breaking of the expected—and opening the doors to the unexpected—hospitality always brings good luck. He knew he was in danger of being kicked out. When he first arrived, I said what a beast of ugliness—and nevertheless this beast of ugliness became sleek and slender to please me. And to let him know that he belonged to me—and that I would never give him away for anything in the world—I hung a chain of bells around his gigantic neck that almost touches the floor—and he was so happy to hear the ringing of the bells in his ears—he stood up on his hind legs for the first time like Silenus the satyr, and I scratched his belly with affection—and he danced with an erection, and his tail swinging. I fell in love with him—and he fell madly in love with me. A beast of joy—half human and half animal. And he became my lover and my spiritual guide. I broke all kinds of expectations under his guidance. He liberated my spirit. I went farther and beyond dimensions I understood as real. He showed me his hairy belly—and I scratched it to feel his warmth. He was warm and gave me heat—maybe because he was carved on a beach—in front of a bonfire—under a full moon, but who really knows how love shoots the arrow of tenderness and impregnates the heart. When I think of the bull, I think of Barney Rosset, so faithful and tender with me. How did it enter his heart to give me this bull which could have raped me but instead opened my life to a new dimension of understanding. What was the origin of this mystery. If not the Eleusinian Mysteries. The mysteries of the maenads—ready to charge from the other great bull—the Bowling Green bull—also green. Lo que madura se pudre. Prefiero ser verde. Verde que te quiero. Verde. Viejo verde. That same year the bull entered my house uncanny things began to happen. I was in Laredo with Manuel Broncano working on the last touches of the translation of *United States of Banana*. Manolo was hosting a barbecue in his backyard—grilling burgers—on a beach—in front of a bonfire—under a full moon—when the phone rang and his face grew contorted with tristeza—and his daughter Lucía en cámara lenta—I watched from a distance—went to him, embraced him, and kissed him. His mother had died in Salamanca. And he had to fly there the next day, early in the morning—and I had to fly back to New York the next day, early in the morning—and early in the morning, I received a call from my brother Juan in Puerto Rico to tell me that my dear, dear mother had fallen and broken her hip. This was the beginning of the end for her. I had just been in Toulouse at a conference where I met a semiotician named Charles Joseph, a younger version of Roland Barthes—and I had told him I would be in Paris for two months—and we should meet there because I liked him very, very much. We became friends in Paris—and when I returned to New York—I enrolled in the Alliance Française where I met a fashionista named Adam Baggy, a younger version of Karl Lagerfeld—and I liked him very, very much—and we became friends. Adam, a buyer for Chanel, was going to stay with a friend in Paris. I had a strange inkling that his friend might be my friend. And I asked—what is his name? It turned out it was Charles Joseph, the friend I had just met in Toulouse. All these connections the bull was making for me—and the combinations of taste and colors—and ruptures and raptures were all his doing. And the awakening of my senses too. The bull led me to the New Museum in the Bowery—and there I got a book by Unica Zürn—and I met Falada and Ambergris—and I immediately ordered from Egypt a perfume made of ambergris and musk because Falada in the *Trumpets of Jericho* got pregnant by inhaling ambergris and musk and gave birth to Ambergris through his ear. Like me, through my ear, this Ambergris fragment.

I went to the Whitney Museum and got Spellbound Oils. Resurrection with its orange gulps of filtered oil looks like mucus orange sunset. Enchanted Dreamers, a white musty smell. Midnight Warrior, I wear at midnight—and I hear bells ringing in my ears—bells of preconception—announcing the revelations of a seven-year itch. I've had up to now two revelations within a seven-year itch. The first was in Visby near the ruins of Drottens. It was two in the morning, and the light was rising. There is hardly night during the summer. Hardly three to four hours of sleep and yet one feels fresh. On one of these nights, I was not sleeping but listening—my ears were contemplating what my eyes were not seeing—if ears can see—and eyes can listen—and I certainly think they can switch roles—and my eyes were listening to a voice from another age—not timeless, more untimely—it had a time, but it was not a time framed in a watch—it was a baritone voice that spoke in a spaceless time—a time untimely.

Ella estaría olvidadiza
cuando él se perdiera en el bosque de sepias.

Seven years later, missing from my cabinet of curiosities was a cameo I had acquired in Rome of a bacchante's face carved in blue stone. I was upset to be missing my cameo. Someone had stolen it from me. Out of envy or greed or lust, it was taken from me. It still belongs to me but it was forced away from me—they know it—and I know it—and everybody knows it—it is evident to everybody that we belonged together—and they are breaking a relationship by taking what doesn't belong to them. It will never belong to them because it didn't grow with them in the love that belonged to me—it was not meant for them to take it away—as a property value—and put a price tag on my love—and to ruin a relationship. I was cut short of a relationship—and my stolen cameo reminded me of that. Someone stole what belonged to me. But who? When I went to look for clues, my cameo, it was there. I took it to my ear as if it were a shell—and I would hear the sea in my ear, but instead I heard a ringing—the ringing of a bell—and inside the ringing in my ears, this revelation:

Porque el corazón al mismo tiempo
te quiere llevar a pasar por mi rosal.

--So, this is what happened.
--What happened?

I got an irritation in my eye. I made an appointment with Dr. Delle Michael. I open the door—and instead of finding my doctor's office— I'm in a hotel suite—and Charlie Palelo, my lawyer who is filing a lawsuit against one of the tenants of Pendejo at Trump Tower, is now my doctor—and he is in bed. How curious, Charlie, is now a doctor. I go closer to the bed so he can examine the irritation in my eye.

--It looks like bubble gum.
--It's the influence of Frenzy.
--You know what this is called.
--No, tell me.

--Frenzy's influenza. It's a stye in the right eye—it's moving over to the left—and if it moves—it will cover the whole eyelid with a wad of bubble gum in one doozy of a big swollen stye. I will give you this cream. Use it for three weeks—and it will resolve itself.

--What does this mean?
--That what you will see—che sarà, sarà—will disappear by itself.

Charlie was underneath the blanket—half naked—with his hairy chest showing—and suddenly—out of the blanket—at his side was Frenzy— and at her side—coming out of the blanket—two seconds later came Floozy and their cats Poofy and Puffy. And at this point, Charlie said:

--You have been deluded. This cream will take the delusion
 out of both eyes. And if it doesn't—look around and see—
 just see by yourself—and just learn how to see.

At this point, Frenzy said to me:

--Are you disillusioned?
--Why would I be disillusioned?

--You've got a stye in your eye. It means you're disillusioned.
 You need to pull an eye lash out.
--I just don't know what is real anymore. Who is that
 woman at your side who just popped her head out from
 under the blanket?

--You know who she is?
--Who?
--Flair's girlfriend, Floozy.
--Hi, Floozy, it's a pleasure to finally meet you.

I look at her through the irritation in both of my eyes, and I say:

--Where did you get your sunglasses?

They are the sunglasses I gave as a gift to Frenzy, and she gave them
to Floozy, but I don't tell Floozy—hey, I gave them to Frenzy. I just say
they are beautiful.

--Aren't they beautiful. Frenzy just gave them to me.
 They're from Punto Ottico, one of the best boutiques on
 Madison Avenue.

Frenzy doesn't believe in private property. She is a communist. She
believes we should all share our property. But a gift is a gift.

--You were trying to buy my love. I gave your sunglasses
 to Floozy, so she knows how much I care for her—with

your love—with the love that you tried to buy me because I can't afford to buy Floozy expensive sunglasses—I gave her your sunglasses and irritated your eyes—creating a big blur of a stye. For god's sake, it's a stye. A stye is just a stye. Floozy is Floozy. And you are you. Things are what they are. A doctor is not a lawyer. And if a doctor who is a lawyer gives you a cream that irritates your eyes even more, why do you listen to a lawyer who is a doctor. Geometry says that divisions are there for a reason—the density of the air changes when you are in certain dimensions that are unacceptable—and it's hard to breathe—if the atmosphere changes—for better or worse—and you— with your red slippers—continue walking naked—through the freezing dermatological skin of the planet that uses blankets when it is hot inside—then, as it is then, as it is now—it is not logical—nor an answer that falls out of its place like a blanket off a bed—it is a serious matter that needs to be discussed by serious practitioners of the art of fooling around when all is easy and it is made complicated by people who are burning the candle at both ends and struggling to open their lids without blinking—and the answer is there on the opened lid. Take this white marble sculpture as a blessing. I have travelled close to the birds with my open arms in the sky radiating innocence to bring you this white sculpture with a ring on each middle finger— and these two powder puffs, fluffy, so you can powder your eyes with these fluffy puffs.

--Was it as bad as *Triangle of Sadness*?
--Worse. Imagine all the vomiting that happened there at the captain's dinner. All that vomiting by different mouths, by different characters, happened to me alone.

I had coffee and two pieces of bread with salt and olive oil for breakfast. So that could not be it. Then I ate a salad for lunch. Maybe the olives were poisoned by an agent of Putin or Pendejo. I don't know which. I came back to the Baltic Centre. My head spinning. I managed to pack

my bag. Then, stupid that I am, I took two Tylenol thinking it was a headache. But it was poison. I go to the bathroom and vomit. Fua. Fua. Good, I said, feel free of yourself. Now you are relieved. But another Fua. And more relief of my innocence that had been deluded. I called Eva Brita to come up to the room. The sink clogged. What should I do? She stirred it with the handle of a comb until it went down, swiped the sink with a paper towel, and said: Come, let's go. We had to catch a plane to Stockholm. In the airport I vomited again while waiting to board. I went to the bathroom and vomited two more times. Fua. Fua. I drank two bottles of water, the worst I could have done because I vomited the two bottles of water. Fua. Fua. I closed my eyes to calm myself. I told Eva—should we go to a hospital. No, she said. This is nothing. Poison. That's all. But how long will it last? I have nothing more inside. And right when I said that. Fua. Fua. Nobody seemed to care. They minded their own business. We landed in Stockholm. We took a train. And then a taxi. And the driver gave me a paper bag just in case. At the Grand Hotel, the spewing stopped, but I was totally dehydrated. I was supposed to take a plane at six in the morning. But I cancelled my flight until the following day to feel clear of the poison. I heard—bang—bang—bang—on the door. Persistent knocking. With frenziness. But it was not Frenzy nor Flair. Bang—bang—bang. Bang—Bang—bang.

   --Who is it?
   --It's Floozy. I have executive orders from Frenzy.
   --One moment.

   --Do you have shells on shelves?
   --Thousands. Right now, they are sleeping. But a couple of
    clams are making love under my hat. I want to capture the
    energy following the sexual act.

   --And for that you put a hat over them.
   --I was protecting their coitus. I didn't want anyone to see
    them making love. I wanted to give them privacy—to do
    whatever they want in a room of one's own.

I raised my hat—and there they were making love—chiqui-chiqui-chiqui—like rabbits on the back of a flatbed truck—and the other shells on my shelves were opening and closing—following the rhythm—of the music of the squeaky mattress—moving up and down—chiqui-chiqui-chiqui—I heard them at night—chiqui—chiqui—chiqui.

   --This is unbelievable. Hard to swallow. Only Frenzy is
    allowed to make love on the mattresses. I will bring back all

the shells to the sea where they belong. Things are going back to where they belong.

--I don't want to go back to where I was born. I don't think Frenzy wants to go back to where she was born. There's evolution on this planet. People leave the origin way behind. Although I am going back to ancient times because I am going to enter an ancient age and I am a golden age girl. You are out of your mind. Have you noticed how all these shells are bald? They don't have hair on top—but they have clams inside. They stick around like you—you stick around like chewing gum to the bottom of a shoe—like Turkish grains to the bottom of a coffee cup—like a stye to an eye—like a stamp to an envelope—and I don't know where to send you. Why don't I send you back to the place where you were born? Do you think they want to go back to the sea when they were left behind by the sea on the shores? They prefer to be here—under my bed—on my shelves— giving the sound of the sea to books—or to objects on display—bringing from the sea—the m-U-U-U-U-sic of the movement of the waves of the sea. That is frenzy. Refugees looking for political asylum. They don't want to go back to the places they were born. Nor do the madmen in the streets. Displacement is a condition as natural as accepting that you are out of your mind.

--I am taking all the shells from your shelves. I am leaving you empty of shells.

--Look what happened to Teiresias when he interrupted the coitus of two serpents with a blow of his staff. He was transformed into a woman for seven years—and then after seven years—he saw the same serpents coupling—and he struck with his staff again—and he was transformed back into a man. When Zeus and Hera were arguing who had more pleasure in bed. They asked Teiresias because he had

A seer is indirect contact with the thing—he doesn't need a metaphor nor a simile. A prophet comes afterwards and makes an assessment—after the fact—he doesn't need to see.

lived as both. Hera said men have more pleasure. Zeus said women have more pleasure. And Teiresias said women have more pleasure. And that made Hera so furious she blinded him. And Zeus said—excessive punishment. Let me grant him the gift of seeing. And he made him a seer. There's a difference between a seer and a prophet. A seer is in direct contact with the thing—he doesn't need a metaphor nor a simile. A prophet comes afterwards and makes an assessment—after the fact—he doesn't need to see. But there are no homeland prophets. They are always displaced like shells on shelves that stick around without the clams inside. Shells are the ears of the sea—they are mysterious and musical—and sad—they are very sad—their sadness comes from being left behind—but they don't want to bring back their bonnies—and they sing:

> *Bring back, bring back,*
> *Oh, bring back my bonnie to me, to me.*

--This is the one I am taking—of all the makers of love—this pair reminds me of you and Frenzy making love. I may go into eternal despair, but I will break this pair apart.

--Aye, Aye, Aye. You're breaking love making—not me. A punishment will come to you—not me. I am going to stop the bad from happening right now. My hat will stop the evil doers from doing evil deeds.

I put my hat in the same place where it was before I lifted it, and Floozy separated the shells that were making love with their clams inside. From now on, this hat will take the temperature of the world and lift goodness up in the air—to shine—once more—like a halo rising on top of the poet's head that is crowned with laurel leaves and emits light over the crown and crowns itself with laurel leaves and grapes and wine and merry-go-lucky:

> *Bring back, bring back,*
> *Oh, bring back my bonnie to me, to me.*

Melody hasn't stop speaking all its notes—in perfect pitch—and it unveils the beauty of Frenzy without the shell—and no clam to eat but a bell that has a jingle and plays the role of the clam displaced from the shell. All of us creatures in displacement—hiding from people like Floozy who want to take us back to the sea where we were born but left behind on the shore—looking back at the sea—and never wanting to raise our voices nor to claim legitimacy—without a clam inside as the jingle in our bell—and charging all our poetic credence on the credit cards of our plays.

In *School for Wives* by Molière, Arnolphe asked Agnes if she knows how children are brought into the earth. By the ear—conception happens in the ear—where you hear the conception in the misconception— the word is the conception of the world. Ringing in the ear, the bells of annunciation. Gargantua was born through the ear of Gargamelle, conception of Rabelais—and Ambergris was born in the ear of Falada, conception of Unica Zürn. On February 5th Sabine Cassel brought to my birthday party Franco Lacosta whom I had met in the street, on the corner of 5th and 57th, in front of Bergdorf, 25 years ago.

--Where are you heading?
--To Bergdorf's Salon.

--Don't go there. Come with me to Sacha & Olivier. Franco-Russe coiffeurs. They'll invent a new hairdo for you based on your whims, exaltations, moody broodings. It will show your personality, sensitivity, charisma. They won't give you a standard hairdo. It will match the hairdos of the skyscrapers. It will become a skyscraper hairdo modeled to your personality and transfigurations.

We walked down to 18th Street from 57th. We stopped on a corner for a cup of bone broth before he left me with Olivier who gave me a Russian Muscovite Kremlin Hairdo, precursor to our times. I never saw Franco again. Although I used to think of him because he was a left-handed Aquarius like me—and he looked like my brother Brascho who had just died. Franco was one of the most gorgeous men on the planet, a model for Karl Lagerfeld back then, which must have been in the late nineties before the Twin Towers came tumbling down like Jack and Jill. Nuria told me she wanted a new look, so I took her to Olivier whom I hadn't seen in 25 years, since that day Franco took me there for a touch of the Bacchantes in my bangs and frenziness in my wings. Olivier recognized me immediately and asked.

--What ever happened to Franco?
--He is dead—I said.
--Oh, no—Olivier said. I adored Franco.
--He adored you. And I adore you both.

Franco wanted Sabine to read his cards. Sabine didn't want to do it because she knew he was very sick and didn't want to see anything bad. But he insisted on a reading. So, she shuffled, and he picked a card. And again, she shuffled, and he picked another card. And again, she shuffled, and he picked another card—and when she read the three cards that he had picked—they were all positive—no sign that he was going to die—or even that he was sick. Well, on my birthday, I was wearing all my unguents. Resurrection behind my ears, Ambergris on my wrists, Midnight Warrior on my left foot and Enchanted Dreamer on my right—and Sabine brings to Mamo's in Soho this gorgeous man whom she wanted me to meet because he was also a left-handed Puerto

Rican Aquarius like me. I could not believe it. It was Franco, the model I had met 25 years before in front of Bergdorf and who had brought me downtown walking like a yellow cab with his tires and mine made legs. Franco appeared like a hallucination, more gorgeous than before and stronger. We had all gone through hell and come back as a resurrection. I often had thought about Franco and Olivier and wondered if they were dead. Some people are so sensitive they can't stand very much reality. A splinter in a fingertip can kill them not a big event like Ground Zero or AIDS. But look, the Resurrection of a scent—like the madeleine of Proust—brought Franco and Olivier back from the dead with the interference of Nuria and Sabine. But why not, Medea rejuvenated Jason's father with a potion. The witch, who didn't like any kind of hitch, rejuvenated Faust. And in Francis Ford Coppola's *Youth without Youth* an old man gets hit by lightning—and after he sheds his burnt skin and loses all his teeth, he grows a new skin—and new baby teeth sprout in his gums. Que malos son los puertorriqueños. If they haven't seen you in a while, they claim you're dead. I remember a dermatologist Maritza Perez in New York who came recommended by another dermatologist, Dr. Fletcher, who was my childhood doctor in Puerto Rico. I once asked Dr. Perez about Dr. Fletcher, and she told me he was dead. But I later found out that he was alive and kicking. Which made me very happy because I adored Dr. Fletcher. So, I was angry at myself for having told Olivier that Franco was dead. I had no confirmation of that fact. It was an invention. And I'm very glad that he came back from the dead to confirm he was alive and kicking. If you don't know if a person is dead, why would you say he is dead—just because you haven't seen him. Maybe Perez killed Fletcher because she wanted me not to see any other dermatologist but herself. But I had no reason to say Franco was dead except his disappearance from my life. And like Franco, Olivier, and my brother, we disappear, resurrect, and rejuvenate with lightning, oil, incense, and love.

Return of the Eternal Sardine

I SAW A POET DRESSED AS A HARLEQUIN in a long white tunic, and what came out of his mouth was the sound of a cello. I was excited to hear the poet. And as I went closer to let him know how much I loved his poem, he came closer to me, and to my astonishment, said:

--Giannina, I love what you're doing right now. I am going
to help you.

I was stunned that it was Charles Baudelaire and that he came to me as I was going to him, and that he called me by my name and told me he liked what I was doing, and that he was going to help me. I had gone to visit his grave at Montparnasse and read the epigraph written by his mother who made her second husband sound more important than her son, the greatest poet of his time who transformed poetry by bringing modernity into it. By modernity, he means—the ephemeral, the fugitive, the contingent, the half of art whose other half is the eternal and the immutable. She practically ignored him—as if he were not important. It read something like here lies the major general of France, senator, ambassador to Constantinople and Madrid, grand officer of the division of such and such, married to Baudelaire's mother, in second núpcies, and after listing these attributes and qualities of the general, it simply states, and here lies his beau-fils Charles Baudelaire. And now we go to Montparnasse to lay offerings on her son's grave as if he were a modern saint whom we come to visit on

Quality is experience condensed in a moment.

peregrinations from every corner of the world—leaving bouquets and thank you notes for his poems that give us so much understanding through the ages. When he was a child, he visited the home of the richest woman in Paris who had the most exquisite collection of toys. Baudelaire was fascinated by it, and Madame Panckoucke said—take one as a memento of me. Now choose. She was expecting him to select a bagatelle like so many children whom she had asked the same question, but he seized upon the most beautiful, the most expensive, the most dazzling, the most original toy in sight. It embarrassed Baudelaire's mother who slapped his hand, saying—no, not that one. Choose another. But Madame Panckoucke, dressed in velvet and fur, said with pain in her heart—let him have it. He knows what quality is. Quality is experience condensed in a moment—experience transformed into an object—a useless object that has magic—transition—it allows experience to communicate the quality of life and the eternity of an instant—it allows a toy to become the object of luxure—magnifique—la luxure. The pleasure it gave him to select this toy—among all the others—was the inspiration he felt—and developed as the voice of a cello that came out of his mouth in les Champs-Elysée when he recited:

> Ma jeunesse ne fut qu'un ténébreux orage,
> Traversé çà et là par de brillants soleils;
> Le tonnerre et la pluie ont fait un tel ravage,
> Qu'il reste en mon jardin bien peu de fruits vermeils.

I can smell the quality of a perfume in an Instagram—an inscription of a moment in an epigraph. What made Baudelaire recognize the best toy—the density of the depths he would develop—the quality of music that would sound like the strings of a cello. The toy gave him pleasure—the same pleasure he got from writing a poem—a poem for his collection of toys—being himself—or transforming himself into the richest woman in Paris who collects toys—poems that have a mechanism that functions in the heart and that mechanism triggers chords that play different moods, movements—and the attitudes and postures of the toys transform this moody poet into an engineer—a virtuoso, a dandy, a dilettante—someone who delays the arrival of other things to come because he is enjoying the present moment. But the arrival of what comes after the present moment comes with the same delectability—and how do you recognize the best wine—the way you recognize the best toy—you taste the quality—it involves memory—you have to compare the taste of the tasteful with the taste of the untasted—you also have to forget—and when you forget the taste—a new taste arrives—the taste of desire.

> *Voilà que j'ai touché l'automne des idées,*
> *Et qu'il faut employer la pelle et les râteaux*
> *Pour rassembler à neuf les terres inondées,*
> *Où l'eau creuse des trous grands comme des tombeaux.*

What is necessary is to shovel and rake the lands that have lost their shape to bring back the nuisance of the origin—or to bring back innocence to the eyes that are weeping—inundated by so many bad experiences or disappointments—and to write innocence which is to build a toy or a sand castle in the land where no one cares is to go blind in the hour of seeing and not be prepared. Judgment without pleasure has no generosity of flavor. Sometimes the meaning of a flower is simply the growing of a concept that has textures in the flavors it tastes. You have taste when you have humor. Without humor you can't have taste. To have taste, you have to allow the senses to appear and disappear. To have humor and taste, you must be light. When you are light, you give light. Sometimes you have it (whatever it is)—you have it but you lose it too—and you miss what you had and want it back but you recognize you had something irreplaceable—and it's unforgettable because it's irreplaceable—and the memory comes back like the poem of Charles Baudelaire:

> *Ô douleur! ô douleur!*
> *Le Temps mange la vie,*
> *Et l'obscur Ennemi qui nous ronge le cœur.*
> *Du sang que nous perdons croît et se fortifie!*

When I was 23 years old, I heard a recording of this poem by a pretentious French récitateur who exaggerated the diction—an affection made affliction—but made me aware of the pronunciation and the diction. I learned it by heart—by memory—the way Baudelaire ought to be read—by heart—to be remembered like a relationship—a poem you recite when you go to bed and close your eyes—and the affection and affliction of the poem opens like an experience you may never have experimented, but you are experiencing it now—and since I learned it by heart—it became part of my affliction—my memory—and whenever it comes back to my lips—wet with wine—the poem appears as a mirage of happier moments that were never happy but that with distance became abundance. I'm not nostalgic for the past. A madeleine doesn't open my senses and transport me to another moment. Nothing substitutes the living moment I am living now—better and fuller than all the ones I lived before because it contains all the others—and even if it doesn't contain any other—it contains my body. Every moment passes with me inside. In *The Blessing,* the poet sees his mother as the chosen one to bring into the world this stunted thing whom she vows to torture for having made her a mother, a role she didn't want to play. I have to understand my mother too. Maybe I reminded her of what she could have been if she hadn't chosen to become what she became—my mother—and maybe she didn't choose to become my mother—it was chosen by a destiny of motherhood that many women don't like and feel forced into—in spite of themselves. Then comes the mistress who abuses the poet too because abusers follow the pattern of abuse—they can see the mother's abuse—and when they become the lover—they become the mother too—and follow the abuse knowing whom they can abuse. They can abuse a child who closes his eyes when he is tortured—and the moment he closes his eyes—maybe he closes his heart too—to the beating, but says with his eyes closed—I deserve better. When he closes his eyes and sees the stars of pain, that child also sees the stars of light—that light can happen too when darkness falls. When I was beaten by my mother, I thought she doesn't understand I have something inside that is different—that I will develop that thing that is different, not because it is different. At this moment of stunted anointment—of stunted reduction to a stunted abortion—of stunted reduction to the size of a microbe. It's very different. To be different. To not agree with the agreement. To disagree is to be beaten. And chosen is disagreement. And chosen is beaten to the extreme of screaming disagreement. Not that it came out of the blue into the disagreement. It came out of the blue to understand the sky. But then it was beaten and called a stunted thing, but it knew it was not stunted. It knew it was beaten to affirm it was stunted. But it knew it was not stunted. It was sour. It had a sour statement not to please or displease others but to make them understand the disagreement that happened right at the moment when the mother—the mistress—beat it into a stunted thing, which it was not. It was not even a thing—it was a song—a poem that came out of its lungs—and that understood that stunted thing had to say what it said—in order to become the canto that blooms and blossoms at the cost of pain.

I don't want to idealize the child either. And that is what poets do. They put themselves as the ones who deserve better—to please the public who is easily persuaded by a poet's suffering—because then they see eye to eye. And they both—poet and public—blame the mother and the mistress—and the stunted world that has made possible this show of cruelty—nailing its fingernails into the stunted arms of the public, the poet, the mother, the mistress. The poet is no innocent rose. He is as cruel as the mother—and his revenge—avenging the curses of the mother and the mistress—is worse than having brought this stunted thing to the earth.

There is nothing lazier than to say I like it. Could you be any lazier than to like it? Who are you pleasing by liking it. Agreeing for the sake of pleasing—of not confronting that there is nothing to like—and plenty to complain about—and to dislike—and to improve—to redo it—to replay it again and again—and to disagree—in the misunderstandings that always happen—as complex issues modify the things that are stunted—and broken—and some of them should not be fixed—but that doesn't mean they should be liked either. Do you mean to tell me that because you like it, I should be pleased? I am not pleased at all because you like it. I doubt very much you're liking it. There is a non-committal laziness in your liking what should not be liked or disliked but allowed to exist without the laziness of sycophants liking it or disliking it. Opinions don't matter. Facts don't matter either. But the worst is your liking it to make it comfortable, pleasing. Who are you kidding? No one is more pleasing and likeable than me—and when I say me—I mean the likeable poet—or the pleasing crowds who, like me, don't understand what they like. They want to please. They don't want to be conflicting. But the problem is created because you like precisely what should not be liked at all.

I am telling you, Claudio, but I am not telling anybody else. It is something I shouldn't even say, but since you're from Argentina, I'll tell you the reason I'm cancelling the appointment today. I'm exhausted. I went to bed at two in the morning—and at four I heard a voice inside me giving an acceptance speech for the Nobel Prize. And it made sense. I would have to wake up and rewrite what had already been written. I mean, transcribe what was written for me so easily. So, I woke up because I had this speech to give and write down—and when I wrote down what had already been written—another thing was transcribed. And it always surprises me that I can never say what is dictated to me because it comes out with a different meaning. You know what I heard then and still feel now—the urgency to do it at the moment it said it should be done. If I didn't do it then, a punishment would come with cruelty. The revenge of poetry would come to whomever stops the flow of energy from manifesting itself. That's why so many avenging spirits exist. Because they have not manifested what they should say when they should have said it. And it comes out anyway but not the way it would have come in the first place. And then it comes with a vengeance and a curse. It is better to put wax in your ears not to hear what comes out of a voice that has voice and charisma—and never says what it should have said—and when it says it, it changes the course of action with a curse. Unless the curse is derailed by a blessing, another voice interrupts the curse, and the course of action calls for a Palinode—to interfere—and start the course of action again. It never starts from the beginning. It starts in the middle because it has all these avenging fists and curses inside that have interfered with the course of action—and have made the canto more cursed but fuller of wisdom and labia—more fit to the purpose of recovery from a pandemic—more unfit to the measures of standardized tests—and fuller of joy and pain. And when I tell you I have this voice that is unfitting to my body—the voice is very young—and I am much older than the voice—so when people hear the voice, they think how can it be that an older body has such a juvenile sound—delinquent too—it is strayed—and it has been astray for years, not finding the tone or the register—or not identifying with the things it hears or sees—of not liking what it hears—of liking too much—and of not having been liked in the same measure—of being disappointed and separated from the source of income—the source that makes fruition grow and overcome hunger and poverty—and these are all measures that are registered in the voice when it sings. And you can hear, when you listen carefully, to all these registers in that voice—and the missteps taken—and the disappointments, and the appointments fulfilled—and not overcome or cancelled. For that reason, I am cancelling the appointment to color my hair pink today—because the appointment with the register of my voice is accomplishing its goal—exhausting my time—bringing to fruition its own time—its own voice—to experience the full measure of a register—not interrupted by appointments to color pink what is black and has a hairy constitution.

Baudelaire told the story of a rat, two boys, and their toys. Sandcastles on the beach—skyscrapers rising from the bottom of the sea—and a hand blows them apart in a whim of gratitude or contrition. The rich boy was fascinated by the poor boy's toy—a rat he was shaking and provoking in a box with a grate. The rat had magical powers. It was alive. Maybe that is what fascinated Baudelaire—that this toy, the rat, was alive and moving. He was attracted to the unleashiness of the crowds. Maybe the rich boy's toy was the one Madame Panckoucke had given Baudelaire—expensive but not alive. It missed the magnitude of experience. Where do you get charisma? Charisma, apart from being gratitude for the living. Some have charisma but miss the gratitude. They never miss anything—to miss implies a disconnection between yesterday and today—among many other things—there is a distance. When the interconnection happens—Electra—electricity shocks the world with charisma. Charisma is experience experimented—drunken wine transformed into a river—it moves mountains and builds bridges—it breaks distances and recovers wasteful time—and brings upon us the

> When I
> fell in love—and I lost
> what I loved—suddenly. I had what
> I loved in a poem, a gratitude for
> the living and the dead. That is
> charisma. The recovery of a
> wasted moment that becomes
> an expression of gratitude.

quality we are always looking for. If we didn't miss our origins, we would all be here in the moment of creation. Creativity has charisma, toys of inspiration, and melodies to open doors. When you are a child, you play with rats or you build sand castles, but you are here. Disconnection cries for help, a tear of frustration, you dry the tear and start playing again. Charisma comes after as a halo—an accumulation of experience—it has to be experimented—worked and lived through altitudes and destructions—one event after another builds energy and passion. When I fell in love—and I lost what I loved—suddenly, I had what I loved in a poem, a gratitude for the living and the dead. That is charisma. The recovery of a wasted moment that becomes an expression of gratitude. Even when the moment is unhappy, if it has grace, it has gratitude. It is free—when it is free—it comes and goes—it doesn't stay forever—what stays is not loved as much as what leaves—what leaves—is then cut and measured—a distance is established. It doesn't belong. It leaves, it leaves you empty—what better than to fill the emptiness with thoughts.

--Would you say charisma is dark power and a halo is white light, a bright future?

--I am not a racist. Darkness or lightness is not a measure of power.

--A halo is a light of purification. After the Black paintings of Goya comes the halo of *La Lechera de Burdeos*. After my book, *Clowns and Buffoons* comes *Pastoral; or, the Inquisition of Memories*.

--Charisma comes from a source. Find the source of the attraction—and you'll get the sorcerer. The problem here is that you want to separate me from the source—that force—that sorcerer. Margot Arce told me—look what she is doing to you. She nailed your photograph to the head of her bed. And I came with a hammer, unhooked all the nails, and ran with my photo.

--But she is coming now to show you the charisma she acquired after having cheated death. What she saw, experimented, missed, reconnected, and forgot. All of these, and none of it together—because it was after life—something that has not even been forgotten— nor missed—nor experimented but transgressed and recomposed into a body made of hell's experience—a body made of the ashes—not of the ave fénix—because it doesn't fly—it comes back to show you more than it could give once it was alive—a will of iron—a will of hell— filled with an accumulation of grievances—and a serial experimentation of mistakes—not arranged—or misdeeds not misdone—it didn't miss the doing—it missed what it had not accomplished in moving forward—it missed experimentation in the accomplishment, but it achieved its goal of coming back to life after being dead.

To come back from hell after being dead and acquire a body that breathes charisma—an attraction born in the experience of returning—and still be dead. This time—as when I met you a long time ago—when you were alive. This time that you are alive—it's fake and rotten news—an appearance of life that is rotten dead—and death will reclaim this appearance that has come to me to reclaim life as it was 30 years ago—and now is dead. No one would claim what is dead is alive. Yet you told me you were alive. It was a lie. You were dead. And it was not a resurrection. When a dead body, the same dead body that dies, uses its primary source as the intercourse of life, it comes polluted with the same coronavirus it died of. And you forgot the reason you came back with the same body—to make amendments to your first constitution. But you forgot the amendments—because the way you cheated death—you have always cheated life. You did not tell the people you cheated all your life that you are dead—that you just want more life—and you want to get it however you can. Cutting short others of their primary source of inspiration, you take their breathing patterns to give your dead body some claim to history, to art, to culture—cheating death of the priorities it had for you.

An angel is very different.

A resurrection is very different—it comes clean—not polluted. But a dead body that comes back after dying of Coronavirus to pollute the earth is not a resurrection. A resurrection comes without pollution—clean of wounds—not hurt—nor forgotten but loved. It comes to lift the spirit—and it goes into the light in a blue halo. But a dead body that comes back from death—never really comes back—it is still in hell but wants more hell on earth—it comes to bring a piece of that hell back to earth. Hell always needs agents on earth to transmit its properties—and they always come with pollution, collusion, contagion. They don't come clean to inspire. They prefer to infect. They are liars. They don't believe in truth. They believe in obstruction of light. And that's why they are contagious. Their contacts are not clean—they have bad intentions—bad faith.

It's not the first time—as you well know—I have seen resurrections. I killed Franco—and a week later, after I told Olivier:

--I think Franco is dead.

Franco appeared in my birthday party with Sabine Cassel. Maritza Perez had killed Dr Fletcher when he was alive and kicking. So, when Jabalí called to invite me to dinner, I said:

--Que malos son los puertorriqueños. Arnaldo Cruz and María Carrión told me you were dead, and Ruth Lugo even sent me your obituary. I said—Jabalí always said she would die at 84 like her grandmother. All a lie. I am happy you are alive and kicking. Of course, let's celebrate your resurrection. Wait until Franco hears another one who bit the dust is alive again.

--I can't believe you're going to eat with Jabalí. She's dead.
--She is not dead. She just called me. She's as alive as Franco and Dr. Fletcher.

--How many people told you he is dead?
--Three.

--Did Jabalí tell you she is dead?
--No, why would she tell me she is dead when she is inviting me to dinner?

--The obituary in *El País* is as good as a death certificate.

--Didn't I just tell you I heard her voice?
--If she called you, it's because she wants to take you with her to hell. To hell with everybody. I have to save you from hell.

--She picked you up in her '76 green Volkswagen Beetle and drove you through the cliffs and abysses. All her life she took the hard road—the difficult path—and everything about her was forced—even her fake Castilian accent and her small voice. She had zero charisma until she came back from hell. She was no longer 84 years old as the obituary had stated. She was 54 again, a bit stocky, well-tailored for a professor, and with a newfound charisma she had acquired from having cheated death.

--It's true she had zero charisma. And she had a small voice like a grain of sand and enormous hands. How did you know that. I have goosebumps. I can't believe you know these things. I never told you about them. Beware of the Dark Lady. The Dark Lady inspires you and makes you sense the whole world in a scent—and then leaves you vaporizing the hours, the minutes, the seconds—and nothing makes sense but she acquires this fortified energy that she steals from you, and leaves you close to dying of love, misunderstanding and in fruition of a work of art. Once she leaves you, you start completing your art. You always miss the darkness, but creativity comes with light. A Dark Lady is a murderess in disguise. It wants to kill what is light—what comes with a flashlight and illuminates her face. She doesn't want anyone to know she is old and wrinkled. She comes to make fruition out of hunger and malnutrition. When you shine a flashlight on a Dark Lady, the Dark Lady retrocedes and walks backward, but she is not supposed to look back at the hell she came from. That is why she is dark. She only comes at night. To manifest her darkness, and her shadows are the agents of discomfort. One can't figure out why after she leaves us in pain, we are yearning for the hell she came from.

--That's how she appeared in the dream. You went to a Spanish restaurant, good, but not the kind of restaurant I take you to, not five stars. It was dark and outdated. She brought a Chilean colleague, a former student of hers whose face was effaced. She had effaced her face. She was sipping sangria without a face. And no one seemed fazed by her faceless face. You looked happy. Jabalí looked happy. And I couldn't believe she had not told either one of you the truth—that she was dead. You were wearing a Dior jumpsuit, grasshopper green, très chic, with pointy white Louboutins. She was trying to guess the brands to steal your style.

--She tried to steal everything from me to the extent that when I was in Newark writing the finale of *United States of Banana*—a thief on the train tried to steal my bag. I said out loud: What is this? The sensation I had was that the thief was doing what Jabalí did to me—encircling me, entrapping me, stalking me to steal from me. It was a very familiar sensation—menacing—and at the same time exciting.

--You exaggerated your mannerisms, unfurling your napkin midair and dabbing the corner of your lips to show off how much style you had acquired since she left you 30 years ago. You were moving your fork and knife as if you were conducting an orchestra of salad on your plate. I peered through the window ashamed I had stooped so low as to spy on you, but I couldn't believe what was happening. I called my best friend Marijana.

--Spare me the details—Marijana said. Get to the bottom of why she is attracted to people who put her down.

--She doesn't know what love is. She thinks affection—the affection one has for a dog is love. So, she confuses affection with dog love.

--I can't believe you are saying that. When Jabalí left me, she said—What I have for you is affection. So maybe it is true that I confuse affection for love. They gave me affection, not love.

--She likes to be put down like a Jack in the box—I said to Marijana. Close the lid—and she jumps up. But this time she's playing with fire. If Jabalí puts her in the box, it will be a coffin, not a Jack in the box coming out to sing:

Pero siempre me gusta vivir,
Ya lo decía.

The next scene is in Spain. There is a mass grave, bulldozers, and thousands of bodies thrown into a mass grave. Wrapped in white sheets. The ones who were good and generous fertilize the earth and sprout dandelions, daisies, daffodils. While the bad ones sink deeper and deeper into the earth—to underground caves where almas desalmadas are howling:

--I didn't do it!
--It wasn't my fault!
--I swear it wasn't me!
--Give me another chance! I'll make it up!

Here there were serial criminals. People like Jeffrey Epstein and Donald Trump who never make amends. Jabalí was there too but compared to their crimes—the crimes of a critic who plagiarized and seduced her students—petty—and even her voice was small and petty—so the gods were not paying attention to her claims. She took advantage of the situation. Jabalí, who was raised in Ponce, knew that huricanes have an eye. And when the eye came, the rest of them didn't know what to make of the sudden calm, but since she was raised in Ponce, she seized the moment and swam straight up like a champion. And even though I knew she was a cheat, I found myself rooting for her as I would for any prison break. I was torn. I knew she'd do more harm, but I couldn't help but admire her iron will when I saw her face break the surface—coughing, sputtering—her little head bobbing up and down in the vastness of the sea. Now she had charisma. She had a story to tell—an experience of life and death—crossing the borders. She could come back and tell what she had experimented. She could have told you:

--I'm sorry. I came back to bring you this experience so
that you can tell the world the story of my charisma. How
I acquired this immense magnetism.

The body was starting to smell. The waves were rising. The restaurant was next to the sea. I can't believe she hasn't said that she's dead. Soon the body will begin to stink. Everyone in the restaurant will think it's the stench of a rotten boar in the kitchen. They won't know it's the stench of a dead critic. Of course, Jabalí won't know she stinks—she died of Coronavirus—she lost her sense of smell. All of a sudden, I hear this voice in my head say—those without roots will fly. I run into the restaurant and grab hold of your foot with all my might—to give you roots—and just as you were about to kick free because you wanted to go with Jabalí, Marijana to the rescue grabs hold of your other foot. We're on a mission to save you—so we put wax in our ears not to hear you screaming:

> --Worse than Tolstoy's wife! She treats me worse than
> Tolstoy's wife!
> --Like a rubber band—Marijana said—shoot her in the
> opposite direction.

We let go at the same time—you fly through the air—and Cupid flies by and catches you like a basketball.

This is very different than when Honorata Pagán appeared to me in a dream and said:

> --I stopped coming to help you because you stopped asking
> for my help. You thought I was dead. But people like me
> never die because we were never born.

And she really helped me by showing me that everything that moves has inspiration, dynamism, life. The bad thing is when things don't move—and they get stuck in a knot—and if they got stuck in a knot it was because Jabalí had my picture in the back of her bed stuck in a knot with nails—and I had to go there—and with a hammer—and with ease—it was very easy—I took the nails out—and ran out with my photograph. A dead body that comes back is very different than a free spirit that is everywhere in nature because it never dies because it was never born. And if it never died because it was never born, it is part of what comes and goes, but is always here like the seasons returning or like the ages of man, which are

seasons
repeating
their structures
and their patterns.
That was the great lesson that
my psychic Honorata Pagán taught me. Things
that are alive never die because they are never born—they are here and
now—bathing in the sun—or playing with a ball. Enjoyment never dies
because it was never born. Instant was never born—it never dies—it just
passes by—you have to grasp it in its becoming—grasp its figuration—
and the meaning of the passing by. Could it be fruition or fortification?
Could it be attainability—the ability to grasp in an instant what never
dies because it was never born? Maybe our imagination is like that—
and our prefigurations don't necessarily come before—they can come
after—because they never die because they were never born—and
our stamina is like that—a prefiguration of wasted time—time is a
waste of time—lost and found in what never dies because it was never
born—our wasteful gestures—the movement of our hands—our jumping jacks—and our jacks in the box—and our prerogatives that don't
walk with bare feet in the sand—and the horizons—vertical on their
shores—and in their manifestations—hilarious—and hilarity doesn't
know that it doesn't die because it is never born—and for that reason it
moves with ease and precision and ahead—frontal to the expectations
that don't die because they were never before nor after but here, in the
here and now, manifesting breath—breathing easy and sleeping easy
because they know that they won't die because they were never born.

Delusion is a past illusion presenting itself as hope.

The agenda of a dead body coming back to life. Whenever you have the past (what is dead) presenting itself as an agenda to fix the present moment by taking us back—to the dead—you have contagion, pest, collusion, pollution, delusion—not illusion. Illusion is a hope. Delusion is a past illusion presenting itself as hope. Hope is something that has not happened yet, but when it happens, and the happening has already died and been buried—and other present moments have come forward and made us live other present moments—and a dead body—a dead moment—comes back presenting itself as if it were alive—and it is dead—and it doesn't tell us that it is dead—that is not an illusion—that is a delusion.

--It is important to wear a mask.
--Of course, it is important. Have you ever smelled the smell
  of a dead body?

--Noxious. Only other dead bodies walking around don't
  smell it—they're immune to their own smelly rottenness—
  they're rotten to the core, but maggots and bitches still want
  to rip a tender morsel off their bones to nourish their entrails,
  regardless of the rotten smell. A dead body must be given its
  proper burial. And even with a burial in a common grave, a
  dead body came back to life to infect us again with a virus
  that is smelless and tasteless—right out of the rib of a Zoom
  meeting which is also smelless and tasteless.

And here comes the sardine again—that stinky, rotten sardine coming back to life—to inflict suffering from the past—with more delusions of grandeur—with its smelly smell—diffused with oils of Resurrection, Law of Attraction, Ambergris, Enchanted Dreamers, Love Force, Exorcism, Midnight Warrior, Higher Power. But underneath all these mighty smells evaporated and rotten was the smell of the stinky sardine of the 20th century—passing itself off as a grand dame of the 21st and infecting us all with Coronavirus. I could smell its smell coming from the underground as Eurydice from hell—and I put on all my enchanted oils—so that they would enchant the sardine—and make it dance in front of me—and I would send it back to where it belonged—back to hell.

That stinky sardine came back to life like the Nose of Gogol—with a pretention—as if it didn't smell like a rotten sardine—as a grand dame—as if it were red caviar served in a Russian roulette—spinning wheel—captain go round. Who is next? Another one bites the dust—poof—dead. And it had a red cape over its black jumpsuit and a dimple in its cheek that used to laugh at all of us when it was alive. But don't forget it is dead. And it is a stinky sardine with the high pretention of a grand dame who doesn't know her place. It's a nose. It pretends to be walking up Madison Avenue, up with the sniff and the snuff of the Nose of Gogol that is a snob that pretends to be higher up than it is. It walks without legs, but it has a smell, and when it smells, it leaves you without smell and taste. It numbs you because the smell of death leaves you numb.

The most intriguing thing about this stinky little thing is how it has acquired charisma. It's the charisma of having cheated death—of coming back with the appearance of a body that is alive but stinks to high heaven. I used to love this stinky sardine when it was alive. It was pretentious, but it had spunk. Now it has delusions. I pity the moment when all the people the stinky sardine has infected with delusions of grandeur wake up from the numbness in which this stinky sardine has made us live as if it were alive walking around without a mask over its nose. And at times that stinky smell spooks us as it did to Pendejo after he learned from the press that he had the stinky sardine inside him—puff—that smell that numbs our senses and leaves us spooked, unnerved, and acting without any sense—senseless but above all tasteless and smelless—smelling spooked—and without a smell. The stinky sardine cannot tell who has it and who has it not—like Gretchen—it loves me and it loves me not. It loves you not. It loves you not. I can tell, but it spooks you and leaves you without a smell smelling a rotten egg.

First, she had to disguise that she was a nose. Then, she had to disguise that she was a sardine. And lastly, that she was dead. And that she had had such an important burial—where Hamlet, Zarathustra, and Giannina had buried her as the symbol of the 20th century. So, when she came back as a manifestation of Coronavirus, she was hiding the triple whammy of her three identities: nose, sardine, dead body. Nose, stuck up—no humility at all—a sardine pretending to be a nose—pretending to breathe—with her nostrils high up—while her little insect eyes could hardly see—so small and with such pretention. Hiding her stink under her red cape—and with that dimple open to the world—she was saying:

--I am better than anyone else. I came back from death.
I cheated death. No one should fear Coronavirus. I beat it
up. You have to just kick it in the butt.

She didn't realize she was the contagion. She didn't know she stunk of death. She didn't know who she was. She was a sardine pretending to be a nose walking up Madison Avenue looking to catch a rich fish in her network. Oh, yes, she knew how to work the web. She was a computer herself, a database of information and gossip. Everything registered as information in that nose of a stinky sardine to catch the rich fish in her net web. Everything was a knot, a web, not a nest. She was kind of a spider web with the pretention of a nose smelling with its nostrils high up. But the moment Tartuffe lost his nose in the Presidential Inauguration she was in for big trouble. She had to hide that she had stolen Tartuffe's nose—and that she was a sardine—and that she was a dead body coming back from hell. She had to hide all three together.

Everybody including me was touching their noses and finding no nose but instead a big hole. We were all terrified of catching a little cold, a little cough. What will we do at the end of the day if we all start coughing and pretending we are a sardine pretending to be a nose—and we don't find our noses anymore in the frame of our faces—because they're all walking up Madison Avenue—smelling of sardines—stuck up—pretending to breathe—and sniffing—catching a fish—a rich fish in their nets—in their holes that can hardly breathe—and they're sniffing and

Here comes the sardine
again, pretending now
to be The Nose of Gogol.
It is not a pretention.
It is what it is.
A fake dimension.
An illusion that will
become a delusion.
It will inflate the
markets as a tick—
and then it will deflate
them with a depression.

coughing. We all thought we were alive, but we were dead. When we could hardly breathe, we protested in the streets and screamed:

--We can't breathe.
--I lost my nose. I can't breathe. But I still have a mouth.
I can catch a rich fish in my teeth.

We were all looking for excuses. If you can't breathe through your nose because you lost it, a blessing in disguise! Good luck! Start breathing through your mouth. Develop a new breathing pattern. We always had the mouth as a second breather. Now it is not a vice president anymore. We will elevate the mouth to the position of the nose. It will continue eating and talking but now it will become the primary income of breathing, smelling, and tasting too. It will multitask like a computer or an octopus.

I was the first one who recognized the sardine in the nose pretending to catch a rich fish. I said—Here comes the sardine again, pretending now to be The Nose of Gogol. It is not a pretention. It is what it is. A fake dimension. An illusion that will become a delusion. It will inflate the markets as a tick—and then it will deflate them with a depression. It is looking at the eclipse. You are not supposed to look at the eclipse. It will leave you blind. And it is not wearing a mask—it's wearing a cape—and thinks it can disguise itself as a sardine pretending to be a nose—and that nobody will recognize the pretention of a dead body coming back to pollute us all. Let me remind you, we are not as stupid as we pretend to be. There is a point of no return. When we will all look at the hole in our faces—and we will miss the noses we have lost—and we will not let a sardine pretending to be a nose degrade us more than we already are—pretending—all of us—that it is a blessing in disguise to lose a nose—because now the mouth has to become a multitasker—and has to breathe through one hole—the one of the trachea—so if now we can simplify our functions—and breathe less through one mouth. Count yourself lucky. A blessing in disguise is coming! Maybe we will win the next election! And when the new president is installed, our noses will appear again, the day after the inauguration. Tartuffe will recover his nose too when he wakes up in the morning and looks at himself in the mirror with his nose in its place—and not smelling like a stinky sardine, full of fear of catching Coronavirus through the nose or the mouth.

Sardine: If they get infected, I am so sorry. They wanted
             to hug and kiss me. I love to be kissed on the top
             of my nose. I was so moved by the kisses and
             the hugs. They thought I looked like a rosebud.
             I did have a peak—the peak of my nose—full
             of enchanted oils. But the bud when it smelled
             had thorns that were peaking—they were on
             the peak—and as I peeked around the corner of
             Madison and 89th—a policeman stopped me.

Police: What are you doing here without wearing a mask?
             The virus is peaking again. And before we could
             foreclose on all the businesses, we saw you running
             around—without a mask—and peaking—and
             sniffing. I have to fine you.

Sardine: Fine with me. You will have to charge the face. I am
             part of that company of noses, ears, foreheads.
             I don't have a dime in my pocket, but my company
             can pay.

Police: Why aren't you wearing a mask?
Sardine: Because I don't want to hide my nose. It is peaking
             high.

Police: You are wearing a blanket around your throat.
Sardine: I don't want to catch pneumonia. It's getting cold.
Police: Show me your identity.
Sardine: Sardine. Nose. Dead body rejuvenated by essential oils.

Police: Are you a resurrection?
Sardine: I am the President. I preside. Over a nation of noses
             that sniff high. They don't want to cough, but
             coughing happens despite us all.

Police:	Are you spiking?
Sardine:	I am spooking in disorder—in disarray—out of balance and place. I am looking for a face. A face where I can dawn a country and breathe again with relief. And not be spooked.
Police:	You stink.
Sardine:	I stink since I came back from hell looking for the nose where I can pose the body of a stinky sardine. Keep looking for clues, detective. You still haven't found my origin. You are tracing me, but I've got many traces and few remitting addresses. Now that you are speaking to me. No one spoke to me before. I got this red cape to infiltrate the company of pleasure. Of mourning I have black underneath—and a dimple to show a wink of empathy towards the living—eyes of an insect—memory of an elephant—and ears of a rabbit. I do run fast. I am tracking your movement—and the pace of your peace to bring hell on earth. Oh, please, bring peace on earth and spook the rest.

And don't forget that the vice president—the mouth—had a fly on the top of his head—just standing there during the entire vice-presidential debate. I wonder if the fly smelled the greasy Vaseline in his hair or the stink of the deadly sardine in the air. Contrary to him and to the monsignor at the Catholic Charities gala who had ants crawling in and out of his white collar—something sacred—the halo of the white collar—not emitting radiance but deadlines and fundraising goals crawling in and out of the collar. Contrary to them, I had no flies nor ants. I had a green grasshopper—una esperanza—on the sleeve of my red jacket when I went to the park to exercise my angles, my postures, and my cadences.

Grasshopper:	My heart has been strained. It has been forced to sing when it wanted to jump.

Sardine:	Sing. Sing a song of jump.
Grasshopper:	Why is there so much acid in the air?
Sardine:	I am toxic.
Grasshopper:	I am green. Evergreen. With spring I put a stop to your toxification. Acidification.

Sardine:	You need me—to make the opposite of me.

Grasshopper:	My hope comes from having suffered in the winter storm of discontent.

Sardine:	Stop jumping. Your jumping makes me dizzy.

Grasshopper:	Look at the grass. It's moving. The snow is green—green fields of grasshoppers—green ivy leaves—green I believes. I have realized toxification happens when you pave the road with a forced energy and you strain it by not allowing the snow to melt without imposing your will. To will is not to hope. Hope has no preamble. Expectation appears with wings—and it hopes in the winter of your discontent with wings—it expects a miracle. When faith appears clinging to a wing of hope, tackiness has a wing strained by hope. But hope has vacillations too—it has doubts—and when it achieves it takes away all doubts of separation because it integrates what is strained with what is possible and appears full of hopes that are giving birth to the moment of hope—and there's no moment after. When the expectation has achieved multiple purposes of hope—at an inch of separation from probability—fruition happens in a second of happiness.

I have become more human with expectations of hope arriving soon. But not soon enough. Enough has determination but doesn't always know when to stop—or how to recognize readiness as an impromptu of tenderness—and when you don't know when to stop—because you don't really know how to make something out of it—you keep hoping it will get to where it wants to get—and you keep pushing for it to give all its hope of attainability—all its attainability has to achieve its expectation—to get to that level of fruition—where it makes sense without having to make sense of it—and without having to force it—because there's no reason to stop hope from achieving its highest hope—its highest attainability—and fruition—and climbing the wall as ivy leaves—as I believes—it hopes in magnitude of degrees—and it climbs higher and higher into expectation of hope and fruition of hope.

Dead Body: How would you recognize a dead body that walks around enjoying the breeze as if it were alive. And why would you discriminate against a dead body. Can't we take over the planet and breed again a new generation? Maybe the new dead bodies that come to life will never die.

Sardine: A dead body that comes back with the same virus it died of is still contagious. It stinks of sardine. But it doesn't smell its stink.

Nose: This new breed of sardines is blind to color. Before they were blind to love—now they are blind to taste. They taste nothing. Their senses are as opaque as their contagion is attached to claims of invincibility—and vacuity—full of vacuous spaces—and blank verses—with nothing to say. Vacuousness is a syndrome of the home run of the new species running around as if it were alive, but it is dead. The species is coming to an end. A new breed is coming to make proclamations.

Bacchus:	I ate three pairs of sardines—my breath stinks.
Frenzy:	Are you in a state of Frenzy?
Bacchus:	Now that I'm human, I have to smell in order to survive. The smell of sardine is everywhere.
Frenzy:	How did it become a plague?
Bacchus:	One lonely, stinky sardine escaped hell—and spread its smell all over town—using coitus for pleasure and fun—and lost touch with reality but not with its base at the rallies. They were mass rocking and rolling their hips, belly dancing—out of sight—out of heart—out of touch with reality.
Frenzy:	A crime against humanity.
Bacchus:	Do the locals have a saying?
Frenzy:	Don't you find it insulting to call them locals when they are natives. The locality is misplaced in another place—and I can't find the origin. But I know that when they referred to them as locals, they are localizing them in a locality—and they are misplacing them—and taking them out of their place—and making them inferiors—demeaning the locals.
Bacchus:	That's what they do with noses nowadays. They sniff when they can't breathe—and they want to smell something—and pronounce their noses full of air that they can't breathe. They use their nose to sniff what they can't sniff. They remember that they could sniff—and now their nostrils are full of empty promises—of broken promises—of when can we breathe again in this toxic atmosphere.
Giannina:	I became pregnant. I gave light to a sardine—that itself became pregnant.
Bacchus:	You are unfocused.

Giannina:	Very aware of my surroundings but misplaced—bouncing back—and striding forward with all my heart.
Bacchus:	Are you aware of the consequences of your actions.
Giannina:	If I had actions, I would have consequences. I already said once—I don't act. So, there are no consequences. The results are not consequences. They make real what is unreal. The dead bodies that came back to life appeared old enough to become who they were before they passed. They appeared again—and no one questioned their credentials because of the incredulity that was going around—no one wanted to question appearances—appearances were not questioned—as long as they appeared as creatures that existed—who cares if they were dead before and came back to life—who would question a disappearance that appears again—and who would dare to ask for proof that they were dead—a certificate of defunction would mean that there is no more function coming out of that body, but a lot of functions came out of that body—and no measure of sleep—the body didn't need to sleep—it killed sleep—it went dead—and when it came back no more sleep was needed to reenergize the body.
Sardine:	Now that I'm so alive—and of a perfect physical specimen and so young—after dying of Coronavirus—defying the deadlines of my condition—and so I am lucky in that way. A bad sardine never dies. And if it dies, it stinks until it finds a way to return and do what I was doing. Repeating the conditions in which my behavior was called reprehensible. All my comrades either smell of death—or they have moths—or ants—or

flies flying around their heads. I am the President presiding over all the sardines that pretend to breathe in Congress through their mouths—and in the Senate through their noses—and they can't breathe because their orifices are clogged by compromises and preconditions. A mouth (a fly) is not a sardine. A fly can fly around the nose of the sardine pretending to be one—or being one of the insects flying around the smell of the rotten sardine. But a mouth—with all its vicious worms rotting its stinky breath—is not the sardine of the nose—a mouth is the voice of the stench propagating the propaganda of the stench—and the kisser of the ass of the nose pretending to be a sardine. Why would the mouth want to have the stench of death of the stinky sardine with all the mocos coming out of the nose—with all the delusions of grandeur coming out of it and not a grain of truth? Does it want to snort like the nose? Does it want to sneeze like the nose? Does it want to pretend to be the mouth of the nose (the speaker of the house) in chambers never forgotten or becoming is the simple identity of a mouth becoming a nose—and pretending to be healthy when it speaks ill of the stinky sardine pretending to become a nose. I don't know what you think of this. But to me it has many fanatics inside. Insiders are insiders. And intriguers are intriguers. They aspire to other positions in the constitution of the body to act with more caution or to amend the constitution. Why does a nose have the power to cut the legs of the multitudes of wages at the knee. I sure know they fear their own Achilles heel. But when they look at their heel, they're not looking at what stinks to high heaven. They are cutting off the movement of the people at the knee. And what does a nose pretending to be a breather of youth overcoming Coronavirus through a mouth full of serpents and vicious dogs pretend to be without a heel and a knee that gives movement, dynamism, and life to the stinky, deadly sardine of law and order—in disarray of disorder—breathing through a deadly sardine pretending to be a nose?

Esperanza: Hope has wings.

Sardine: And then when I turned on Madison and 89th, the police tried to exterminate me during a raid. They were looking for the fly that stood on the vice president's head. And I complained about my substance. I drank a tank of gasoline—nothing makes me tipsy except gasoline in my tanks. This fervor I have to always return to sender makes me a predator—I precede—predate—I stand up—I run—I am not thorough. I bring velocity, and when people achieve, sometimes they achieve with me. But then I wreak havoc—without wanting it—it's just that I am salty. My luck is not green like yours. It is compromised by a virus. To return from hell, I had to forget that happiness is a state of mind that has fruition. I am not the happy kind. I am salty and bring pain.

Esperanza: Whenever you see green, you stampede, predator, you possess. Oh, I feel good, there is music around—bees buzzing around—a sound of happening. Some weird happening was misunderstanding my state of accomplishment where I could stand on my six legs and accomplish the hope I came to achieve. After missing the death you left behind—without tracking my innocence— because you were predating all my predecessors. You wanted. Who knows what you yourself wanted. Pleasure was the happening, and your achievement was regret—red with wings—and sleepless nights—and I wouldn't say corruption but decadence without remorse. You flew away for more than 30 years—and then—poof—dead—like a tick on a dog's skin. But the return to defeat has made me rise in the middle of the stage to bring hope. What hasn't happened yet—what is not going to turn sour—and what has no regret. The intentions of my hope are not to get what I want by stealing what the other has—or getting as much as I can—only to fly away—and come back from hell to wreak havoc. But to bring hope which has not been compromised—which is not a predator and doesn't empty your memory—doesn't evaporate proportions—gives dimensions—and creates music and bans the bewitched. Bewitching is kind of admitting you are not free. And then when you become free—because the predator predates you—and takes you to that unreal state of memory—where everything predates time—there are so many things you want to understand—that when predating leaves you—you become obsessed with what is happening all the time that precedes time because it comes with an achievement in its melodies. And when it arrives with precision, that's the moment of climbing and jumping and rising. Why is it that negation is essential to creation— as if a Yes depended on a No—to stamp with innocence its affirmation again—as if good needed bad to step ahead—to have the obstacle as the steppingstone of the achievement. No, it is not a necessity to have hunger in order to give food. The emptiness has not to predate the vacillation or the accomplishment. The emptiness has not to predate the inspired state of accomplishment—done deal and sealed with a stamp—without reference to the past—and memory not following any leader. It was a misstep to stand high and ahead when nothing

was forfeiting the life we lived together. Oh, how
romantic and nostalgic. Why do regrets bring
misunderstandings. It was, and it is not romantic—
and it was, and it is not a misunderstanding, and
it is stepping up to claim what is stolen—what
has always brought delusions of grandeur. If you
feel vertigo, it is because you are claiming a piece
of hell—and earth is earthy—not hellish—it is
rough and it is dense—and it has what it has—not
descriptions for description's sake—the eyes were
not made to describe—they see—they don't
describe the things they see—they retain them—
and when the eyelids close—they see them in the
thought that passes in the brain like Eucalyptus
under the nose. In order to wreak havoc on earth,
you have come back from hell, but I will bury
you again and again. This year I am celebrating
every new year of every religion, custom, and
memory—every new year of every continent—
and an hour ahead—or twenty hours after—after
I go to bed—I clean the havoc the sardine brings
with essential hopes to bring to earth—the earthy,
healthy, wealthy winds—and inspirations to
bathe away reprehensible behavior. But whoever
reprehends has reprehensions and pretentions
of being something else—a grand dame—with a
grand piano—and high heels—going up Madison
and 98th with an attitude of fortune stolen from
misfortune. Don't listen to the tune of happiness
when it is mixed feelings that claim another
sardine—a New Year. If it is a misstep, I will get out
on the next bus stop and hop on the bus of the next
New Year. Good luck! Keep hope alive!

And when the detective, Patrick O'Dwyer,
arrives with the police to find out who murdered
the sardine and sent it back to hell where it

belongs, they will find that it is redundant to
find the murderess because even though I killed
it—throwing it against the wall and breaking its
tick—the tick ticking inside the sardine—they will
find out the sardine was not breathing through the
nose—nor the mouth—because it was already
dead—and even though I murdered it—and threw
its ticking head of a tick against the wall—I cracked
opened its cranium—and it shed plenty of blood—
confused and diffused through its red cape of little
Red Riding Hood—no innocence in that blood but
a dimple in the cheek that is empty with a rotten
smile. And the detective, Patrick O'Dwyer, had
to claim it was attempted murder, but it was not
a homicide. It was a double whammy because
it was already dead. The murderess—Hope—
Esperanza—is free to continue spreading its oil of
Eucalyptus. The nose was not breathing before it
was murdered—and the mouth was open, but it
was dead before it was killed again by Hope. The
remnants of the sardine pretending to be a nose
will be held in the Capitol for a week—flags at
half-mast—because the stinky sardine was dead.
Before it was killed, it killed more than 1.1 million
Americans and 7 million people worldwide. Before
it was killed, it was already dead. Nobody will be
accused of killing what was already dead. A green
light will shine forever in the sky!

Foreshadowing of the Sardine

WHENEVER I SEE COMPUTER WIRES entangled in knots, I have for the purpose of the good will of the world to dissolve the knots, the grievances, the fights, the bad energy and leave the wires empty of themselves—leave them empty of bad breath, bad communication, disease—and bring them to a state of being in which they feel liberated. It is exhilarating—the liberation of wires, the unraveling of a knot—or of many knots that should not be knotted together—and whoever lets them be knotted unconsciously or carelessly it's because they're in knots—and they reveal their knotting attitude toward life. Some always go tit for tat—and tit for tat is a knot with plenty of wires. Some knots take time to dissolve—they are not only knots—they are grievances and grudges held dear for a very long time—complexes—and disorganized energy put in front of us as barricades to defend what they hold dear in their dear, dear treasure chest of their hearts. They miss the point of putting things in their place. Of liberating the energy of each piece of furniture. A human trouble is a human disarray—a purpose unlimited with obstacles created by knotty people who don't know how to break the knots that are breaking apart all kinds of connections with the human course and progression. I had just celebrated my birthday on February 5th 2020 not knowing Coronavirus was around the corner when in one of my many dissymmetrical, asymmetrical windows a dense oily shadow without any musicality or radiance appeared. When I lived in the Parc Vendôme there were many weird episodes and otherworldly encounters—and they had reasons to appear in that old crusty building where so many old crusty Broadway actors and musicians had lived and died—you felt their presence or the aura of their struggle for survival in certain appearances that disappeared. It was the past superimposing on the present with more weight than it should have, weighing me down, and I had to move out of there. But here, in the Jean Nouvelle, no one has died yet—it is a younger crowd—a crowd of millennials—and there is no weight on my shoulders—the past doesn't exist here. Finally, I said, I can breathe. This is the type of place where I feel in control of my happiness. My happiness will be my driving force. But a shadow from the past appeared in my bathroom window—and the shadow was stuck like a wire full of knots with obstruction, obfuscation. Not anger—it was not anger I saw—it was yellow—not the yellow of the sun but the yellow of hell. The sardine had appeared again. I had just gone to Santa Maria Novella for unguents and incense—and by chance they had a new product—a rose scented holy water which I splashed all over the obstructed shadow. Tess said:

> —It's a winter shadow. It's not a sardine shadow. It's a
> shadow that will appear every February because it's cold
> and there is condensation from the heater and interference
> from the wires in the outlets. It makes for a stuck-up
> shadow appearing to present a melodrama to you who
> have no grievances and are always looking for the fifth leg
> of the cat.

I mean, I was hungry, cold, and anxious—and there was no outlet for my anxiety but to fixate on the wires and the shadows. That is true. That is how it was, but there were other reasons. The shadow was there presenting itself as the foreshadowing of the sardine. And the arrival of Coronavirus had been postponed by Pendejo for another month, so I had no reason to throw holy water hysterically at the window. And when I woke up in the morning, I realized what I threw at the window was oil not water. I had confused the bottles in the dark, and, in my confusion, I made a mess of the window. The oil had created yellow spots—yellow streaks as if I had urinated on the window. But by doing so I had delayed the arrival of the stinky sardine. And I was preparing myself with essential oils to ward off the return of the eternal sardine and kill its effects for a little while. And after I saw the shadow in the window—which turned out to be the shadow of the eternal sardine returning—claiming the lives of millions of people—all of a sudden, forgetting that 30 years had passed—and that maybe I had forgotten her or felt hurt that she hadn't call me at least to talk about the happy widow—the reason why she had stopped talking to me was because I had called her a happy widow in *Yo-Yo Boing!*—the next day after the shadow of the sardine, my cousin Kia sent me a text message that she wanted to see me. Her daughter, who was born on my birthday long after the episode of the happy widow, was living in New York and wanted to meet me. I could not believe the return of my cousin—after the shadow in the window—and the return of the eternal sardine—and we didn't know then that Coronavirus was heading here with the speed of cholera. My uncle José Firpi had given me a sculpture of a gigantic turtle—and I embraced its marble shell—I climbed over its shell to protect me and rang the bells of the bull. I don't have to explain why I said my cousin was a happy widow. Happy widows are happy not because they are widows but because they embrace every moment of happiness they encounter. They are not disrespecting the past but embracing new arrivals. I will not forget the scene in *Satyricon* when a guard, who was watching over three crucified men to make sure their families didn't remove their bodies from the stakes, left his post to console a grieving widow who had buried herself alive to be with her dead husband. The guard gave her water, food, and more than water and food, honey. When the guard returned to his post the morning after, he saw one of the crucified had been taken down from the pole and carried away.

    --They'll kill me!—the guard cries. Kill me or I'll kill myself!
    --Don't worry—the widow says. Take my husband who is
      already dead and put him on the stake. The dead can be
      crucified. But you are alive.

That moment, wonderful moment, she became a happy widow embracing the present not the past. We would meet on Saturday at midnight to hold an exorcism. We would burn a green candle with sage and palo santo and invoke our higher powers. Franco would dance bringing forward whatever good wanted to come out of Earth. Earth wants to give something for everyone to receive, and everyone was receiving. If they were expecting more, more would come. If they wanted less, less would shrink them in olive oil, and they would become wrinkled raisins. There was a feather, a black feather, and I would use the black feather to fan the flames of palo santo and sage—higher and higher—into the multitudes of our aspirations—to fan the sprouting of flowers—more blooming—more pluming—more and more plumes of smoke—with the feather—la pluma—sprouting the plumes of creation—to give rise to countless aspirations that aspire higher than becoming an aspirin to calm a headache—but to open possibilities—to open doors—to forget about the buts, the regrets, the contrarians and the no's because the no's were all opening their mouths—and out of those mouths tongues of fire were also coming out and sprouting. It was like a blaze of fire—burning inside—like lava—and I don't like all the likes that are like another thing but are not the thing that is becoming the thing without the likings. All the likings are crutches, but walking happens without metaphors or similes. I passed the McAlpin and looked inside wondering what it would have been like if my brother were still alive. I lived there when my mother gave me the news that Brascho had died. I was outside, looking inside, and all of a sudden, a student, the same age I was when I lived there comes out of the revolving door with her mother—very affectionate—the student was saying good bye to her mother who was going to hop on a bus—I stared at them with tenderness in my eyes. They must have felt the love because they smiled at me—and the mother said--Hi! I am visiting my daughter. She's a student at NYU. I said to her—I lived here when I came to New York. I was a professor at Rutgers. You remind me of my mother and me. When you came through the revolving doors, I thought: it's the eternal return of the same—as the seasons come again every year—so do we come again to ingratiate with what is here. There was no GAP here. In the basement was a tavern that served the best burgers—and the walls and vaulted ceilings had glazed terracotta tiles by Frederick Dana Marsh depicting the maritime history of New York—a landmark destroyed by the GAP which also took over Chock Full o' Nuts on the other side of the McAlpin, across from Macy's. Their grilled cheese was dirty delicious. A rabbi who loved me dearly used to bring me coffee in the morning and a bagel with cream cheese—he would leave them at my door in a paper bag—he knew I was sleeping late. But when I woke up every morning, my coffee and bagel were waiting at my door—to keep me alive and floating in the air. He knew I was fragile and had nobody who took care of me at that time. I only cared about singing my song, making it simple to last a whole life long. Some people have said to me: You are too sheltered. Sheltering stifles creativity—you should experience everything—the good, the bad, and the ugly. Mind your own business, busybodies. Not everybody is the same. And it is true, I have always been sheltered. By rabbis, nuns, grandmothers, mothers, and lovers—and many times in deed the sheltering stifled my creativity—but I am still hungry with expectations—and even when stifled in a desert—without water—but with mirages of water—I was expecting the rain and it came again with more strength, speed, and sleep. I heard a young man in his early twenties coming out of the subway at Columbus Circle—singing in Spanish un cante hondo as if his body were dwelling inside his voice—not the voice inside the body but the opposite. I thought of Lorca's duende. So immediately I started a conversation.

--¿Eres español?
--Si.
--¿De dónde?
--De Valencia. Estoy aquí para adquirir experiencia. Me
  encanta Nueva York.

When someone says he loves New York, you or I or anyone who has been living here knows that he must be new here because after a while you would not say: Me encanta Nueva York. You would start feeling the pressure of making a living in an inhospitable place where no one would miss you if you dropped dead in the street. This guy still has duende and innocence. I too had said once: Me encanta Nueva York. In fact, I wrote a book about the love I felt for New York, *Empire of Dreams*. Afterwards, the love evolved into a marriage—and the city disillusioned me—with all its love affairs—not being loyal to anyone—and not missing me when I am away. He reminded me of me. Me, me, me. The duende and the canto hondo. And the fact that his body was inside his voice, and there was suffering in the voice. I'm not talking about the song but the voice. And I realized that he was singing not to feel cold— singing was his heater—he was getting warm as he sang—and it was a way of being connected to his roots. He was alone in this inhospitable place and didn't speak English. I was feeling alone too—and cold—and his song warmed my bones. When he finished singing, I clapped and invited him home for a drink and from that moment on, we became inseparable. Every week Manuel Sacristán and I would have lunch in the cellar of the Plaza Hotel. Of course I would pay. But he warmed my bones and recovered my innocence. The suffering in his voice was not a personal annotation—it was the suffering of the culture that he carried in his bones—a gypsy in New York. And a poet too, a singer with sensibility. And taste. He understood la luxure, magnifique, la luxure. Manuel wanted to make people feel good. And, if they were feeling low, he would lift their spirits by playing the spoons on his elbows and kneecaps—and the bad mood would dissolve in the glass of wine we drank together or in the song we sang together. It was all about dreaming loud. And when his mother and grandmother and sister came to New York to pick him up, they came to my home for dinner—and all that we did was enact our happiness as we sang and ate and drank and danced. To think I met him in the street—innocence in the street— song—in the street—love—in the street—tenderness—in the street. And also, conversation and company and food in the street. All these things that Manuel gave me and never asked anything in return but poetry and adventure in the street. Trust in the first place—not being afraid of meeting a stranger in the street. Confidence—not thinking of ulterior motives—trusting in serendipity. My friend, come back in 20 minutes. I am not 30 years old anymore. I have to put some make up on and glitter my eyes to decorate my wrinkles with twinkle little stars that you will see but dismiss with a smile, saying—good try. But it still shows. But you'll wink at the wrinkles disguised by little stars that twinkle—and they'll bring tears to your eyes not of sadness but of life. She's trying—at least she's trying to avert the wrinkles of time—to avert bad times. Oh, please, disguised as a freckle, or a twinkle, or a wrinkle, I will recognize you, bacalao, aunque vengas disfrazao. I am in prime time. I was rejuvenated by Fortunata who ate an egg—the yolk of an egg—sunny-side-up in front of me, and it made my eyes twinkle like when I was thirty years old. And I giggled. Trouble-free, clueless, carefree, duty free—free for all—at the mercy of graciousness and gratuitousness. Innocence is not a vanity product that you buy in a store.

Innocence is not stored nor restored. Innocence is born with you, and it grows inside you becoming you all the time you are yourself—and you show the wrinkles in your eyes—and twinkle, twinkle little a star.

I also met Hasib in the street. I got into his cab. He took my hand through the window and read the lines. He said:

> --Architecture is about the teeth of the foundation. Does
> it have good bones? You are about the lines. Follow the
> lines always. Many don't know how to read the lines. They
> skip the lines. They miss the underground, the levels of the
> tones. Each line is key. It opens doors. I say it opens doors
> but what it opens is the sky. Give me a call. Take my card.
> I'll be your spiritual adviser.

It took me one month to find the nerve to call Hasib. I could explain what happened but I would miss my next encounter with Hasib in Newark. In a plaza with a gigantic star in the center. The skies were weeping. It was 5 o'clock, cold and dark, in the middle of March—remembrances of winter and forecasts of spring—in between—on this rainy day, he massaged my eyelids and said:

> --I am healing you.

Heat came out of his belly to warm my belly.

> --Reading your lines. You were in love?
> --Does it matter?

> --It hurts. You know what hurts. When love has opened
> multiple possibilities. You realize how strong you are. And
> then love leaves you empty. And you realize how weak you
> are. They are states of the same mind. The weak and the
> strong produce results. And in between we wonder. What
> can we do when we don't feel any longer because love has
> killed our disposition? Like a bamboo you and I bend in
> the middle of the storm. We swing to both sides. We are

loose teeth, but we have very strong bones. A very strong architecture of bones. This is not the moment for a good fight. Good fights are tasteless. They don't bring good moods. They want to keep fighting tit for tat. If you want to understand you can't explain. Explanation doesn't expand the sky in the horizon spreading marmalade in a toast. As I encounter an orientation, as I coordinate a meter and a centimeter. You must levitate and land without falling out of love with a grace pinned to your bones that makes you feel safe, which is not to say in control of the situation.

--In the center of it all.
--Between the pentagram and the star.
--You are healing me. Go ahead.

--A miracle is an apparition of a supernatural order—and when it passes as an event—you don't have to believe in it—it is always looked at with suspicion—no one would believe the supernatural arriving and installing itself. Everything we know as certain becomes uncertain not because doubt is installed in certainty but rather because uncertainty can become a certainty. We can exist in this dimension of disbelief not because we don't believe but because a new existence—an existence we never allowed ourselves to believe—pulled apart our systems of belief. And I insist—it's not because we disbelieve. We are believers. But now uncertainty—a new dimension of uncertainty—not illusory—it has no illusions of grandeur like the ones of the sardine—it has taken us to a different dimension where we don't recognize ourselves anymore. We don't exist only to eat. Our moods don't swing but they are not stable either. They congregate and express their dimensions. There are plenty of dimensions. We go from one stability into another instability—and we are not stable in our instabilities.

--What do you make of this?

--Why do I have to make something of this? We will not
try to make something of another thing that doesn't make
sense. Or that we want to make something out of it because
without us making something out of it, it would disappear
into oblivion. Or it needs our meaning or our interpretation.
Or it needs us to make something out of it because by itself
it doesn't make anything. Maybe it makes a lot of sense. It
doesn't need us to make something out of it. That is what
it doesn't need—that we get involved with it—and make
something out of something that doesn't need for us to
make something out of it. Why can't we just look at it
and be wowed by it. Is it so hard to admire for the sake of
looking at its lines—at its movements—its way of weaving
and moving and intertwining and breathing and creating a
monument without us having to make something out of it.
We get involved with it because we want to be involved—
and that the thing makes something out of us. Not us—
something out of it. It is the thing in itself that is making
something out of us. We are getting into a dimension where
there is no identity as definition of ourselves. There will be
no narration because there will be nothing before that will
be the point of departure—and the after that will come
before—perhaps—will become completed before. And
nothing will be before nor after, but here to be grasped with
the hands. We will be able to exist without worrying about
existence—existence will not exist—not even in memory.
Another existence that doesn't claim to exist will intervene
and grab us by the hair. We will claim liberty, and then we
will claim no more of the habits we inhabit. We will lose
our habits and our references—where—how—because
of what. Let me make sense of it will be history in pampers
looking to simplify the issues that never became because
they never had to make sense of it. We thought *Life is a
Dream*. We were *Waiting for Godot*. We left the *Doll's House*.
We existed in cliches. We chewed a lot of convictions. And
we were never convicted because of our convictions. We
were full of dogmas and cliches, full of ourselves. Now we

The nymph
is pointing her finger
to that precise place
in the middle of
the Baltic Sea: Visby.
Where I had found
my happiness.
Where I belonged.
And nowhere else.
I belong
to the nymph.

will not believe what has happened. It will take us by the back—pull us by the T-shirt. We will scream: where are you taking us? I cannot say what it will be like. It will not be the future nor the past nor a present tense of nomination.

I met Serapa in a café in Visby. She smiled and asked me if I wanted to be initiated in witchcraft—if I wanted to be a witch. I told her I wanted to fly with a pen like witches fly with a broomstick in the sky. Every day we would meet for coffee after I already had a coffee with Vilma Velázquez on the stairs of her jewelry store. I met in the Baltic Center a chef from Tel Aviv named Ett Rum who told me I would write there, but two weeks had passed and I had not written a word until Serapa showed me her broomstick.

--When I fly in the air with this broomstick, you will write
  with your pen.

I need velocity to capture in a blink of an eye a century or what I have been dismissing and delaying all this time. Velocity and ferocity are how my pen flies with a broomstick in the sky.

There were 16 Maenads in a shell surrounding a nymph who looked like the Venus of Milo, a sensitive nymph that Yoko Ono and I found in the window of a laundromat across from her Dakota apartment. The nymph was in a drunken stupor of dolce far niente reclining her naked body in the shell with her long wavy hair draping the curves of her body. What is this nymph doing in the window of a laundromat? Nobody knows who she is. She has to be recognized. In the window looking out, making circles in the water with her fingertip but pointing to a specific place in the middle of the Baltic Sea. A little island named Visby. That is where I have to go. The nymph is reminding me. She was taken hostage all the way to New York only to be found in this laundromat where all the dirty linen is cleaned—to remind me I have to go to Visby. The nymph is pointing her finger to that precise place in the middle of the Baltic Sea: Visby. Where I had found my happiness. Where I belonged. And nowhere else. I belong to the nymph.

I had been ill, and Serapa had willed me in a dream, a dream that was a visionary like herself. She had willed me her good wishes for a quick recovery. And the good wishes had appeared in the middle of a dream that was not a dream because it had a veil and it had to be unveiled. I unveiled the cover of the dream, and inside was a sculpture of two hands and arms that were offered to me as my healing. They were made of marble—white—and there was a ring on the middle finger which seemed to me to be saying: Fuck You! But that's only part of my interpretation. And I also see good will in its delivery through the air by Serapa who flew all the way from Visby to deliver this sculpture with a ring on its middle finger saying: Fuck You! And maybe good-bye. But also, congratulations because I was granted a prize, and all of Serapa's friends and colleagues were there—and it took me by surprise because I was in pajamas when the prize was delivered to me—and without a drop of makeup. Which means I was not making this up. It was real. And I woke up astounded by the prize and the photographers who came to take pictures of me with the prize in my pajamas and without makeup. I was singing a song by Becky G:

Nos metemos en la cama,
Sin piyama, sin piyama.

So, when I was walking with Yoko Ono, and I saw in the window of a laundromat the shell with the nymph inside, I saw the objective correlative of my dream. I thought this is the marble sculpture Serapa delivered to me. It had not arrived in my house. Only in a dream. But now I had found the sculpture of the dream. It was not marble. It was an open shell—not that different from the marble sculpture of two arms and two hands that had travelled through the thick and the thin of atmospheric changes—and when it had arrived in New York—it was lost and found in a laundromat. I told Yoko I had to get that nymph. It belonged to me. But the Chinese woman behind the counter said:

--Not for sale.

Yoko Ono said to me:
--Don't worry. I'll get it for you.

I had forgotten about the nymph. Totally forgotten. Not forgotten. But I had lost hope that I would ever get her. It was not for sale. But one day, the day of my birthday, Yoko came to my house and delivered the nymph, which has been resting in my bathroom for more than three years now. She arrived here the year before the pandemic. This year, with a warped sense of time and an arrested libido, as Mona Mark would say, I went to Visby. And when I returned to New York, Yoko Ono gave me a beautiful arrangement of flowers. I asked her:

--How did you get that nymph for me?
--I don't remember, but I'll let you know if I remember. I'll
try to remember.

She made use of her memory and sent me a text message that said:

--I got it at a laundromat right behind my apartment. The
owner said—not for sale. But I felt the nymph didn't belong
there. And that nobody cared for her. I said—Can't you see
she doesn't belong here? You don't even care for her. And
after some negotiations, she agreed the nymph didn't mean
that much to her, so she sold her to me.

Yoko did not remember that I had noticed the nymph first or that I was with her when the Chinese woman said—not for sale. The nymph's eyes are blank. Lost in space. She doesn't have eyes. The holes are haunting, a ghostly apparition of some kind. She got lost. She got trapped. Now she is free. Yoko also told me the laundromat had disappeared during the pandemic. She had delivered the nymph right before the shutdown. Strange, strange story to remember and to deliver the sculpture of a shell with a nymph inside pointing her finger to Visby.

--Sweden is becoming everyday more like Puerto Rico.
--But at least you put your hand over your heart when you
hear your national anthem. That means that your heart is
beating. I don't know where my heart is.
--You look like a ghost roaming the streets of Visby without
any goal.

--I have a goal. I am looking for the nymph that took my heart and never returned it to where it belonged. I knock on doors. I ask—Have you seen a heart beeping. It is my heart. It was taken hostage by a nymph. I don't know how I exist without a heart. I hear other people's hearts in their smile. Their eyes say so much. My eyes blink at them in admiration for what I don't have. I blame the heart for everything that has happened to me ever since. It beeps outside of me. As an alarm clock. Warped in time. 2011. The year I finished *United States of Banana*. The year I was expulsed from Visby for no reason—for reasons of the heart. My heart beeped as an alarm clock everywhere I went. And people thought I was too noisy. But I couldn't help it. I couldn't control my love for Visby. And they decided not to allow me to come back until I dimmed the alarm clock of my heart. I don't have that kind of discipline. I am loud in love. I am outspoken. I scream when I am in love. I dress in red.

--But now you dress in white.

--I am a ghost of the one I was. My heart was stolen. It hardly beeps anymore. You see that nymph. It is a sculpture, a white marble sculpture of two hands and arms. It is not real. It beeps like an alarm clock every time I say I have to go to Visby—the alarm clock sounds—it beeps out of my heart. It is my heart alarmed of myself, looking for me, wanting to get back inside me again. As if it were so easy to get the heart back on track. To get the body in shape after the pandemic. Or to get Sweden to belong to NATO.

--Sweden is becoming everyday more like Puerto Rico.

--Ever since my heart got out of myself. My laughter beeps the way my heart used to sound. People don't mind when I laugh. They mind when the alarm clock sounds as an alarm—blinking—an interference—electric wires are

intercepting our conversation—watch out—a spy is
coming. You don't know who is a spy nowadays—only the
ears and the eyes and the lips that hear more and see more
and say more than has been said and seen and heard. Maybe
Sweden is becoming every day more like Puerto Rico, but
I would never exchange Greenland for Puerto Rico.

I was dressed all in white, como una santera, including my white jingle
boots. A woman came to me and said:

--Cool boots!
--Christian Louboutin.
--They're not Louboutin if they don't have red soles.

I raised the boot to look at the sole out of curiosity because I didn't
know that all Louboutins have red soles, and to my surprise, even
though they looked as if they would not have red soles, they did have
red soles. We laughed wholeheartedly at the frivolity and at the surprise
that surprised me more with laughter.

--Where are you from?—she said. You're not from here.
I don't know where you're from. But you're not from here.
--I was raised here.
--I live here. I don't know where you are from. But you are
not from here.
--I am from here.

Her friends joined the chorus of deniers that I was not from there,
repeating that they didn't know where I was from. At that moment
I even doubted my identity and asked them:

--Where do you think I'm from?
--We don't know where you come from. But not from here.

I was frustrated. Doubting of my nativity. And thinking—how can
I prove to these bitches that I am from here. The worst two were from

Bogotá, not from here. They were laughing and murmuring at the way I was dressed all in white como una santera—at my hair dyed pink—at my nails, green—at my age, perhaps—at my lack of familiarity. But why did they come to harass me with the refrain.

   --We don't know where you are from. But you're not from here.
   --I am from King's Court. I grew up here.
   --I am from King's Court—said the ringleader very
    aggressively. And you're not from here.
   --What's your name?
   --Corali Betancourt.

My eyes blinked with joy.

   --Corali, are you still una loca divina? Estabas siempre con
    una nota bien alta. Stoned on pot, cocaine, hashish —you
    name it. You had an entourage of four gay guys who
    carried you on a litter into Hashish. I had five-inch platform
    shoes. Yours were seven inches with jingle bells. They called
    you Hot Lips. We wore maxi dresses tight to the body. We
    were the most popular girls in town. And we both had our
    court of followers.

   --¡Gia!
   --¡Yo te adoraba!
   --¡Y yo a ti!

Her friends were put to shame when Corali recognized me as her friend. How many times she had been at my parties in King's Court where I would serve champagne and grapes, mountains of grapes. Even from childhood I had been an initiate of Bacchus, one of the Bacchantes. I always loved Bromius since I was very young. I had parrandas with mariachis, and Corali Betancourt, another Bacchante, came with jingles on her bellbottoms and platform boots, and we sang our lungs out, pirouetting around with Good Cheer, Lady Radiance, and Festivity—the three graces and the nine muses.

> Locals-localization of the
> discrimination and
> segregation of the majorities
> into a localized place
> as if locals were less than
> tourists and foreigners
> invading the native.

I heard my brother Juan arguing with the hostess who told him that she would allow him just this one time to eat with me, but that the restaurant was not for the locals, only for hotel members and guests.

--But I live here.
--You're a local. We don't serve locals.

When I heard locals, I thought of the Native Americans assigned to reservations—after being the natives of the land and the firstlings—and how those who came first now come last. So, the tourists are more important than the natives—a propagation of an absurd colonization—a confinement of the natives to become less in their own land to the extent that someone colonized from abroad could expulse my brother from the possibility of having breakfast in the resort where he lives. And he was pro-statehood, in favor of Ricky Rosselló. But at that moment, even a conservative estadista like my brother became aware of the discrimination executed in front of everyone—and the humiliation, and he asked:

--Where are you from? I don't know where you are from.
 But you are not from here.
--Malawi.

--Don't you know you're used by the colonizers so they
 can hide behind the color of your skin. Puerto Rican Lives
 Matter! What do you mean by locals. Since when are we
 locals. Before we were minorities. But minorities became
 majorities. Now the locality is misplaced in another place—
 and I can't find the origin. But I know when they refer to us
 as locals, they are localizing us in a locality—and they are
 misplacing us and taking us out of our place and making
 us inferior—denigrating the locals to again minoritize the
 natives—to underline our underprivileged status of being
 less in our own land by becoming locals—localization of
 the discrimination and segregation of the majorities into
 a localized place as if locals were less than tourists and
 foreigners invading the native.

It always amazes me when a conservative like my brother has to come
to terms with the fact that he too has been discriminated against and
treated as an inferior citizen in his own land. We decided to go else-
where because the tension became too big and no one was feeling at
ease in their own skin. I told my brother what happened to me with
Corali Betancourt. I asked her:

--Are you still una loca divina?
--No, I found Jesus—she said.
--God help me!—I said.

And I moved away from her, not to escape religion, but I had chores
to do. I went to my room to pack the bags. The flight was overbooked
because of Covid. They always have an excuse why the flight is packed
or delayed or cancelled—never because of bad planning and greed—but
because of Delta variants this time. They offered me another flight on
Saturday instead of Thursday. I said yes—and the hotel said I could stay
if I changed rooms. I packed my bags and realized I was missing a white

silk shirt with a silver braid on the breast pocket. I reported my loss to management. I thought of a maid who told me to leave my room. But I didn't accuse anyone. I suggested instead perhaps the white shirt was confused with the white towels and mistaken for laundry. Please, check it out, I said. I missed my shirt. I thought of the good times I had shared under the skin of that shirt—and how I had breathed better under that skin—and I had made a whole mystique—and a whole memory—lost and found—not in the laundry amidst the white towels that could have been confused with it but in the memory of the meticulousness of my mother who gave extreme importance to clothes—and how cautious I had been not to spoil my shirt with dirt—not to spot a spot of dirt on my white shirt—and if I spotted it—I would have to shout it out before my mother found out. Once I had a white shirt that I spotted with ink—and I put it in the washing machine afraid my mother would find the spot, but the ink went viral and spoiled not only the whole shirt but the whole load and devastated mi estado anímico because when I had my first communion I was also dressed in white and I went to Elsita Tió's house—and she had a Labrador Retriever Tito who was full of pulgas y garrapatas—and he gave those pulgas y garrapatas to me—and my mother almost drowned me in the bathtub, trying to rid me of pulgas y garrapatas, and pulled my hair—and it was abusive— and she was screaming that I ruined the white dress—and nothing is as important as the whiteness of the white—because believe me white shirt— white dress matters—if you want to preserve your life—and you are drowning.

I called Margie Lugo, and she said—call Quenepa. She took a photo of you in El Viejo San Juan next to the statue of Tite Curet Alonso who wrote the song La Lupe immortalized, *Puro Teatro*. I called Quenepa who sent me the photo right away. And I went back to security and showed them the photo of me in the white shirt. I said: This is the shirt I'm missing. I looked up Brunello Cuccinelli on the internet. Here's the advertisement. Here's the price. But it's not the price. It's the missing. It's my mother and my father who are not here. It's my childhood. It's Rosebud. And by the way I'm not the kind of person who reminisces. I like to forget a lot. But I look at the essentials. And when I miss the core. I look at my umbilical cord. I was having an interview with Carmen Dolores Trelles that morning. I didn't tell her anything about my missing shirt. Who cares. A shirt is a shirt. But when you miss a shirt, a cloud appears in your head. Look what happened when Tartuffe lost his nose—Trump came into power—and then none of us could breathe—and Coronavirus left us without a sense of smell—senseless we were walking with a warped notion of time and space. Survival and biotechnical issues became our sole calculations. We even tried to control the weather. We won't be able to walk at 4 o'clock because it will rain, but it didn't rain at 4 o'clock. The storm that was predicted was a shit storm, so that we would invade our homes with more products and things that prepared us for the storm that never came. Other times they are right. A volcano in the Canary Islands—what a beautiful spectacle—unpredictable. Lava has always been a force in my poetry. Carmen Dolores came on the dot at 11:30. We held the interview, and then we went to the Colegio de las Madres to pay a visit—a homage—to the nuns who had raised us. Then I went to visit Pacotazo and had dinner with him in Old San Juan. It is so boring to narrate like this—how is it that novelists can stand it—the straight line of following a pattern—and the homogeneity of it all. The ceremoniousness of it all was what got me from the beginning—how Pacotazo made things that were small, big—and how he made himself the largest of all—and how when he put himself on top he was condescending from below—and how his envy was not only chronic but pathological—and how his claim to knowledge was a chronic case of pathological envy that couldn't help but manifest itself in spite of having read all the books in the world, which he has not read but which he claims to have so—just as he claims he knows French, German, Swedish, and Greek, but whenever I had a friend in my house who spoke French, German, Swedish, or Greek, he kept his mouth shut like a mouse because he doesn't know French, German, Swedish, or Greek. And he speaks English lousy. I don't claim to know English—it is not the language of my childhood—and it doesn't laugh the way I laugh. But he does laugh the way I laugh. We are from the same town and country. He has two hundred teeth on the top and two hundred on the bottom—and he always drinks at night and cooks divine because he likes ceremonious acts, which I like too, because they give me structure—and he is a thinker—and he thinks that if he were not born where he was born on a little island,

Philosophers have poets inside. Those poets become characters like Socrates or Zarathustra.

he would be as famous as Socrates, excuse me, as Plato—as if both were not born on an island—and he thinks Socrates is a nobody, but without Socrates, Plato would not have the dialogues—he would not have the character because Socrates is what makes philosophy bone and flesh—what makes it a work of art. He always complains that he is not famous because he was born small on a small island—and he thinks small—small of others and of himself too. Small-souled. He says the poet has readers not a public. Wrong. The poet has so much public in the Republic that he is expulsed from the Republic. Socrates has a public, his whole town is his public. What would have happened to Plato without the public figure of Socrates—from youth to old age—looking and finding conversations to misinterpret and take out of context—through the word of mouth—the words of others—and the inspiration that goes in conversations, in banquets, and in public bathrooms. Of course, poetry has a public. It has public bathrooms. And it goes public. The poet is a public figure that goes around intervening in public spaces. He comes out as a public citizen in a public place to say what he has inside. Philosophers have poets inside. Those poets become characters like Socrates or Zarathustra. You hear their thoughts moving very late at night—and there are revelations—revelatory statements that the philosopher finds under his pillow. When I was in Paris, after I had eaten pork blanquette—and that is why I didn't pay attention

to a very important dream in which he stabbed me in the back. Este
Pacotazo, I said then, me tiró una puñalada trasera.

--Are you insinuating I am a coward?

--Tiras la piedra y escondes la mano. The dream should
have advised me to get away from envious people like
you, but at the time, even though the dream was so strong
that I felt the knife in my back for two weeks, I thought it
was because I had eaten pork blanquette not that it was
a premonition. I knew you were going to betray me. It is
written all over your forehead: Chronic Case of Pathological
Envy. Then you brought up the case of Espinoza and how
he was expelled from the synagogue when he was only
twelve. And you looked at me, with a smile.

--You were expelled too—from Rutgers. Forty years ago,
you were expelled. And before that too, you were expelled
in childhood from the Coro de niñas de San Juan when
adolescence arrived. And when old age comes, not yet, but
right there at the corner, you will be expelled again. Three
times expelled. From school, marriage, and work. Expelled
three times from fruition and growth. Expelled from love.
I was expelled too—seven times—way more than you and
Espinoza together.

--Why do you brag about your expulsions?
--To prove my exceptionality. I was expulsed seven times—
way more than you and Espinoza together. Nevertheless,
I am a member of the Academy.

And it was so petty—after I'd been honored by Cambio 16 in Spain and
by the North American Academy of the Spanish Language—neither
of which I had ever expected—to then receive a rejection letter from
my best friend from high school to whom I had given so much. Every
time he came to New York, he stayed in my house—and I adored him—
until the betrayal—the stab in the back—from my best friend from

high school who in a fit of envy could not stop himself from writing me a letter of rejection, congratulating me on the international prizes I had won but nevertheless regretting to inform me that on the island which he blames for his lack of recognition, I will not be honored by the Academy.

--Will you forgive me?
--You are already forgotten. For that, blame the island
 where you were born.
--Perdón.
--Que te perdone Dios. It is not my role to forgive nor to
 bless nor to curse. A Dios lo que es de Dios. Y al poeta lo
 que es del poeta.

The next day that lasted seven weeks I was abducted by martians. So, when I say it was a day that lasted seven weeks you can imagine how the calendar was altered, and how my mind changed after I won the Cambio16 prize: *You Are My Hope.* I had no time to look around at the spaceship, very cold. The furniture was white, skinny, with shapes newly taken out of a bone, fragile and broken, white like teeth. My memory stopped thinking. There's a memory that thinks when it remembers, slow, what took place at a certain period in a certain time. The abduction took place that evening on Little Island. But nothing is certain when seven weeks are condensed in one night in which instead of growing old, I went back in time, recovering all the periods of my life that had made me lose consciousness of what I would never know. If you think you know, I never thought I knew until I entered the spaceship, then I learned what I never knew, and it is better to skip this chapter than to get a glance and a grip of this reality. Nurses, I call them nurses because they were dressed in white. They could have been nuns or doctors, what do I know. One of them was called Lark. She sang in the middle of the night, checked my pulse, and took my blood, every single day of the seven weeks condensed in one night in which I grew young again. I saw Lark as a manicurist painting my nails, taking my blood, pinching me, and poking for more blood. Sometimes she didn't find my veins, so she poked me again and again until she had to call another manicurist to find the vein because her pinching had soaked me dry.

--Do you understand what we are doing?
--Interrupting my book.
--We are changing your blood. To make you young again.
 We are radiating you with youth. Remember, 49 days in one
 night in which your body will rejuvenate.

They wanted me to explain to them what they were doing. They wanted me to know that I consented. That I gave them the right to do what they were doing. Because I had signed an agreement giving them the right to do what they were doing. But I signed the agreement because they insisted:

--This is serious.
--What makes you think that I'm considering it otherwise.
--It is more serious than you think. Take it seriously. It is not
 a joke.

My humor advises me with wisdom to distance myself from people who like to take my blood. My wisdom says to distance myself from serious matters or serious people who take themselves too seriously, more seriously than the matters of the war in Ukraine, and in my body poking my veins and swabbing my nostrils. All remissions are settled for later but you are cured of all afflictions. So don't talk about losing your innocence or your originality because you are getting back with refills your virginity and your youth. But the poking and the exams and radiations—external and internal—lasted for seven weeks condensed in one night in which I grew young again. And it set my clock backwards, in remission. I wondered, with all the time I have wasted in my life, waiting, if this was a moment of finding where the trunk of the fir tree was so that I could bend it and seat Pendejo on the top branch where the maenads would find him, on the top of the tree, shake him down, and tear him to pieces. The time of jubilation is back. I have to take back what is mine and was taken from me to recover. Why recover. Question everything you say but not as right or wrong. Question how it rings in your ears. My ears, I have to tell you, see far away, see so far away, with speed, what a camera, surveilling all the speedy matters, sleeping, dormant to what is happening to me, allowing the interceptions in my body with scalpels, robots, and anesthesia—to forget—and allow it to happen—and forget—and think that it is not you who is allowing the instruments to attack you—you are not feeling it because you are dormant, but when you wake up, you will feel the awakening of pain from the attack when you were sleeping—and it is for your own good—to revitalize you. I will not badmouth the martians. I loved them. They inflicted pain on me for my own good—or so they say—and others tell me—be grateful for the martians, they made you young again and they saved you from a matter that was serious. So now play a record and enjoy life as it is on this planet.

The martians said one thing before they returned me to earth:

--We want you to sign this new agreement. We don't want you to talk about death again.
--I swear. I will never talk about what is killing me or about what has killed me in the past.

--Nor about pain. We don't want you to talk about pain anymore. We want you to sign an agreement that you will not talk about death nor about pain.

--I already signed with my blood when the manicurist was painting my nails gold that I knew what you all were doing, and that I agreed to what you were doing.

--We made you young again—that is what you need to know. And what you consented to. But now you have to agree never to talk about death because you are young again. And youth doesn't want to talk about death.

--Is talking so important. I thought it was not important at all. So why are you making word of mouth a consent in an agreement.

--Because talking about death is important.

I have faith now
that finally the sardine
has been laid to rest—
after it was killed
by Hope—by me—
it came back and
wreaked havoc.
My abduction was
a consequence of
that riot act—
of that insurrection.

--Censorship is important. More important than camaras
surveilling my steps. More important than abduction
by martians who took 49 days of my human life and
condensed it in one night to make me young again.

--We would like you not to talk anymore.
--I will not consent to that.

--Take water when you have a desire to talk. Take gallons
of water. That will cure your desire to talk. You can watch
all what you want. As long as your tongue remains in
remission.

I am convinced it all had to do with the Cambio 16 Prize I won: *You are
My Hope.* And don't forget I had killed the sardine. I had killed what had
wanted to kill me long ago. After the abduction by the martians, I said
to myself—no more talking about death—never again. And I will never
talk about it nor dress in black—this I promise you. Nor will I say—this
makes me sick! Words mean what they say. Even when they have no
intention to harm you. Nor to put you in harm's way. The fact that I was
abducted had to do with me killing the sardine. Me, Hope, the hope that
still flourishes in the world—dimming light in the sky—green. A green
light still beaming in the sky. The triumph of Hope over the sardine, but
even though the sardine was killed, it spread contagion. Or maybe my
abduction had to do with me—Hope—grieving the death of the sardine.
I promised I would not talk about death anymore. Especially, when a
green light continues beaming in the sky without blinking an eye nor
winking. But there are consequences, results, interferences. Without
logic or reasoning, things appear and wink an eye, and you understand
that you are not alone in the universe—that the stars are winking an
eye—in response to the green light beaming in the sky like a big smile
and a loud applause. And when the dance happens—and the mysteries
take place—and the rites claim their right to take over rallies run by
nonbelievers. I believe, I have hope, I have faith now that finally the
sardine has been laid to rest—after it was killed by Hope—by me—it
came back and wreaked havoc. My abduction was a consequence
of that riot act—of that insurrection. And when I returned to earth,

I promised I would not talk of what happened when the abduction modified my conduct and made me again a vehicle of good—if good exists—I say—and nobody taught me this—I learned it from my own experience—singularity is not a product of plurality but of exceptionality. That I remain in seclusion—outside of myself—looking at my surroundings—and sometimes entering into a monad. I find a place in myself where I have not been away but close, and I feel a certain tenderness for the fawn skin, the yellow parapluie, and the crown of ivy that Bacchus wears while Pendejo cuts his curls, takes his wand, and puts him in jail. I have been there—locking, unlocking—knocking—singling with my finger and saying: that's it. Breath came out of my kerchief—the one I had on my desk—the one that had gone with me to the hospital when the martians abducted me after the insurrection. I saw it breathing, the kerchief. First, I thought—since I am Cartesian—I breathe, therefore, I exist. But it's not my nose breathing nor bleeding from the dry heat. It's not that I blew my nose and found no nose. I found my kerchief breathing on its own—and out of the wind not dust but Bacchus—my genie had appeared, not out of a bottle. I had gone to the Americas Society to hear Gabriel Bouche Caro's premiere of a song cycle based on *Book of Clowns and Buffoons* in *Empire of Dreams*.

> *No, no fue el juego,*
> *no, no fue el fuego.*
> *Todavía, no tengo puñales en mis bolsillos.*
> *Tengo estrellas.*

Written at the same age the composer is—28 but 40 years apart—and tears welled in my eyes. I was sniffing—my nose high—erect. I relived that moment in which I was writing those poems. It was as if we were one, the composer and me—me at the age he is right now—and he picked the poems I wrote at his age—the age he is right now—and I relived that moment and released myself—and tears swelled in my eyes—and I was afraid my nose was going to bleed but it didn't. I raised my chin straight up—and since the music was loud—as loud as the soprano singing my poems—they could not hear my sniffing. My genie had appeared. For the first time, I saw Bacchus as a figure coming out of the kerchief that blew air. The kerchief became the god. And when I saw that figure big—a giant figure in the shape of a kerchief—I figured it all out. Gabriel had told me the story that he had fallen asleep on a beach in Crete and when he awoke, he saw a giant coming out of the water. I said—a giant, like ten feet? No, he said—a giant the size of the Empire State—Afro Greek with long curly hair—far away in deep waters—up to his waist—and he was coming to the shore but he made a sudden turn and disappeared. And this was real. This was not something I invented. I saw that giant. This inspired me to go to Crete where I saw mountains slope like the amphitheaters of Athens with different gradations of thought—where the mountain meets the sea—right there in front of me—and with different degrees of magic, freedom, and separation—with silence and exclamations in between. I was there with Michi, Tess, Magnus, and Helena. We were dreaming—and the hills were alive for three static and ecstatic weeks. Giuliana hosted a birthday party for Sabine Cassel, and as I've always said, I feel like Ditirambo. If I have the chance to admire and give compliments and felicitations, I do it. Giuliana—I said—I like your collection of globes and maps—and these two cherubs are beautiful. She said, I will give you a cherub. Do you want one? Yes. Of course, I love cherubs. She goes to get me a cherub. Michi whispers to her—who knows what she told her—and Giuliana returns without a cherub and doesn't speak to me for the rest of the party. I was confused, shattered. Somoroff said—Michi stopped an angel from coming to you—that's not good. I was stunned. A cherub not given. A promise not fulfilled. A deed unaccomplished. We all sang happy birthday to Sabine—and Michi looked at me sideways, happy that she had stopped a cherub from coming to me—a delivery undelivered. She stops things from happening. I don't know what she told Giuliana, but my intentions were fresh, innocent, clear. I had no intention of getting anything—just of admiring—of being Ditirambo, exclamations, interjections. But if you offer me something beautiful, why do you offer what you then don't deliver. I see Francesca, the ex-wife of Alfredo, who has an angel with giant wings painted on the back of her fur coat. Here is the angel delivered to me. Francesca says come with me. She takes me to a church and there is Alfredo waiting at the backdoor with two black bags of clothes they were donating to Sant'Egidio. We take the stairs down to the basement to deposit the body bags, and when we come up, I light two candles— one for my mother—and another for a nun Carmina Rosselló who had taught me *The Little Prince* when I was a student at el Colegio de las Madres. And I knew Francesca with wings was doing a deed that was more than charity for beggars—she was saving my life from the wings of the cherub undelivered—she was saving the message—and delivering the wings so they could fly—and the handkerchief could breathe—and Bacchus—Ditirambo—exclamations and interjections—and this has been my life—full of exclamations and interjections—full of delivery and expediency—though no authority—and as I turn my back I see Bacchus waiting to embrace me, but instead I embrace his warmth and feel his presence through a rim, a ruffle of a leaf, a kerchief breathing on its own. What god before this one have you ever heard say—I come to make progress. To advance not to delay. The court always delays the case because they believe in locking you up, in delaying your cause. This god is interested in advancing. He wants to leave you mindless—not knowing who you thought you were because that person who you thought you were is the one who is not allowing for you to become who you will be—and it might even surprise you who you will be if you allow your mindless powerful power who directs your intuitions not to neglect the senses but to bring them to the stage. The senses should all be brought to the stage. You should trust your senses as you should discover new senses, genders, genres. And get the spectator off the stage—too long has he been taking selfies from the stage—looking down at experience—at experimentation—thinking behind the selfie that he can be protected from participation because he wants the exclusivity of watching without participating in the rites, in the orgy of collectivity. The spectator expects too little of the advancement of humanity—keeping himself apart—looking through the iPhone—not participating in the orgy of the senses—to watch without being seen. Bacchus has a voice—a voice that is everywhere in nature—you hear the voice in the wind—and when you hear it—you look everywhere—because we are admitting that we are innocent—having heard nothing like it before—it comes from everywhere and nowhere—from all and none—it speaks in tongues of fire—and when it speaks it reveals all the hollowness—and the round, the square, the triangle of sadness, the plenitude of nowhere—the elements in the voice—the intrusion of the intruder. He doesn't defend himself. Those who defend themselves too much delay the advancement of humanity. Methinks thou does protest too much to block the advancement and to always delay the advancement with the traffic of the argument that creates violence in the driver who always has to blow the klaxon because the argument never advances, it creates clutter, and now a days the garbage is left in the sidewalks for days on end—creating more clutter—and delaying more the progress of the world. The fact that I have cheerfulness doesn't mean that I am in a state of untroubled contentment. I am not interested in what will happen next—or who is the audience I'm writing to—addressing—pitching—as an advertising consultant—nor in the result—nor in the numbers of the polls—nor in the positive nor the negative. When people ask me: What do you write about? I shrill. As if there was an about in my life. When I was born—did I know what this was about—what would become of me—or how do I solve conflicts when they arrive at the due moment they come—unexpectedly—that is what I write about—the un-expectancy of life—and the misdemeanors of what appears—infallible or fallible—without a voice over narration running its air conditioner to smooth what is rough, bumpy, and unsettled. In this un-expectancy I insert the magical determination of a poet making beauty out of what is sad or happy because it is neither sad nor happy but beautiful. The incompleteness of history as a movement never reaches its limit, only the limits of transformation. In this transformation humanity dwells—thinking it is definitive because it is becoming acquainted with the transformation and doesn't want a change anymore, but for better or worse change happens. We are made of changes and transformations. We deal with them—we get used to them—and then we miss them—even when they were not good for us—because they didn't make us grow. If it hurts and makes you grow—it is good for you. If it hurts and destroys your possibilities, it is what it is. But does it allow the growth necessary to sense the pulsing of the nerves that are touching the right cues to achieve perfect pitch. I don't think of myself as an achiever. I think of myself as a living melody trying to achieve a perfect pitch—and a cue—having no idea of the end. To create a genre the way Galileo discovered the Medicean Stars is different than to create a movement. Petrarca created a movement. Rubén Darío created another movement. Breton created a movement. And generations are a product of time. The Generation of the 27. Or the Beat Generation. Movements and generations exert their power at a particular point in history, while genres exert their power as a phenomenon in space. The creation of tragedy by Aeschylus is the invention of a prototype—or a model that has been used from ancient times to our time. Dramatists still go to this model like designers to the prototype of a chair with four feet and a seat to sit on for generations to come. A new genre is not a movement—or a generation—dated—but a shift in thinking that has a structure—a location—a territory. That territory was the Oresteia where a paradigm shift happened when the furies agreed to transform their fury into blessings. The source and the sorcerers are the same. The power is there in the in the No of furies—and in the Yes of blessers. In the No of their curses—and in the Yes of their blessings. To create a new territory where paradigm shifts happen, you have to create a new prototype that can be reproduced for generations to come. You don't need the baggage of history and the pestilence of culture to create the transition. You need a partera—to hum the enchanted words—and a witch or furies to change their curses to blessings—the knots into nests—and there you will have the shift in a nest full of eggs. You can say the language is out modeled but the invention works because the shift happened in society—and the new genre captured what happened and how it changed. It captured the change in the prototype it invented. And it figured out how the change worked—and it changed with the work—what works—that is not the work but the pleasure involved. It is not about the years spent in making the prototype but the passion that produced the change. The prototype is achieved as a phenomenon that appears, makes a turn, and changes the way of making things—it changes the thinkings—it inserts in the thinkings not a method but a pattern—with many structures—many ways of making the prototype in different locations in time—sometimes with ineptitude—other times waking late at night—not working at all—and not always changing shifts but shifting always the paradigms of time. As time has said once and again, things happen in time—and the repetition of this lie has been perpetuated by the storytellers of fiction, but things don't always happen in time. And when they have a method—the method is broken—and there is a space where the things broken that find no method find a structure—not of analysis nor of theory—no theory is allowed—because they are all destroyed by the method they use in their analysis. What is needed is

We don't need storytellers.
We need soothsayers.
I never said I am a storyteller.
I said I am a soothsayer.
I say the sooth.

to start creating in the void where nothing works. What is needed is to find that void—that the analysis tries to fill with theories—so that we don't find the gap, but it is necessary to be acquainted with that void and to not fear that space where nothing works the way it used to because that is the place where possibilities take place. To make the shift, you must inhabit the void and confront the terror that happens in that void where nothing works—where music starts—where pleasure invites the muses to come along to inspire the void to shift its course to the space where new shifts can be attained. We don't need storytellers. We need soothsayers. I never said I am a storyteller. I said I am a soothsayer. I say the sooth. When you say this doesn't work, at that moment, you start shedding the works of others and start working for yourself. If you go on working in the void—there where nothing works—starts the shift that moves this work forward. Imagination starts where nothing works. Where people say: Nothing works—this is a disaster. I say: I'll take it from here—I'll make a work of art that doesn't work but creates beauty. Listen, I used to worry when people thought I don't work, I'm lazy. I used to apply work to my method of understanding. And it never worked. When I applied a method to my madness nothing works because a method is part of a plan to exterminate creativity. To cut everything with the same scissors. To make me inclusive—not exclusive. I am exclusive. I am creating a work that doesn't work. It should not even be called a work. Work is the problem. The word work doesn't work. Even when it creates a work. It creates a problem inside the work. We have to stop using the word work because work implies a production that has an expiration—a bankruptcy—and it always loses its job—because work implies replacement. Capitalism believes everyone is replaceable. But time is not a limit of productivity. To produce is not our limit. Don't listen to those who tell you: I'll make it work—I'll apply a method to your madness. That's where everything goes wrong. When a method of logic dated and expired comes to offer you the help to expire and not to create the genre you aspire to create without a method. To apply productivity to your creativity is to apply expiration to breathing. Breathe through the void. Don't give up when you meet the Furies or the Sirens. Know what happened in the past and change the outcome. Transform the energy of the Furies—from curses to blessings—and give them a land where they can bless the coming into being of new babies. When you create a genre—which is not a movement—because it has no past—and if it has a past—its past is pregnant with a future bigger than its past—its past is its post-creation—only a point of departure—it created modes of thinking. A genre has in itself movements, generations—and after all these concepts expire in time—the genre—that is an artifact—that is a fact made shift—it doesn't belong to a date—it is not dated—it includes all the expirations that expire in its belly—and it is still pregnant with new beginnings. It allows transformations, revolutions but in itself it is a discovery, an invention—like the stars Galileo discovered and dedicated to Cosmo de Medici.

I dedicate this book to Tess O'Dwyer, on her birthday, June 2, 2024.

Giannina Braschi is an award-winning American poet, novelist, and radical thinker who writes in Spanish, Spanglish, and English. Her masterworks include the epic poem *El imperio de los sueños/Empire of Dreams*, the iconic Spanglish novel *Yo-Yo Boing!*, the geopolitical tragicomedy *United States of Banana*, and the multi-genre epic *PUTINOIKA*.

The U.S. Library of Congress calls Braschi "cutting-edge, influential, and even revolutionary," and PEN America recognizes her as "one of the most revolutionary voices in Latin America today." Her texts have been widely adapted and applied to theatre, chamber music, graphic novels, painting, photography, artist books, short films, industrial design, and urban planning. Her life's work is the subject of the anthology of essays, *Poets Philosophers Lovers: On the Writings of Giannina Braschi*, edited by Frederick Luis Aldama and Tess O'Dwyer. Braschi's numerous accolades include honors from the National Endowment for the Arts, the New York Foundation for the Arts, Danforth Foundation, Ford Foundation, Instituto de Cultura Puertorriqueña, and PEN America. She has received lifetime achievement awards from the North American Academy of the Spanish Language, Cambio 16 in Spain, and her native city of San Juan, Puerto Rico. Terms frequently associated with Braschi include Postcolonial Literature, Latinx Philosophy, Postdramatic Theatre, Hysterical Realism, McOndo, and Post-Boom. She goes simply by poet.

Milton Keynes UK
Ingram Content Group UK Ltd.
UKHW050858270924
448840UK00017B/194